The Love Lie

*To my family for their unconditional love,
my friends for their overwhelming support,
and my fans for their incredible enthusiasm.
Thank you from the bottom of my heart.*

The
Love
Lie

CHAPTER ONE

sam

YOU ARE *such a great guy and I'm sorry to do this to you right now, but—*

No. Sam shakes her head. *Don't apologize.*

The past few weeks with you have been absolutely magical, and I will cherish these memories for the rest of my life—

Blech. She gags at the thought. *Too over the top.*

I've really enjoyed getting to know you, but I need to focus on myself right now, and blah, blah, blah...

Sam sighs. *Too selfish. I'll lose the audience.*

I never wanted to hurt you, but we can't get engaged. It wouldn't be right to either of us when I know in my heart that you're not my perfect match.

Sam grins. It's excellent—succinct, to the point, riding that line between kind and unapologetic, and, added bonus, it features the show's tagline.

Go, me!

Now...

She drops her head back against the seat and tilts her face toward the sun as a cool, salty spray tickles her cheeks. Glimmering cerulean water surrounds her on all sides, the quintessential image of the Maldives. Lulled by the humming motor and splashing waves, she takes a deep breath to soak it all in. Most people would probably be nervous right now, but Sam is perfectly at ease as the speedboat carries her closer and closer to the man whose heart she's about to break.

It's a showmance, she reasons. *Emily said he already agreed to the plan. And he was probably just here for the likes anyway.*

No harm.

No foul.

No use worrying when for the first time in she can't remember how long, she has a few minutes to just sit and be.

Forty-eight hours ago, she'd been crammed into a cubicle, elbow deep in financial spreadsheets, lucky to catch a brief inhale of garbage-infused New York City air on her way into and out of the office.

Now, she's in paradise. Blue skies. Pristine white sand beaches. Endless ocean views. The only thing missing is a freshly blended piña colada, heavy on the rum. But still, a great trade up, even if it comes with a few unavoidable consequences—namely, the fact that she's on her way to turn down a perfectly nice man's proposal...in front of ten million viewers...while pretending to be her identical twin sister on national television. Oh, and this skintight sequined ivory gown the producer forced her into isn't helping either. The fucking thing is getting itchier and itchier by the minute in this heat. But that's beside the point.

How the hell did she end up here?

It's a long story.

Eight weeks ago, her mother caught the attention of the *Wake Up, America!* hosts while standing in the studio audience sporting a bedazzled sign that read *#EmilyAnnNeedsAMan*. The clip went viral, and somehow, against all reason, her twin sister, Emily, ended up as the lead on their favorite reality TV dating show, *The Love Match*, set to have thirty men fighting for her heart. Except unbeknownst to Emily, her ex-boyfriend slash love-of-her-life Jake was one of the producers of said show.

Naturally, things got a little dicey.

Flash forward six weeks to Sam's arrival on location in the stunning Maldives. She and her parents were supposed to meet Emily's final two suitors before the proposal, but instead, due to a delayed flight, Sam missed the entire first day of filming, got pulled into a dramatic late-night reunion with her sister, and then slept over in Emily's suite. The second the cameras were gone, her twin broke down and explained how she'd fallen for Jake again. Not ideal, considering she was supposed to get engaged in two days to another man. (*Side note—thirty hot guys had been fighting over her, and she went back to Jake? The guy who ghosted her at eighteen? Seriously?*) Sam must not have been the only one annoyed by his mere presence, because before her arrival Jake had been fired and kicked out of the resort. Emily was desperate to go after him (*Again… really?*), and Sam might've said no if not for one tiny detail —while Emily was on a complete communication blackout during filming, one of her doctors called explaining they needed to get in touch with her. Sam was her emergency contact, and though she tried and tried to get through to Emily, she was both blocked by Jake and stonewalled by the producers. The only way to get her sister access to a phone so she could check in with her doctor sans cameras was to get her out of the resort, and there was only one way to make that happen.

A twin swap.

Cliché? Yes.

Doable? Absolutely.

Call it jet lag, call it sisterly devotion, call it complete insanity, but Sam would do anything for Emily, which is how she ended up here, on this boat, on the final day of filming, on her way to break a man's heart. Not that she minds, really. She gets a free week in paradise out of the deal—her first vacation in years—and breakups are sort of her thing. She's perfected the art of letting them down easy…or ripping them a new one, depending on what the situation demands. Yesterday had been a soul-crusher kind of day. Ethan, Em's runner-up, was a grade A asshole and tearing him apart in front of ten million viewers while she kicked his ass to the curb had been a complete delight. But Cooper, the Midwestern cowboy about to propose to her on a private island in the Maldives, is apparently a sweetheart, so she'll be gentle. Well, as gentle as an up-and-coming New York City investment banker knows how to be...

Nice. Nice. I can be nice. All I need to do is channel my inner Emily. Sweet. Soft spoken. Kind. I'm the good twin. I'm—

"Emily!"

"What?" Sam snaps, totally breaking her zen—not that it takes much. She's always been the spice to Emily's sweet. Some things just never change. But she's supposed to be her sister right now, so she takes a deep breath and puts a pleasant smile on her face before she turns toward her producer, Nina Chen.

The woman is a petite five-foot-two, but her personality packs a punch. Beneath that saccharine smile, punk-rock hair (half of her black tresses are buzz cut close to the scalp), and combat boots, lies a cunning assassin. It takes one to know one. The moment Sam set eyes on the producer, she knew she'd have to be on top of her game to keep Nina fooled. The woman's entire job is to pick people apart, manipulate them, and capitalize on their weaknesses to make entertaining TV. Sam knows because she's spent hours being entertained by said TV, but this time she's not watching from the comfortable position on her egregiously large bed (at least when compared to her laughably small city apartment). She's in the thick of it, which means now is not the time to lower her guard.

In two more hours, filming will be done. She can relax then.

I'm Emily, Sam thinks as she switches her tone to something humble and apologetic. *Be Emily.*

"Sorry." She smiles meekly. "I zoned out. Did you need something?"

"Just checking in. We're almost there. How are you feeling?"

Like I was born for this shit. It takes everything Sam has to keep the smirk off her face. Instead, she swallows nervously. "Good. Great! Maybe just a little anxious…"

"Really?" Nina smiles conspiratorially and lowers her voice. "After what I saw in the dream suite, I thought you'd be eager to get engaged."

As a fan of the show, Sam is aware of the infamous "dream suite" dates. When only three suitors are left, the lead gets the opportunity to have an overnight date with each one sans the cameras. AKA, it's time to get freaky. Except, she knows her sister and Emily doesn't do freaky. That's Sam's department. So she has no idea what the hell Nina is referencing, and in their little tête-à-tête before the swap Em never mentioned it.

She's going to have to wing it.

Sam shrugs, playing up her nerves, and offers a vague, "Yeah, well, you know…"

Nina's eyes fill with sympathy. "Are you afraid he's not going to propose?"

"What?" Sam rears back.

He's going to propose.

He *has* to propose.

The whole reason Emily signed up for this show in the

first place was to promote her budding jewelry business, Emily Ann Designs, and being turned down on national television is *so* not a good look. Not that turning down a certified heartthrob's proposal is that much better, but still. Sam and and her sister spent hours preparing the best way to let Cooper down easy, focusing on the personal growth and female empowerment that defines Em's brand. Once she makes it through the initial breakup, Sam's messaging will be on point and sure to gain the viewers' support. The speech is a practical rallying cry for the business, and now she's being told it might all be ruined? By a freaking cowboy? Who does he think he is, turning her sister down? Emily is a complete catch. He's lucky he's even getting the chance to propose to her, lucky to be breathing the same air, lucky—

Sam breaks off and turns suddenly toward Nina. Wicked sparkles flash in the corners of the producer's eyes.

Oh, she's good, Sam thinks, suddenly remembering that this woman was one of the assholes who refused to let her speak to Emily during filming, not even when she explained the need to pass along private medical information. *But I'm better.*

The only thing that anyone who works for this show cares about is ratings, and there's only two ways to draw in the viewers—drama or romance. People want a heart-stopping love story or a jaw-dropping explosion. Anything in between is utter crap.

So Sam looks at Nina innocently and offers an amused

laugh. "Wouldn't that be funny? If he told me he didn't love me, and he couldn't propose, so we just hugged it out before deciding to be friends?"

"Hilarious," Nina drawls as her lips twitch with a frown. Sam works to stifle her grin. *Gotcha.* The producer clears her throat. "Should we go over the schedule one more time?"

"Sounds great."

Sam smirks and drops her head back again, soaking up the sun's warm rays as Nina drones on about hair and makeup and the plan for the day. It's not rocket science and she's heard it all before, so she mostly tunes it out, choosing to instead focus on the five free days she'll have to enjoy her network-provided, over-ocean bungalow when all this is through. It's customary for the show to pay for the lead to have a few extra days in the final location, normally shared with her new fiancé since the two then have to part ways until the live finale three months later. But in Sam's case, she'll be blissfully solo, just the way she likes it. Sure, she'll have to spend most of her time answering emails, fielding phone calls, and doing the grunt work of an investment banking analyst (this is an unplanned, totally impromptu extended vacation after all, and her boss is undoubtedly already losing his mind because she's been offline for an unheard-of forty-eight hours), but at least she'll be doing it with an ocean view.

Too soon, the boat slows to a stop in the shallows of a gorgeous beach bustling with activity. The executive producer, an ice woman named Trish with her white-blonde hair tied in a severe bun, whispers with the director, an utter romantic named Fred with a wide grin on his lips, in the shade of a tent filled with various television screens. Three cameramen wander the shallows in search of the perfect shot. Local artisans scatter rose petals in a path along the sand, leading to an elaborate platform covered in tropical florals. Two drones hover overhead, undoubtedly ready for filming. There's a table arranged with food and drinks, though no one seems to be paying it any mind. The cowboy is nowhere to be found, not that Sam really knows what he looks like seeing as they've never met, but she's assuming it will be hard to miss a six-foot-two redhead with six-pack abs, if Em's description of the man is anything to go by...and Sam is sort of hoping it is, because, well, yum. Eye candy. But Nina steps directly in her line of sight before she has a chance to scan the rest of the area.

As if reading her mind, the producer comments, "Cooper won't be here for another hour. Weren't you listening? It's time to film your pre-proposal interview."

With that, Nina hops over the side of the boat and lands with a splash in the shallow surf. Phil, her personal cameraman, follows. Sam glances down at her floor-length ball gown with a frown. *What the hell am I supposed to do?*

She could ask Nina, but why give the woman the satisfaction? Instead, she takes advantage of the thigh-high slit in the ivory material and gathers the skirt in one hand before launching herself over the edge of the speedboat.

A horrified cry pierces the air.

Too late, Sam thinks with a smirk as her toes touch cool water then sink satisfyingly into the sand. There's a small splash, but none of it reaches the fabric bunched around her waist. Half the crew probably gets a clear view of her thong, but whatever. She has a killer ass and she knows it.

"The fuck, Emily," Nina mutters and shakes her head. "I was just about to get someone to help you down."

Sam shrugs. "Oops."

"Oops?" Nina deadpans. "It took us an hour to pick out that dress this morning, and I don't have time to find you another."

"Relax, Nina," Sam coos. Then she reaches back and snatches her heels from where they're perched on the side of the boat. "It's all good."

A glower passes briefly over the producer's eyes, but she clenches her jaw and holds whatever retort she wants to say inside.

Pushing the woman's buttons is too much fun. Sam smiles sweetly and adds, "Don't I have an interview to get to?"

Nina glances up at the sky as if praying for strength, then simply sighs. "Follow me."

Ten minutes later, Sam is arranged on the flower-covered platform with a camera in her face. Off to the side there's a large fan to provide the perfect "ocean" breeze.

Nina stands behind the bulbous lens with her clipboard, and the interview begins.

"How are you feeling?"

"Are you ready to get engaged?"

"Do you miss Ethan?"

"Are you excited to start your life with Cooper?"

"What do you love most about him?"

"Do you think you made the right choice?"

"Are you sorry for sending Ethan home?"

"Will you move to Cooper's ranch?"

"Did you find the love of your life?"

"What does your happily ever after look like?"

It's an endless stream of leading questions designed to force Sam to lower her walls by catching her off guard. The topics jump confusingly back and forth. Nina asks her to repeat certain things, then asks the same question twice as if to trip her up and elicit a different answer. By the end of the session, Sam's half-delirious from the whirlwind and can hardly even remember anything she said. But Nina's smiling, so undoubtedly somewhere in the madness, she provided the perfect twenty-second sound bite for TV.

They move on to some filler footage and Phil directs Sam around the small platform.

"Can you stand here? But look there. Not quite so serious. How about a smile? Soften your lips. Straighten your back. Can you lift your chin just a little bit more? Now think about love while you stare out at the horizon. Okay, maybe not love. Let's try...chocolate cake? Skittles? Ice cream?"

It's exhausting.

And a bit depressing, if she's being honest.

As a longtime fan of the show, she's always known *The Love Match* is nothing more than a Hollywood-crafted vision of true love. The corny dates. The over-the-top drama. The cheesy one-liners. And yet...the emotional aspect always seemed so authentic. By the end of every season, the central romances inevitably warmed her shriveled, bitter heart. The proposals pierced her cynical walls. So being here and actually seeing how much of the story is staged for the cameras is a total disappointment, like finding out Santa Claus isn't real. Sam's already over it, and they haven't even begun.

As if on cue, Nina lifts her fingers to her comm. "Cooper's on his way? Great. We just finished up. Is Keith ready? Send him over."

The middle-aged host known as America's favorite father figure emerges from one of the production tents in a three-piece suit and a full face of makeup designed to appear natural on-screen. He marches across the sand with what can only be described as a resting bitch face, meaning he's either extremely focused on the interview or extremely over his twenty-second time filming a season finale, and Sam's leaning toward the latter. Still, her heart flutters as he approaches. After so many years watching him help the leads of the show navigate their love stories, she's a bit starstruck. Keith Holson is really here. He's really on his way to talk to her. Sure, he thinks she's Emily. And yes, she's planning to turn down the proposal, so, no, he isn't about to send her off into the sunset of her very own happily ever after.

But it's still pretty fucking cool.

Though it gets a bit less cool when he stops right next to her without even bothering to look in her direction, let alone say hello. The director starts the countdown. At ten, Keith finally makes eye contact. At seven, he puffs out his chest. At four, he widens his lips into what Sam had once thought of as an endearingly lovable smile, but now recognizes as a hollow, made-for-TV grin. It doesn't reach his eyes, and the realization leaves her a bit sad, even if by one he looks exactly as he always has on TV. When the camera starts rolling, he launches into a prepared diatribe about romance and it's all Sam can do not to roll her eyes.

I'm Emily.

I'm nice.

I'm— Ugh.

Who am I kidding? I'm Samantha. I'm a New York City asshole who never takes shit from anyone, but right now, I need to sweetly turn down this proposal without revealing my inner bitch so everyone watching stays in love with my sister and wants to buy her jewelry.

Easier said than done.

"Are you ready for the rest of your life to begin?" Keith asks, his tone so dramatic she almost wants to laugh. It's his fourth time asking the question, and this time he must get the intonations right, because the executive producer gives a thumbs-up from the production tent, and the cameras finally switch to her.

"Yes," Sam says plainly.

From the side, Nina snorts.

"How about a little more enthusiasm this time?" Fred calls and they signal to go again.

"Yes!" Sam half shouts.

"Okay, too much enthusiasm," Fred comments and Sam rolls her eyes. "Let's tone it down just a touch."

"Yes."

"Yes."

"Yes."

"Yes."

She repeats the word so many times it actually starts to sound weird, like an alien language rolling uncomfortably off her tongue. The meaning is completely stripped.

"Try smiling."

"Not like that."

"You're giving me serial killer right now. Less hostile. More cheerful."

"Imagine you're a fairy-tale princess."

For the love of god.

Sam grinds her teeth and takes a deep breath, attempting to strip the daggers from her gaze. It's time to channel her inner Cinderella. No, not the meek, subservient one, but the total boss bitch who defied her wicked stepmother, snuck out of the house to crash a ball, entranced everyone before hightailing it out at midnight without a backward glance at the lovestruck prince, and then offered her horrible stepsisters a soul-crushing *fuck you* by sweetly supplying the second glass slipper after the first one broke. No matter how kind people want to paint her, Cinderella oozes the sort of take-no-prisoners attitude Sam can't help but admire.

You can do this.

You've got this.

"Yes," she finally says.

"That's the one!" Fred cheers.

With the cameras still rolling, Keith gently takes her by the shoulders. "Then turn around."

"Wait!" Fred shouts and Keith freezes with his hands on her bare skin, palms slightly moist in the heat. It takes everything Sam has not to writhe uncomfortably as the cameramen shift positions to get ready for the arrival of her winning suitor. Nina explained earlier that they shoot the proposal itself in a single take to capture as much true emotion as possible, so genuine relief fills her heart at the knowledge that this lesson in patience is almost over.

After a few minutes, Fred gives the signal and Keith applies pressure. Sam slowly spins around and—

Holy shit.

She freezes. Her heart flips. Just like that, the cameras and the crew all fade. The world around her blurs until the only thing in perfect clarity is the man striding confidently toward her. Even though Sam spends her days surrounded by men in suits, she's never seen a single one who looks as good as Cooper Kelley does right now. Black slacks hug his thick thighs and a matching jacket stretches across his broad shoulders. The formality of his crisp white button-up and dark tie are offset by the straw cowboy hat settled low on his head. Her gaze drops to the scuffed and worn leather boots kicking through the sand. She's used to overgrown boys flashing their fat wallets, but he oozes the sort of rugged masculinity that can't be bought. It's in the casual way he saunters closer, not rushing, sure the world will wait, as if fully aware of the choke hold he has on everyone around him.

And dammit, she *is* in a choke hold—unable to breathe, unable to think when he finally lifts his head high enough to clear the shadows from his face.

Sam gulps.

His jaw is so chiseled it might as well be cut from stone. Red hair curls out under the brim of his hat. His skin is the perfect shade of sun-kissed that can only be achieved by long days spent working outdoors. He crooks his lips in a lazy half-smile, bringing out the dimple in his right cheek, and Sam's knees go weak. When he sweeps his gaze over her dress, tracing every line of her curves, a flush spreads across her whole body. The moment those crystal-clear emerald eyes meet hers, it turns to an inferno.

She may actually whimper.

I could kill Emily right now. Just murder her.

Sure, Em said he was handsome. And okay, her description of him as a six-foot-two redhead with six-pack abs was technically accurate. But so is describing the sun as warm. Sam had been expecting a good-looking cowboy. Instead, she's facing a god.

Her throat goes dry.

She's woozy, parched.

The man is sex on a stick and all she wants to do is lick him.

What? No.

Well, maybe.

Okay, yes.

Yes, licking is definitely on the list of things I want to do to him.

Cooper comes to a stop about a foot away, and it's all she can do not to drool. The hotness overload leaves her lightheaded. He opens his mouth and she tries to concentrate on what he's saying—she really does—but all she can think about as she watches his lips move is how they'd feel pressed against her skin. Every inch of her body is on fire from the fantasy playing out in the back of her thoughts. But just as those imaginary lips begin to work their way south, she realizes he stopped talking and she has no idea what he just said.

Stupid overactive imagination.

Sam blinks into the lengthening silence.

Focus.

Focus.

The cowboy drops to one knee and takes her by the hand, his fingers rough and calloused. The slight scratch sends a pleasurable shiver down her spine. Those hands have been places. They know things. Just like that her thoughts are off and running once more, wondering exactly what they can do as he lifts her fingers to his lips. The gentle kiss leaves her breathless, and that's before he offers a wicked grin Sam can feel all the way to her core.

Her muscles clench.

"So what do you say?" he asks, looking up at her with those captivating green eyes, his Midwestern drawl turning her bones to noodles. "Will you make me the happiest man in the world?"

Only one thought enters her mind. "Sure."

When he slides the ring over her finger, reality hits.

The proposal. The TV show. Her sister.

Fuck!

PANIC FLOODS those large golden eyes, and for the first time that morning Cooper finally understands what the hell is going on. Why her gaze filled with heat the moment she saw him on the beach. Why the sight of it stirred a similar reaction in him. Why she looks exactly the same but feels entirely different.

He's spent the past six weeks with Emily. He's kissed her on camera and he's joked with her off-screen. He's held her in his arms. He's dug his fingers into her thighs while she wrapped her legs around him. He's done just about everything someone can do when pretending to fall in love with another person on national television, and more so, he's become her friend. Which is all to say, he knows Emily.

And this sure as shit ain't her.

Hello, Samantha, he thinks as the wheels visibly spin in her gaze. Cooper understands her panic. Emily would have told her the plan before they made the swap. It's been figured out for days, ever since that fateful night they shared in the dream suite while the cameras were down. Instead of the night of passion the show intended, he and Emily were finally able to tell each other the truth—that they cared for each other in a completely platonic way, and nothing more. So rather than cement their relationship, they used the hours to plan their mutually beneficial exits. He was going to propose. She was going to let him down easy. He'd walk away as the obvious lead for the next season, securing the publicity he's so desperately hoping will help his family's ranch. And Emily would walk away with her head held high, her jewelry business thriving, and her future open for the man who truly held her heart. It was a win-win situation, now completely undone by a single, clearly stated word.

Sure.

Unfortunately, he's far too intrigued by Sam to be annoyed. Why did she say yes? Why did she go off-script? And why, oh why, did his heart lurch the moment she did?

Sam opens her mouth to speak.

Alarms he doesn't understand go off in Cooper's head. While he made a promise to his mother to always be a gentleman, he knows if he doesn't act now, he'll lose his chance to get answers. The show will be over. This woman will slip through his fingers. And the spark warming his chest for the first time in six years will sputter out. So he does the one thing he knows will keep her from talking.

He yanks on her hand so she falls into his lap and

slides one arm around her waist in an exaggerated dip. She gasps softly, taken by surprise. Her eyes flash with undeniable interest. Using the opening, he slides his fingers through her hair, grips the back of her head, and kisses her with everything he's got.

At first she goes rigid.

Cooper almost stops. The last thing he would ever want to do is kiss a woman against her will. But when he starts to retreat, she grabs the collar of his shirt, arches her neck to deepen the angle, and pulls him closer.

Hello, Samantha, he thinks again, this time unable to stop a grin from twisting his lips as he sinks into the kiss. Her lithe body presses flush against him, her frame petite but not at all fragile, perfect for, well, things he shouldn't be thinking about when a dozen cameras are watching him from every angle, just hoping for a show.

Still, he doesn't pull away.

There's a subtle taste on her lips he can't quite decipher, one he needs more of as he slides his tongue against hers, sucking on the flavor. Memories stir, of fragrant flowers and fresh air, as if he's galloping across the springtime plains with nothing but the sun and sky and open land stretched before him. A cool breeze brushes his cheeks, like a promise of wild, untapped freedom.

"Cut!"

Sam doesn't pull away. And well, shit, he's not going to be the first to break, so Cooper just keeps moving against her pillowy lips, intoxicated by that sweet elixir.

"Cut!"

She pulls him infinitesimally closer as a quiet groan escapes her lips. He digs his fingers into the soft curve of her hip.

"Cut!"

Sam shifts her face just enough to deepen the kiss, her mouth opening wider in invitation. Cooper pulls her hair taut, taking the lead and arching her head where he wants it, eager to accept. Then—

"Cut!" Nina shouts for the fourth time, but she must've obtained a bullhorn, because the sound comes blasting across the beach with the force of a hurricane. "For the love of god, cut, before we all self-combust. It was a hundred freaking degrees before you two started going at it like dogs in heat. I'm sweaty enough as is."

Sam rears back, slightly dazed. She drops her gaze to his mouth and darts out her tongue, licking the taste of him off her lips before she swallows. It immediately makes him think of other places he wouldn't mind having her tongue. Heat rushes through him like a bolt of lightning, straight to his groin.

No, I wouldn't mind that at all...

Before the situation becomes embarrassing, horror floods her eyes. She sucks in a breath and narrows her gaze as if in accusation, then shoves him hard in the chest. Of course, seeing as he's twice her weight with about a foot on her, instead of the push moving him, it only serves to send her flying backward. With a yelp, Sam crash-lands on her ass by his feet.

"Graceful, Em." Nina snorts. Then louder, she calls,

"Let's get a close-up of Cooper putting the ring on her finger, some wide-angle shots, and then the season is a wrap, people!"

"Wait!" Sam gulps, cutting her face toward the producer. "Can we do that again? The proposal, I mean. I can be more enthusiastic, more energetic, more excited, more—"

She looks to him for help.

Cooper shrugs. "I thought it went pretty well, myself."

Sam bares her teeth like a lioness, and it's all he can do not to laugh out loud. He can't explain why he finds her obvious exasperation so amusing, only that he does. And the devilish cowboy inside, the one he thought he'd left behind a long time ago, can't help but keep pushing those beautiful buttons. So he rubs his thumb over his bottom lip, and then pointedly displays the pink lipstick he knows is staining his skin.

Her eyes flare with heat.

He wishes he could tell if it were fury or lust, but she turns her attention back to the production tent before he gets the chance. Honestly, he'll take either one.

"One more time," Sam pleads. "Please."

"We don't need it," Nina says.

"But—"

"You were perfect, Emily. Absolutely perfect." The producer turns to the side and snaps her fingers. "Makeup, get over here. We need—"

Sam suddenly gasps.

Her hand goes to her forehead.

She teeters.

Is she—

Before he can complete the thought, her eyes roll back and she gracefully crumples in on herself. Still kneeling, Cooper catches her easily...a little too easily, almost as if she planned it that way. The suspicion is confirmed a second later when she slyly peeks through a single cracked eyelid before going dramatically limp in his arms. He coughs to cover up a snort and glances to Nina. The producer rolls her eyes, clearly not fooled.

"We have an hour of filming left, Emily, and you're not getting out of it that easily."

The woman in his arms doesn't stir.

Nina scoffs, but after another few seconds it turns to a sigh. "Can someone get her a glass of water, please? Now!"

While the crew scrambles to find a bottle of water, Cooper studies the freckles painted across Sam's ivory cheeks, utterly fascinated by the woman in his arms. He shouldn't be surprised she's resorted to the world's most poorly acted fainting spell—Emily described her as a fearless go-getter prone to dramatics—but he doesn't understand what she thinks it will achieve. They already filmed the proposal. It's done. Over. *Finito*.

A fact confirmed when Nina dryly announces, "Oh, well. If she doesn't wake up, I guess we're done filming for the day, and we'll all have to come back here tomorrow to get the last few shots we need."

Sam's eyes fly open. "I'm up."

"I thought you might be."

"I'm ready."

"Good."

Sam offers him a grateful look before she stands back up and brushes the wrinkles from her dress. Simple as that, he understands why she did it. She needed a second to breathe, to plot. There's no more panic in her gaze as the makeup team rushes over to clean them back up. There's only stubborn determination. She has a plan—that much is clear. He just wishes he knew what the calculations spinning beneath her furrowed brow were trying to say.

Because suddenly he's the one who's panicking. While they kiss and hug and smile for the cameras, capturing the last few romantic shots needed to complete the picture of a happily engaged couple, his anxiety mounts. Sam is all business. They've switched places. The focus never leaves her eyes. The heady vixen is gone. And without that distraction, the reality of his actions finally sinks in.

Shit. Cooper grimaces. *What did I just do?*

The same thing he always did.

Think, son. His dad's proud voice echoes up from the depths. *For once in your life, think beyond yourself. This isn't about you. It's about this ranch. It's about this family. It's about how much your mother went through to bring you into the world so you could carry on this legacy. Show some respect. Show some gratitude. Get your ass out of the clouds and your boots back on this dirt where you belong. She doesn't have much time left, and I'll be damned if the last thing she sees of her son is all the opportunities he's thrown away.*

That conversation changed everything.

For better.

For worse.

And even though six years have passed since his father spoke those words, it could have been merely weeks. He knows what his father was thinking while he stood on the front porch, lifted his mug to his lips, and silently watched his son drive away on another harebrained adventure. Why bother speaking when everything he needed to say lived in those chastising eyes?

To his father, the show is just another selfish attempt to chase a foolish dream, to put himself before the ranch, to run away.

But he's not a kid anymore.

He made mistakes. He owns them.

This is different.

Every year, the taxes increase and the cattle become more expensive. They're maxed out on government leases. Maxed out on investments. If something doesn't change, and soon, they'll have to sell some of the land. And maybe to some people, that might sound reasonable, like no big deal. As one of the largest cattle ranches in the United States they have roughly two hundred thousand acres of it, after all. But his father would rather die than lose even a foot of what's been passed down to him. It's not just dirt. It's generations of blood and sweat. It's everything his father has worked for and his father before him, back and back over a hundred and fifty years. It's a legacy, and a burden, and a gift.

It's everything to his father.

And though the man might not believe it, it's everything to Cooper, too.

When Trish first called to offer him a spot as one of the suitors, he laughed in her face. He couldn't take six weeks off to play Prince Charming for some Hollywood executive who didn't know the first thing about his life. It would be fall on the ranch. There were calves to wean, fences to mend, and endless preparations to make before winter buried them in snow. She could find another cowboy to play hero on TV, one of those assholes with shiny boots that had never seen the inside of a pen. He wasn't interested.

"I don't want another cowboy," she told him. "I want you."

"All due respect, ma'am, I don't really care what you want."

"You should."

"And why's that?"

She didn't answer. Instead, she took a deep breath, clearly pivoting the conversation. "There are thousands of cowboys in this country, Cooper Kelley. Aren't you curious how I found you?"

"I know how you found me."

That fucking video had become the bane of his existence. He'd been in town running some errands when a summer thunderstorm struck, soaking him through by the time it was done. Before the drive home, he stripped off his shirt and tossed it into the bed of his truck. The second he settled his hat back on, a series of catcalls filled the air. Cooper had turned to find a tableful of his mother's old friends outside the local coffee shop. The women in town had teased him ever since he was a boy, and they'd keep doing it until he was an old man, he was sure. It was easier to roll with it, he'd learned, than to fight it. So with a roll of his eyes, he offered them a friendly grin and tipped his hat.

"Morning, ladies."

And that would have been it, had a scream not pierced the air. Cooper spun. A young woman chased after a baby carriage. It rolled into the street. A car sped closer. He acted on instinct and jumped for the stroller. What he didn't realize as he hastily pushed the baby out of harm's way, was that one of the teenagers who worked in the coffee shop was filming the whole thing. She posted it to some app, and forty-eight hours later, every news station in the country was calling him, asking for an interview with the "six-pack savior" as he'd been dubbed. And hell if he'd ever live that name down. He said no to all of them, just like he was going to say no to Trish. Until...

"I know you think I don't know anything about your life, and maybe I don't, but I do know this," Trish said before he could find a polite way to hang up the phone. "Last year, the cattle industry had a three percent decline, and it was the smallest herd size in over sixty years. Reports predict a total collapse of the industry by 2030. And even if it doesn't fall apart, every article I read in preparation for this phone call says cattle prices are declining while maintenance costs are rising. Now, I don't know much about your ranch, but my guess is you're feeling the squeeze right alongside everyone else."

"I don't need your insights into how to do my job."

"Of course not, but can you answer one more question for me? And then I'll let you go and never call you again."

"All right. One more."

"Do you know how much someone with five hundred thousand followers on Instagram can charge for a single post?"

"What does that matter?"

"Ten thousand dollars. For one post. If you arrange a sponsored post every week, that's half a million dollars right there. Not to mention brand partnerships, paid appearances, podcasts, book deals, and more."

"I still don't see your point, ma'am."

"Five hundred thousand is the average number of followers a top-four suitor on the show walks away with. If you make it to the finale, that bumps to seven hundred and fifty thousand. And if you get selected as next season's lead, it jumps to two million. Think about that, Cooper Kelley, before you turn down my offer. Your ranch needs money? Longevity? A new angle in a failing industry? I can give it to you. All you need to do is take a six-week vacation around the world. Are you still sure you want to say no?"

"What makes you think all those people would have any interest in me?"

"I've been doing this a long time. I know a leading man when I see one. The real question is do you?"

No, he didn't.

He still doesn't. But that hardly changes the facts. She caught him hook, line, and sinker with her argument. Numbers started spinning the second she finished talking, and weeks later, they're still there dancing across his thoughts, impossible to ignore. Anyone willing to spit in the face of an easy million dollars for posting a few photos is a fool, and Cooper isn't that. He can do a lot with that sort of money, for the ranch, for his family. His father will never understand, but that doesn't matter. Results matter. Which is why he agreed to the deal with Emily, especially after the producers made it clear he would be handed the role as the next lead on a silver platter.

And now he's gone and ruined it.

Well, shit.

Cooper is so in his head he hardly realizes time passing. Suddenly, the beach is gone, the boat ride back to the resort is over, and he's outside the front door of a very familiar over-ocean bungalow—Emily's.

Except it's not Emily's anymore.

It's Sam's. And his.

It's theirs.

Because they're engaged. And supposedly in love. Why wouldn't they want to spend the next five days in paradise sharing the same room together?

Again... *Shit.*

"Here's your itinerary," Nina says as she releases some

papers from her clipboard. Sam quickly reviews them while Cooper stands beside her, mute. His heart thunders. "We booked a few excursions for you guys while you're here, but feel free to call the front desk to adjust the plans. Trish, Fred, and I will be in the bungalow next door for a few days, courtesy of the network, so holler if you need anything. Here are your phones out of purgatory and your wallets. Everything else is inside. I'll be in touch in a few weeks with some follow-up, so don't lose my number. Otherwise, you're free."

Free.

The word clangs around his head like a gong gone wrong, so loud he can't think. He stands there, immobile from the reverberations.

"No need to be shy now," Nina says, rolling her eyes as she looks between them. "I saw the aftermath of your dream suite, remember? And an hour ago you just about set the beach on fire, so go, enjoy. It's not every day you get a free week in paradise."

She gives them both an encouraging push. Cooper stumbles through the door. Sam does too. They stare at each other as it closes with a gentle *click.*

Free.

Free?

He's never felt more trapped in his life. And that's before the petite redhead beside him furrows her brow, places both her palms on his chest, and gives him a good, hard shove.

CHAPTER THREE

Sam

"WHAT THE HELL WAS THAT KISS?" Sam snaps before she thinks better of it. She's been playing the good girl all day and she's over it.

Cooper, for his part, looks shocked as he stumbles backward. It doesn't last long. One blink and he's in control again as he leans casually against the wall and crosses his arms over his chest. And dammit if that doesn't pull his suit jacket taut in all the right places, highlighting the rock-hard muscles practically bulging out of the fabric...rock-hard muscles she had her hands all over earlier that day...rock-hard muscles that held her as if she weighed nothing at all...rock-hard muscles that—

So not the point.

Sam cocks a brow. "Well?"

He smirks as if to say, *Challenge accepted,* and raises his own brow. "What the hell was that *yes*?"

Temporary insanity from hotness overload, not that she'll admit it to him. She shrugs. "An accident."

"So was the kiss."

She scoffs. "So you *accidentally* pulled me into your lap and your lips *accidentally* landed on my mouth and you *accidentally* didn't let me go for five minutes?"

"Yup," he states, letting the *p* really pop. She narrows her eyes. He grins. "Just like you *accidentally* kissed me back."

Okay, that *was* an accident. She doesn't know how it happened. One moment she was reaching up to push him away, and the next her fingers were twisting in his jacket and she'd yanked him closer.

It was his fault.

Did he have to look so delicious? Even now, when she wants to wring his neck, she can't help but admire how the black suit brings out the brilliant emerald of his eyes and how the curve of his cowboy hat highlights the cut edge of his jaw. She wants to rip it right off his head...for more reasons than one.

Gah!

"You knew the plan!" she retorts, launching this fiery ball of blame right back into his court. "You could have given me a minute to course correct before launching yourself at me like some sort of heathen."

"Aren't you the one who, quite literally, threw herself into my arms?"

Again with the technical details. She rolls her eyes. "I fainted."

He barks out a laugh. "Sure, you did."

"That's neither here nor there. We're talking about you, and—"

"And why *are* we talking about me?" His gaze cuts into her like a knife, making her freeze. "I'm pretty sure we should be talking about you. Samantha."

Shit.

Shit. Shit. Shit.

Logically, yes, she knew she'd have to confess the truth eventually. But not now. Not when she's fighting tooth and nail for the upper hand in an argument she knows she has no right to win. To even wage. Obviously, this whole messed-up day is entirely her fault. If she had just said no like he and Emily planned, none of this would be happening. But she didn't. And she's determined to share the blame if it kills her. Because it's his fault, too. His fault for being so goddamn attractive she lost her ever-loving mind right when she needed it most. Screw genetics. He knew exactly what he was doing with that smolder.

If being a woman in a man's corporate world has taught her anything, it's don't admit defeat. Don't show weakness. And always, always stay on the offensive.

So instead of doing the normal thing—the (*yes, okay*) right thing—and apologizing, she lifts her chin in an arrogant tilt. "How'd you know it was me?"

"You might look exactly like your sister, but there's one thing you've got that Emily doesn't." He pauses to rake his gaze over every inch of her body. The slow perusal starts at her toes, then glides higher with deliberate intention, the path of his focus burning like a warm caress. By the time he finds her eyes, her lungs blaze from lack of oxygen, and it takes all her effort just to breathe. "Claws."

She grins, trying her best to cut the tension currently causing her cheeks to flame. "I take that as a compliment."

The wicked edge of his answering smile has her thighs clenching. "You should."

Don't think about sex.

Don't think about sex.

No matter how hard she tries, she can't stop from picturing her legs wrapped around him as her nails dig into his thick shoulders, like, well, claws. She can't help it. When she sees something she wants, she takes it. Always has, always will—except now. Now, she has to tell her inner sex kitten to take a back seat because he's her sister's ex. He's a freaking cowboy. He's her—*I can't believe I'm even saying this right now!*—fiancé. He's too attractive for his own good. And most importantly, she will not let him win whatever this power struggle is between them.

No fucking way.

She'd rather spend the next five nights masturbating any thought of him away than let this cocky asswipe get the best of her.

Except…

The image of his hands gripping her thighs and her fingers scratching down his back invades again.

That goddamn smolder.

His smile deepens, as if he knows exactly what's going

on in the back of her mind, and then he shrugs. "Besides, you don't kiss like your sister."

"Eww," Sam whines. The passionate embrace she'd been imagining is wiped away in an instant as nausea curls in her gut. "Eww. Eww. Eww. We've never kissed the same guy before. This is...incestuous. I feel dirty."

As if taking glee in her disgust, he keeps talking. "Emily kisses like a gentle summer rain, soft and warm and comforting. You, on the other hand, kiss like a fucking tornado. You're out to destroy."

She doesn't know what to make of that, but she definitely knows she doesn't want to hear more. So Sam sticks her fingers in her ears and sings, "La la la la. I'm not listening. La la la."

After a moment, he gently encircles her wrists and pulls. "Relax, Cujo."

"Cujo?"

"You know, the dog who gets rabies and goes on a killing spree in that movie?"

"The St. Bernard?" She wrinkles her nose. "They drool."

"*That's* what you're taking offense to?"

"Oh, I'm fine being an attack dog, but a St. Bernard? Really?"

"You'd rather be a rabid...?"

"Spaniel?"

"Too friendly." He shakes his head and grabs his chin between his fingers as he sizes her up. Then he snaps. "Got it. Doberman pinscher."

Sam thinks for a moment before nodding. "I accept."

"What am I?" He grins. "No, wait. I've got it. A golden retriever."

"No." She frowns and folds her arms across her chest, studying his open expression until it hits her. "Husky."

He rears back. "A husky?"

"Yeah, they're cute and they know it and they use that power to be mischievous motherfuckers."

"So," he practically purrs and tilts his head to the side. Beneath the rim of that cowboy hat, his expression can be described as pure sin. "You think I'm cute."

"And a mischievous motherfucker."

His lip quirks just enough to bring out a dimple in his left cheek. "Guilty."

"Which brings us back to that kiss," she says, jamming her finger into the center of his very broad chest. "And the fact that you knew exactly what you were doing."

"If you say so, Cuj."

Then he shrugs.

Shrugs!

The gall...

Why is this turning me on?

She hates arrogant men. Hates them. Every one except this one, apparently, because he seems as though he just might have the goods to back it up if that kiss was anything to go by.

I need to stop thinking about it.

Easier said than done. It was a good kiss. The best she's had in months. Years. The best ever?

You're still thinking about it.

Yes, she is…thinking about his mouth practically devouring her, and his sturdy arms wrapped around her, and his tongue just barely delving between her parted lips.

Is it hot in here?

Sam gulps.

For once, he doesn't seem to notice his effect. Instead, he lets out a frustrated breath. Then he lifts his hat and runs his hand through his luscious red hair before settling the hat back in place. A nervous habit, she assumes.

"Instead of focusing on what happened, why don't we figure out what to do about it?" He sharpens his focus on her. "You have a plan. I know you do."

"Obviously, I have a plan."

A beat of silence passes.

"Which is…"

Sam sighs. The plan sounded a lot better back on the beach, when it was sunny out and they were in the open air and he wasn't so close. Here in the shadows of a rapidly shrinking private bungalow, with her finger still on his chest, she isn't so sure.

Wait—why is my finger still on his chest?

She tries to order her arm to drop, but instead her rebellious palm flattens against him, feeling the defined curve of his pec. She swallows. He arches a brow. She yanks her arm away as if burned.

Focus, dammit.

"My plan," she starts, but has to pause to wet her annoyingly dry throat. She crosses her arms and stuffs her treacherous fingers under her armpits to keep them in place, then proudly straightens her spine to get back a semblance of the upper hand. "My plan is to pretend we're engaged for the next five days while we're stuck on this island and in this resort with the crew. I'll fill Em in on everything when I get home, and the two of you can then announce your breakup at the live finale. The distance was too much. Outside of the show you realized how different your lives are. She didn't want to move to your ranch and you couldn't leave. Yada yada. All understandable reasons for a split. She'll walk away with her business and reputation untainted. And if you inform Nina of the split with some time to prepare, I have no doubt the showrunners will offer you the lead next season. They definitely aren't going to offer it to that tool I sent home yesterday. It's a win-win, exactly like you both wanted, just a few weeks later than planned."

He purses his lips as he thinks over what she said. But it's a good plan—the only fix, and they both know it. Still, he cocks his head to the side.

"There's only one problem as I see it," he murmurs, tone serious. "We have to spend five days together. Five days sharing this bungalow. Five days playing engaged..." He trails off with a deep exhale. Just as a concerned line forms between her brows, he breaks the tension with a sudden twist of his lips. "Think you can keep your hands off me for that long?"

His gaze drops to where her wayward palm has landed back on his chest and he snickers.

What the hell?

When did that happen?

She snaps her hand back—*This is getting ridiculous*—and sneers. "You know, my sister told me you were the nice one. *A complete and total gentleman,* I believe were her exact words. But I see you, Cooper Kelley. I. See. You."

"And what exactly do you see, darlin'?" he murmurs, laying his accent on thick and leaning closer.

Sam doesn't shy away. She's no shrinking violet. Instead, she follows suit, not stopping until their noses are a hair's breadth from touching. "A wolf in sheep's clothing, but don't worry, buddy. It takes one to know one, and my teeth are bared."

"Aww. That's cute. But I'm not a wolf, Cuj," he whispers. The touch of his warm breath sends a ripple down her spine. Her every nerve stands alert, buzzing underneath the surface of her skin. A sudden gleam enters his eyes, laced with promise, with innuendo, with challenge. The dimple in his cheek deepens. "I'm a cowboy. Think you can handle it?"

"Oh, I can handle it," she promises as she slides her hand up his chest, deliberately this time, letting her fingers drift over hard muscles and hot skin, all the way up to the back of his neck. Desire flashes in his eyes. She smirks and snatches that hat off his head, before taking a step back. Then she plops it right down on hers, holding his gaze as she says, "The real question is, can you?"

Not giving him time to answer, Sam spins on her heels and marches toward the bedroom door. Halfway there, fully aware of his eyes still on her, she reaches back to unzip her dress.

You want to play, cowboy?

Let's play.

The sequins have been scratching her all day, and it's nothing but a relief as she wriggles the straps from her shoulders. The material drops straight to the floor without even a hitch in her step. Cool air brushes over her exposed skin, sending a wave of goose bumps across her flesh. She's in nothing but a thong, high heels, and his hat.

Cooper sucks in a sharp breath.

Sam grins.

"I'm taking the bedroom," she calls over her shoulder, not bothering to glance back as she slams the door in his face.

CHAPTER FOUR

cooper

WELL, *fuck me if that isn't the sexiest thing I've ever seen.*

Two minutes since she slammed the door and he's still rooted to the spot, picturing the round curve of her perfectly grabbable ass. He wonders if she even knows what it means in his world to take a cowboy's hat—*that you want to take him for a ride.* And damn if that doesn't sound like a wonderful proposition. Too wonderful. He's hard as a rock and though half of him wants to charge after her and call her bluff, the other half—the sane half— is exactly what she said. Too much of a gentleman to invade her privacy like that.

So instead of barging into her room, he takes another minute to collect himself before walking stiffly into the living area. He'll make it into her bedroom soon enough, he has no doubt. There's too much fire between them to last five days in the same suite without combusting. But he sure as hell won't be the one to break first. So tonight, he'll have to make do with the couch.

It's comfortable enough, but no cushion in the world is soft enough to stop his fidgeting. Every time he closes his eyes, all he sees is her bare skin in the moonlight before she disappeared behind the door, nothing but a slim white strip of fabric to block his view, and the challenge in her eyes as she settled her hat on his head. To say his balls are blue by the time he falls asleep is the understatement of the century. He may as well be a Smurf.

I'll play your game, Samantha Peters, he thinks just before consciousness slips away. *But I sure as shit don't plan on playing fair.*

The next morning, Cooper wakes with the dawn. A lifetime of rising alongside the sun is hard to overcome. It's ground into him. Innate at this point. But it works in his favor. He sits for an hour drinking coffee and secretly plotting while pastel colors dance over the sea. By the time he hears a rustle on the other side of the bedroom door, he knows exactly what to do.

Before Sam emerges from the room, Cooper strips off his shirt, pants, and socks, until nothing remains but his boxer briefs. Then he walks through the sliding glass door and onto the small deck suspended over the water. After pausing just long enough to stretch his arms over his head to awaken his tired muscles, he dives headfirst over the side. The water swallows him like a warm embrace, almost on the wrong side of refreshing compared to the frigid Nebraskan rivers and lakes he's used to. He drifts there for a moment, completely at peace as the world slips away. There's no current trying to drag him downstream, no weeds trying to pull him into murky depths. He can see all the way to the sandy bottom as the ocean holds him close, rocking him side to side with the gently flowing tide. It's so different from home—so marvelously different he wants to soak in every second. Who knows when or if he'll ever be in a place like this again?

No matter how much he wishes his motives for joining the show were purely about the ranch, it was about this moment right here too. He can't lie. The chance to travel was just as much of a draw. Since the day he was born, he's known exactly where he'd be for the rest of his life and exactly what he'd be doing. It's an odd way to live. Growing up, he'd listen enviously to his friends speak of their lives like uncharted maps, no set destination, no chosen path. But as an only child, his destiny was the ranch whether he wanted it or not. Oh, he'd rebelled, of course. Ran away from home at sixteen. Joined the rodeo after high school. Went to college and threatened to never come back. Then his mom got sick. She'd needed him. So he came home, simple as that. He worked beside his father. He learned the business of the ranch, not just the hard labor. And he loves it. He really does. The horses. The cows. Sunsets over the open fields. Stars as far as the eye can see. It can be backbreaking, but also exhilarating. And when it boils down to it, the ranch is home. It's deeper than a legacy. It's in his blood. Yet no matter how hard he tries, beneath the weight of the responsibility hides an itch he's desperate to scratch—to see the world, to be free.

Trish had been Eve with the apple when she made her offer to do the show, and he'd been Adam, unable to stop himself from taking a bite. They'd gone from Los Angeles to London to Paris to Rome to the Okavango Delta—places he thought he'd never see outside of his dreams—and selfishly he still wants more.

Maybe my father was right after all.

The thought makes his chest burn.

Or is that just his lungs from lack of air?

All at once, Cooper surges to the surface. He flicks the water from his hair and focuses back on the bungalow to escape the nagging doubts. Movement catches his eye as Sam pads across the living room. She peeks casually at the empty couch, then looks around curiously. She's the exact distraction he needs.

It's go time.

Cooper swims back to the edge of the deck. Forgoing the ladder, he places his palms on the wood and hauls himself out of the ocean in one smooth motion, perfectly aware of how his muscles flex and strain. He doesn't look up as he tucks his feet underneath him and pushes to standing. The sun shines overhead. Droplets glisten over his mostly naked frame. Water courses down his bare chest. He brings his hand up to smooth his hair out of his face. With his bicep flexed beside his head, he finally looks up to meet the eyes he knows are on him.

Sam stares at him, her mouth agape, practically

drooling. His lips curl into a grin. She immediately snaps her jaw shut and scowls. He crosses the distance and slides the door open.

"Good morning," he chirps.

"You planned that," she accuses flatly.

"Planned what?" He lifts his brow, the picture of innocence. "The water's great. You should try it."

"Don't you have a bathing suit?"

He shrugs. "Figured this works just as well."

"Sure you did."

Her gaze rakes down his chest hard enough he can practically feel the passionate scratch of nails. She pauses on a location distinctly south of his belly button where his wet boxer briefs cling to him almost indecently. A hungry look flashes in her eyes. She gulps. And he wants to gloat, but instead the intensity of her stare makes him twitch... down there. Suddenly, he's not as in control of the situation as he thought. But Sam either doesn't notice or is too flustered to seize the advantage because she just snaps her gaze up as a warm blush fills her cheeks.

"I don't have time to swim anyway."

"Why not?" He frowns. "There's nothing on our itinerary for the day. I checked this morning."

"I told Emily to leave my laptop and phone with the front desk when she left. I need to grab them and get to work."

"Work?" He pauses and pointedly stares back out at the glistening ocean before arching his brow. "In a place like this?"

"My boss probably wants to fire me for disappearing on him like this, so yes, work, if I want to still be employed by the time these five days are up." She sighs and rubs her forehead, so much more flustered than the woman he saw the night before, all confidence and defiance.

Cooper crosses his arms and leans against the doorframe, his curiosity piqued by the change in her demeanor. "And what do you do for work? Emily never said."

"I'm an analyst at an investment banking firm," she replies distractedly, obviously still running through some sort of list in her mind.

Cooper whistles. "Fancy."

He means to sound teasing, but it must come off differently because she snaps her head up with the wrong kind of fire in her eyes. "Yeah, well, we can't all shovel cow shit for a living."

"Ooh, Cuj. That one hurt." He presses his palm to his chest as if wounded, unable to fight the grin that widens his lips. He can't help it—he likes her bite.

But her expression immediately softens. "Sorry, that was an asshole thing to say. I'm just stressed."

"Who wouldn't be stressed, waking up in a place like this?" He casually takes in the private suite that probably costs three grand a night. "I mean, really? This is the best the network could afford?"

She snorts.

"Besides," he continues. "I do shovel cow shit for a living, among other things."

He's been elbow deep up a cow's asshole more times than he can count, not that he's going to tell that to her. Ranching definitely isn't glamorous. But it has its moments, like waking up before dawn during the first frost of the season to watch the entire sweep of plains glitter like diamonds with the rising sun, or witnessing a newborn calf rise on shaking legs to suckle from its mother for the first time. She lives her life in a cubicle. He lives his outdoors, no walls to cage him in. And when he goes on vacation in a place like this, even if it doesn't happen very often, he can appreciate it instead of waking up anxious to bury his face in a screen.

Yes, Cooper knows exactly what city folk like her think about his line of work, and it doesn't bother him one bit. He wouldn't trade places with them for all the money in the world.

Which is why he just shrugs and finishes his thought with a simple, "I take no offense to the truth about honest work."

"You're too nice." She winces. "I really hate that I said that, and I'm sorry. I don't actually think that way. My mom owns a flower shop and my dad is a police chief, and from what I've seen of the world, they deserve to make millions a lot more than every jerk in my office, including me."

"Want to make it up to me?" he asks suddenly, not really sure why, except he can't bear to think of her wasting her time in a place like this buried in a computer.

She's immediately suspicious. "How?"

"Have breakfast with me."

"Breakfast?"

"We can go to the restaurant in the main building since you're headed there anyway. You have to eat, don't you? I'm starving."

Her lips twist into a wry grin. "Well, an early-morning swim will do that to a guy."

"Don't knock it till you try it."

"Is my underwear a requirement?"

He holds up his hands apologetically. "House rules."

"That's too bad." She sighs and stares longingly outside before turning those overly round doe eyes on him. The innocence in her expression instantly fades, replaced by wicked delight. "I'm not wearing any."

The words are a sucker punch straight to the groin. They land with a physical weight that leaves him exhaling sharply in pain. Sam simply grins and spins on her heels before marching back into her bedroom with an offhanded, "I'll be ready in five."

Fucking hell. Cooper shakes his head and water droplets go flying in every direction. *Does she always have to have the last word?*

His balls might not survive it.

His heart definitely won't.

Because he likes it. Likes the fire in her eyes. Likes the silent dare. Likes the confidence. Likes the challenge.

He's not sure who the first woman in the room had been—worried, and stressed out, and panicked about what her boss might think. But the second version of

Samantha Peters—the sultry, biting ball-breaker—he likes her too damn much. And if all he has to do to bring that woman out is piss the first one off a little, well, he's definitely the right man for the job.

He's never been afraid of a little hard work.

sam

AT LEAST I *don't shovel cow shit for a living,* Sam thinks for the twentieth time in about two minutes. *God, why did I say that?*

The snobby, self-entitled words are branded on her soul, absolutely searing. Any ounce of superiority she thought she had over the jerks in her office is officially gone. She's an asshole, same as them, looking down on the rest of the world.

Except she really hopes that's not true.

It was that stupid word. *Fancy.* Or maybe not so much the word, but the mocking way Cooper had said it. As if the thought of her in the banking world was a joke. As if she didn't belong. In hindsight, it's clear he meant it as nothing more than a teasing jab. He had no way to know how deep the knife would cut. But the moment he said it, she heard another voice in the back of her mind—the one she's spent the better part of six years trying her best to forget.

You think you're my girlfriend?

You're a fucking charity case, Sam.

A pity lay.

And honestly, I'm running out of shits to give you.

Spencer's words echo across the void, still as sharp as the day he said them. She doesn't miss him. She doesn't even hate him anymore. It's not *him*, but what he said that sticks with her, because the jabs taught her an invaluable lesson. That she could build her life around someone, that she could give him every bit of herself, could make him her world, and in less than a minute he could take it all away. Men aren't dependable enough to act as a foundation. The only thing a woman can count on in this world is herself.

Sam closes her eyes, scrunching her face up tight.

Stay focused.

She buries the memories. She blinks them away.

With her arms crossed, she stares hard at the closet full of Emily's clothes and suddenly wonders what the hell she's going to wear. Swapping places meant swapping everything—wardrobe included. And while she grew up in Georgia, the frilly, lacy, ruffled trappings of a Southern belle like her sister make her physically ill. She can't remember if she's always been this way, or if New York just vaporized the sweet tea from her blood. Give her a power suit. Give her stilettos. Give her a pencil skirt over a peplum blouse any day of the week, a smoky eye over smocking. That soft, feminine look works for Emily. It works for a lot of women, and good on them, because the absolute last thing Sam wants to do is to slip on an approachable sundress and suddenly appear like someone who might actually offer to give a lost tourist directions to the subway when she's running five minutes late for a meeting and it's their own fault for not being able to figure out a freaking grid system. It's not that hard!

God. I really have turned into an asshole.

She groans, grabs a muted floral cover-up—the only beige thing she can find—and makes a silent promise. Next week, she's going to help one of those poor lost souls get to Times Square if it kills her. And she's going to buy a whole bag of groceries for the homeless vet who lives outside her building. She and Winnie usually take turns giving him food from the apartment on their way out, but he deserves more. And...she might even feed a pigeon.

Nope. I've gone too far.

Sam slips into a pair of beaded flip-flops and glances back toward the living room, envisioning the cowboy waiting patiently on the other side of the wall.

I probably owe him another apology while I'm at it.

She sighs. The only thing she hates more than actually being wrong is copping to it. Losing gives her hives.

Being gracious isn't a crime, Samantha.

It's her mom's voice this time and she rolls her eyes. The woman is a perfect Southern belle—a stay-at-home mother turned flower-shop owner who runs the local garden club and always has an ear in the town gossip. A true steel magnolia. Soft and feminine and the bedrock of the family. And while she's been trying to turn Sam into a lady her entire life, the lessons never stuck. As if they were two halves of one whole, Em got all the magnolias and Sam got all the steel.

She groans.

The flowers on this dress mock her as she yanks open the door.

You're not Emily, they whisper. *You're not the sweet, kind, strong, loving woman who is supposed to be wearing these clothes.*

She straightens her spine and lifts her chin.

No, I'm definitely not.

Sam spots Cooper across the hall. He's waiting with his arms crossed over his broad chest and one knee bent, his foot up against the wall. That white T-shirt strains across his muscles. Worn light-wash jeans hug his thighs. Boots poke out from underneath the hems, and his bright red hair is in wild disarray without the cowboy hat to hold it down. It's not messy, though—it's effortlessly tousled, mussed up in the sexiest way as loose strands curl over his eyes and around his ears, just waiting to be smoothed back. But it's the shit-eating grin on his face that stops her cold. One glance into his devilish eyes and any thought of being the bigger person goes out the window.

"You haven't by chance seen a cowboy hat lying around anywhere, have you?"

Sam reaches to the side and snatches it off the dresser before nestling it onto her head with a grin. "What? This old thing?"

A spark lights his gaze. "It looks good on you."

"Maybe I'll keep it."

"It's bad luck to take another man's hat," he says. That dimple digs a little deeper into his cheek. "Unless, of course, you're planning to keep me too."

Sam scowls and marches across the room to plop the offending item on his head. "Not a chance."

"Aww, I think there's a chance, Cuj," he counters as he resettles the hat on his head, and dammit if the sight of it doesn't twist her insides. She shouldn't have given it back. It's like sprinkles on a cupcake—a little extra touch that makes him all the more delicious. "Breakfast?"

She rolls her eyes. "Let's go."

The moment they step out onto the pier, he takes her by the hand and twirls her around until she lands pressed up against his side with their clamped fingers against her hip.

The first thing she notices is the sheer size of his hand.

The second is a little flutter deep in the pit of her stomach.

And the third is an electric bolt of red-hot rage.

Oh, hell no.

A flutter?

Is that seriously happening right now?

A flutter!

Hell. No.

She doesn't do feelings. One-night stands? Sure. The occasional fling? Yeah. Friends with benefits? Absolutely.

But feelings? It's a hard line—one Sam's not about to cross anytime soon.

She tries to rip her hand free, but he's made of freaking iron. The arm wrapped around her waist doesn't even budge. Her rage intensifies.

So does the flutter.

Grrrrr!

She tugs again. He squeezes her fingers, completely unperturbed. "Someone might be watching."

It's a fact.

But the way he said it also makes it sound like a dare.

She's never hated her competitive spirit more than she does in this instant, but even so, she relaxes against him and lets him guide her forward. He smirks and flexes his hand. The tip of his thumb slides precariously close to the bottom edge of her bra.

It does NOT make her heart lurch in her chest.

No way.

Not even a little.

"One inch higher," she hisses through her forced smile, "and I'm hip checking you off this pier. I know how much you love to swim."

He leans close enough to brush her cheek with his nose. Warm breath hits her skin, and a trail of goose bumps ripples down her spine. "If I go down, Cuj, I'm taking you with me."

She shrugs. "You can try..."

This earns her a dubious glance. Which, okay, yeah, he's practically a giant compared to her and it would take him little effort to toss her like a rag doll into the ocean, but there's one attack that can down even the burliest of men.

Sam reaches subtly with her free hand.

She prepares her thumb and her pointer finger.

When he's least expecting it, she strikes.

His ass is shockingly firm—the man is a freaking Adonis—but she still manages to grab a sliver of loose skin through his jeans. Freshly manicured nails at the ready, she pinches with everything she's got.

Cooper yelps.

Actually yelps.

The hand around her waist snatches back as he jolts in pained surprise. Sam takes the opening to dash out of reach. "...but you have to catch me first."

With that, she's off.

He recovers almost instantly, but she's shockingly quick, and shockingly scrappy. Halfway down the pier, she flings her flip-flop up, snatches it midair, and chucks it over her shoulder. Then grins when a gruff *oof* fills the air.

I hope it hit him right in his smug freaking fa—

An arm suddenly snakes around her waist. She cries out as he sweeps her clean off her feet as if she weighs nothing at all. A hand digs into her hip, another curls under her legs, and before she knows it, she's somehow been flipped over his shoulder with her ass precariously close to his face.

"Put me down," she demands haughtily. At the moment, attitude is all she has.

He barks out a laugh. "Not on your life."

"Put me down," she repeats, but this time she slams her fists against his back, kicks her feet, and squirms as she's never squirmed before.

His stride doesn't even falter.

"Put me down!"

She goes for his butt again, but he bounces his shoulder to dislodge her hand. "It's adorable you thought that might work a second time."

"Cooper," she demands.

"Yes?"

She doesn't need to see his face to know he's grinning. The arrogant lilt of his words is enough.

They stop at the edge of the pier.

Crystal-blue water glitters below.

He snakes his hands up her thighs, reaching for her waist. She knows exactly what he's planning to do, so she twists his shirt in her fists until she's got a secure grip. She's not going down without a fight.

"You don't want to do this," she warns.

"I really think I do."

Fingers clench around the small of her waist. He lifts up, and for a moment she's weightless, then—

"I leave you alone for twelve hours," someone calls from behind, the sound filled with gentle reprimand.

They both freeze.

Sam only met the producer three days ago, but she recognizes Nina's voice even before she lifts her head to find the woman fifteen feet behind them on the pier dressed in a black minidress and combat boots. She has her hip cocked to the side and her arms crossed. A bemused expression lights her brown eyes. "What the hell are you two doing?"

Sam opens her mouth, but nothing comes out. Cooper, too, is noticeably silent. An awkward moment passes before Nina arches a brow.

"Is this some sort of weird foreplay?" She narrows her eyes, taking them in. And then shakes her head. "You know what? Never mind. I saw the dream suite. I'm not sure I want to know what weird shit you two might be up to now that I no longer have to film it."

Again with the dream suite... That's the third time the producer has mentioned it—what *happened* in there? Sam would have bet money that her sister refrained from that level of intimacy with any of the contestants during the show, especially with Jake nearby, but with the way Nina is talking, she's suddenly not so sure. Part of her is impressed—*Go, Em!*—but a far more annoying part of her is undeniably intrigued. Emily is practically the definition of vanilla, which means if something kinky went down, it was because of the man currently holding her like a sack of potatoes over his shoulder.

Just like that, the pesky flutter returns.

He slept with my sister.

He had what was apparently a very memorable, totally insane, off-camera night SLEEPING WITH MY SISTER! STOP FUCKING FLUTTERING!

Cooper chooses this moment to finally lower her to

the ground, and by *lower* she means let go just enough that she slides down the front of his body, every inch of her against every inch of him, feeling every ridge of his washboard abs on the way down. The moment her feet hit the pier, he clamps his arm around her waist again and digs his fingers possessively into her hip bone.

The flurry turns to a frenzy.

I'm supposed to be Emily.

We're supposed to be in love.

He's supposed to be touching me like this.

Get your head on straight!

"We were on our way to breakfast," Cooper explains.

Just to show herself she can, Sam grabs Cooper's hand and pulls his arm farther across her stomach so he's holding her from behind with her entire back pressed against his entire front. She threads their fingers together and holds him in place so his corded forearm rests just below her breasts, close enough she can feel the heat from his skin. Then she gives Nina a wink. "We worked up an appetite."

"Yeah, I don't want to know," the producer murmurs offhandedly, as if uninterested, yet her gaze lingers on their clasped hands. A little spark Sam can't quite place flashes in Nina's dark eyes before she grins. "Though I guess it can't be too salacious if you're out of your room already. Most couples take at least twenty-four hours before showing their faces in the bright light of day. One even spent their entire five-day vacation in the suite. It's why we left your schedule clear for today."

An uneasy feeling stirs in Sam's gut at the implication. Cooper must feel the same because he wraps his other arm around her and squeezes her tight, nestling his chin against the top of her head. The loving embrace is a silent show of unity—it's also annoyingly comforting.

"She wanted to get room service," he explains, then dips his head closer to nip teasingly at her ear. Heat ricochets down her spine, flamed further by the deep rumble that vibrates against her back as he chuckles softly, and then whispers, "Insatiable girl."

Before Sam can react, he pulls back and lifts his head toward Nina.

"But we have our whole lives, after all. And this is only my second time seeing the ocean. I begged her to explore."

Sam glances up at him.

Is that true? It's only his second time seeing the ocean? It makes sense, with him living on a landlocked ranch. Still, she grew up on the beach. Mornings fishing on her father's boat. Afternoons splashing in the waves. Evenings sneaking out to drink beers by the light of the moon. It's hard to imagine growing up anywhere else. The very idea makes her want to learn more.

And that's a dangerous, dangerous proposition.

Rules, Sam immediately realizes, hating the way her heart has momentarily softened. *We need some fucking rules.*

Rules will take emotion out of the equation. Sam is a businesswoman and this is a business arrangement. A transaction, plain and simple. She doesn't know why she didn't think of it sooner. Rules, a contract, some sort of guideline—it will give them characters to play, a script to follow, just enough separation to fortify her mind against his touch. If she and Cooper are going to survive the next five days together, they need to sit down, negotiate the terms, draft up an exit strategy, and remove any and all questions from the equation. She wants a clean and clear reminder that every time he gets too close, it's for a game, a cover-up, and none of this is real.

Rules.

Sam grins.

It's a genius idea. So genius, Sam is too busy congratulating herself to fully register what Nina says next.

"You want to explore?" the producer asks, eying them up and down. "Why don't you come with us? The network booked Trish, Fred, and me a yacht for the day as a little end-of-season treat. It's too big for just the three of us anyway. You're more than welcome to join. It'd be fun to spend a little time with you both outside of the show."

As nice as the invitation is, Sam can't think of anything worse than being stuck on a yacht with her accidental fiancé and the television crew they're trying to fool. They need to go to breakfast. They need to establish a game plan. And then she really, really needs to get her phone from the front desk.

Unfortunately, before she has time to say any of this, the cowboy tightens his arm around her waist and chimes, "We'd love to."

CHAPTER SIX

cooper

THE EXPRESSION on Sam's face when she snaps toward him is priceless. It takes all of Cooper's effort to hold back a shit-eating grin.

"Great!" Nina says, too quickly for the fuming woman in his arms to mount any sort of defense. He could honestly kiss her—the producer...obviously. "We leave in about twenty. Go get changed into bathing suits and I'll tell Trish and Fred to grab you from your bungalow on their way. There's food and drinks on board, so just bring yourselves. Oh, and Em, your flip-flop is over there if you need it, you know, as another projectile missile. Just don't throw it at me this time." She grins. "Later!"

As soon as Nina is out of earshot, Sam shoves Cooper away and rounds on him.

"We were supposed to be going to breakfast," she seethes. "We had a deal."

"We are going to breakfast." He grins. "Breakfast on a yacht."

She throws her hands in the air. "I need to get my computer. I have work to do."

"According to you, your boss is already pissed. What's a few more hours?"

"That wasn't the plan."

"I improvised."

"Look," she says and jabs her pointer in the center of his chest. "Other girls may fall all over this alpha-male thing you're doing right now, but I'm not one of them. I'm a grown-ass woman and I make my own decisions. I don't need a man to do it for me. And when I make a deal with someone, I expect them to make good on their end of the bargain. Got it?"

His chest immediately deflates, the fun seeping away like the air from a popped balloon. That's not what this was about, and he doesn't want her to see him like that. He might have had some trouble following the rules in his past, might have spread his wild oats a bit, but he hates the sort of man she's talking about—the sort that believes a woman is just an accessory on his arm, and not a living, breathing human in her own right, with her own hopes and dreams outside of his needs. If this push and pull they've been doing is giving her the wrong impression, he'd rather fold than raise the stakes.

"I wasn't trying to force you. You don't have to come," he answers honestly. "If you think it'll cause big trouble with work, go get your laptop and do what you have to do.

I can make an excuse with Nina. But I'd like to go, if you don't mind. I wasn't lying when I said I've only seen the ocean twice in my life, and the first time was six weeks ago from the mansion in LA when we started this whole thing. Life on the ranch doesn't leave much room for travel, or maybe that's just my father, but if I don't jump on this opportunity now, it might never come again. *That's* why I said we'd go, but you're right. I shouldn't have answered for you."

The ire in her honey eyes cools.

A curious little flicker shifts her features—one he recognizes, a little glimpse that reminds him of her sister. They do have the same face after all, and after six weeks with Emily, he likes to think he knows a bit about how to read it. But he doesn't know which part of what he said has Sam intrigued. The mention of his father? Of the ranch? Of his somewhat sheltered life?

She doesn't elaborate.

A beat of silence passes while she studies him, and this quiet, pensive version of her has him spooked. He's not sure what she sees in his eyes, but whatever it is, it's hitting a little too close to home.

So in an exaggerated drawl, he adds, "Of course, it would be a little odd for a newly engaged couple with their first taste of camera-free freedom to separate at the first chance they got. So what do you say? Want to come with me?"

She rolls her eyes with a scowl. "You're insufferable."

"Some might call me charming."

"Who?" she scoffs. "The cows?"

Cooper snorts. *Got me there.*

Sam smiles triumphantly. He can practically see her add a tally to her side of the invisible scoreboard. Then she loops their arms together.

"I guess we should go get changed."

When they get back to their bungalow, she disappears inside the bedroom while he hastily dons board shorts and slides. Right as he's settling a University of Nebraska baseball cap on his head—*Go, Huskers!*—a gentle *click* draws his eye. Sam steps out in barely-there cutoffs and a faded pink T-shirt. His breath catches at the sight of her toned legs and the glimpse of two rounded cheeks as she leans to the side to grab her sunglasses. He swallows, his throat suddenly tight. Oblivious, she reaches up to twist her hair into a bun, revealing two thin blue straps tied behind her neck. He knows a tiny string bikini when he sees one, and damn if he isn't curious what's hiding beneath that shapeless cotton shirt.

"Would you look at that," Sam says as she takes him in. "A bathing suit."

Her snarky comment snaps him from the daze. "Wouldn't want to overwhelm you in front of the others, Cuj. I know how distracting you find my other choice of swimwear."

She glares at him.

"That's not a denial."

She rolls her eyes.

"Still not—"

A knock cuts him off. They share a knowing glance. Cooper offers his hand in a silent truce, and she takes it before yanking open the door. Trish offers a firm nod and Fred a warm grin, their opposite personalities on display. During filming, Cooper heard some of the assistants refer to her as the Ice Queen, and he can't help but think the name fits. Her platinum hair is pulled back in a tight bun, her features are inscrutable, and her white button-up dress is cinched all the way through the collar, not giving an inch. Oversized sunglasses hide her eyes, but he just knows that frigid blue would make him shiver. By her side, Fred is like the perfect foil, his white teeth on brilliant display against his dark skin, his eyes soft and welcoming. His cutoff T-shirt screams relaxation, and his voice is unfalteringly sincere as he says, "So glad you two could join us!"

While they exchange some small talk—*How was your night? How's your room? Isn't this weather great? Have you ever seen water so beautiful?*—Cooper loops his arm over Sam's shoulders to draw her close. They are, after all, supposed to be engaged. But that doesn't explain why his fingers keep brushing up and down her arm of their own accord, drawing long soothing strokes across her skin. Or why his thumb hooks under the edge of her sleeve, just to feel more of her. Or why his face turns ever so slightly to the side so he can smell the coconut shampoo in her hair. He's itching to slide his palm into the back pocket of those cutoff shorts and feel the supple curve of the perky ass she teased him with the night before.

When Trish and Fred pull slightly ahead, lost in some argument about edits for the show, he can't seem to stop his hand from finding her hip, then gliding lower, and lower, until—

"Rules!" Sam suddenly blurts.

He jerks his wayward fingers back to her shoulder. *The hell, man? Control yourself.* "Rules?"

Her chest expands as she draws in a deep, uneven breath. He may or may not drop his gaze to look, may or may not study the electric-blue strings disappearing beneath pink cotton, may or may not find himself fantasizing about what it might be like to draw that shirt over her head and find out what's hiding underneath...

Come on!

He snaps his face forward.

"Rules," she repeats, her voice stronger this time. "For this. For *us*. I know I'm supposed to be Emily and we're supposed to be engaged, but I'm Sam, and we're not. I don't know anything about you. You don't know anything about me. We need to set some boundaries or the next five days could get...blurry."

"I don't know what you mean," he says innocently, as if he weren't just picturing her naked and didn't almost grab her ass in broad daylight.

She arches a brow pointedly in his direction, then sighs. "You and my sister just faked an entire relationship for a TV show. What did you guys do?"

"I don't know." He shrugs. "When the cameras were up, we made out and held hands and did all that stuff.

Then when they went down, we just didn't. It wasn't that complicated. There was no fire between us."

Like there is between us.

"Yeah...no," Sam murmurs, as if hearing the unspoken implication. "That's not going to work."

She drums her fingers on her mouth for a moment, drawing his gaze to her pink lips, then folds the plump lower edge between her teeth.

Christ.

He snaps his face forward again. "Rules might not be a bad idea."

She gasps in mock shock and covers her heart with her palm. "Did you just agree with me?"

"Don't let it get to your head, Cuj."

"Too late." She grins, then holds her hand up and sticks out her thumb. "Rule one. No kissing."

He rolls his eyes. "We're supposed to be engaged. And big as it is, I don't think that rock alone will convince them."

She shifts her hand, providing them both a better glimpse at the engagement ring on her fourth finger. The two-carat cushion-cut diamond is nearly blinding in this sunlight, encircled by a row of smaller diamonds and set on a platinum band. When he first saw it, he thought it was a bit gaudy. But then he suddenly flashed back to this moment with his mom. They'd been sitting next to each other on the couch—him watching football, her flipping through a magazine—when he glanced over to find her studying a jewelry ad.

If I was going to pick out a ring, which one do you think?

For that girl you're seeing now? she'd murmured without even glancing up. *None of them.*

He'd snorted. But inside, an urgency had tightened his gut, because she was there and lucid and he didn't know how many more nights like that he had left. So instead of letting it go, he'd pressed. *Humor me.*

She'd sighed and shifted on the couch, something serious passing over her expression before she paused and tapped a diamond. *This one, so everyone within a mile radius will always be able to see she's yours.*

He'd completely forgotten about the memory until he sat down with the jeweler in front of the cameras, the scene a formality, just another romantic moment bought and paid for by the show. He hadn't even been thinking about Emily when he picked it, since he knew she was planning to turn the proposal down before he even had time to drop to one knee. He'd been thinking of his mom. Looking at it now, he can't deny the woman had good taste. The ring, so similar to the one she once picked, looks stunning on Sam's elegant finger.

"Gorgeous as it is…" Sam sighs. "You're right. How about no kissing on the lips, then?"

"Done. Forehead okay?"

"Sure."

"Hand?"

"Yup."

"Shoulder?"

She swallows. "Okay."

"Neck?"

"Too intimate," she murmurs as a flush creeps up her pale cheeks. Damn if he doesn't like the sight. "Okay, so, rule one—no kissing unless it's on my forehead, hand, and shoulder."

"Or mine," he cuts in teasingly.

"Or yours."

"And rule two?"

"No touching my boobs or butt."

"Likewise."

She ignores him. "Rule three. We'll follow through on everything in the itinerary to maintain the ruse, but the bungalow is our safe space. In there, we're just two strangers who happen to be sharing a room. No pretending. We'll keep that to public places."

"Makes sense."

"Rule four." She's on a roll now. "Nothing too personal."

"What do you mean?"

"I don't need to know your deep dark secrets and you sure as hell don't need to know mine. We keep it surface for the next few days. Let's just agree to have fun."

"Okay..."

"And rule five." She stops walking and turns to look up at him. They're about ten feet from the yacht. The others are already on board. "When these five days are up, we never see or hear from each other again. You and Emily will coordinate your breakup for the live show, and you'll leave me out of it."

He frowns. "That seems extreme."

"Those are my terms. It's the best way to make sure my sister's business isn't affected by my mistake, and the best way for you to get what you want for the ranch."

"You're sure?"

"Positive." The smile she gives is sharp enough to cut. Suddenly all he sees is a shrewd businesswoman with steel in her veins. But rather than scare him off, it just makes him curious to know why she has an iron shield so at the ready.

"Okay, Cuj," he says somewhat reluctantly, but what choice does he have? "You've got yourself a deal."

She holds out her hand.

He takes it.

An uncomfortable pang reverberates around his chest as they shake on it, but the deed is done. She drops his fingers as if they're on fire and leans down to slip off her shoes. Cooper follows. They place them in the provided basket and then turn together toward the pristine white yacht towering overhead. It's three stories tall and almost obnoxiously large for five people.

"There's one more thing I have to know," she whispers.

"Shoot."

Sam looks up at him and narrows her eyes. "What the hell happened with my sister in the dream suite?"

It's the last thing he's expecting, and a laugh barrels up his chest before he can stop it.

Nothing.

Nothing happened in the dream suite. But Emily sure wanted to make it look as though something had, so they spent half an hour throwing stuff on the floor and gasping as loudly as they could for the cameras all while trying not to crack. The result had been a veritable crime scene—something he knows the producers lapped up the following morning, which is probably why they keep bringing it up.

And he could explain this to Sam.

He could be honest.

But he won't be.

Because what's the fun in that?

"Oh, Cuj," he murmurs as he wraps his arm around her waist and pulls her tightly to his side. "You're not ready for that story yet."

sam

THE DEEP RUMBLE of his voice is pure seduction. Her heart lurches in her chest as he offers a devilish grin.

You jerk.

Not ready? What does that mean—not ready?

What the hell happened in that dream suite!? The more she's left to wonder, the more and more obscene the fantasies she conjures become. Did they break the bed? Were there handcuffs? Toys? What did he do? She can't stop picturing herself in all these wild scenarios, because, well, she and Em look exactly the same, and honestly, she hasn't had a good lay in a while, and—

Stop.

Heat flares up her throat to spread across her cheeks. It's not a blush—she is NOT blushing. And her nipples definitely haven't peaked. And the flutters deep in her belly are hunger pangs. Nothing more.

Sex hunger pangs.

Her inner bitch is a backstabbing sloot.

STOP.

"Are you two coming?" Nina calls as she leans over the railing above.

"Yup," Cooper answers.

Sam wrestles her raging hormones to the ground, and walks with him over the gangway and onto the yacht.

"Shot?" Nina extends a tray.

Sam takes both and downs them one after another before Cooper can even lift his hand.

The producer widens her eyes with a grin. "Is fun Emily coming out today?"

More like reckless, sad, numbing-her-pain-with-alcohol Samantha, but she fights the urge to correct Nina. Her sister has never needed booze to be fun. The most fun Sam can ever remember having in her life are the nights the two of them used to spend doing nothing—watching movies, playing cards, chitchatting while they painted their nails, belting out songs as they rummaged through their closets to try on clothes. Nothing has been the same since she left home for NYU. Nothing has felt as joyful, as *right.*

But that's life. Who is she to complain? Playing happy has become second nature and this is just another role, another day.

So aloud, all Sam says is, "Hell yeah!"

"Where can I get a beer?" Cooper asks with a laugh.

"The bar is back there." Nina jabs her thumb over her

shoulder, then hooks her arm through Sam's. "But the party is over here."

The producer leads her through the main cabin, up the stairs, and out onto a sundeck. Trish reclines on a lounger with her phone to her ear, lips pursed. Fred is out cold by her side.

Sam turns to Nina with a raised brow. "You call this a party?"

"I do now." The producer grins and hands Sam a margarita before clinking their glasses. "Cheers!"

She takes a sip, because why not, and tries to figure out what Em would do in this situation. Probably sit in one of the chairs and pull out her sketchbook. But seeing as Sam has absolutely no artistic talent and is in desperate need of a distraction from the hulking redhead sauntering her way like a panther on the hunt, she turns to Nina instead. "Hot tub?"

"Let's do it. Cooper, you in?"

Sam stifles her groan. The last thing she needs is him, half-naked, wet, and oozing rugged masculinity right by her side.

"In for what?" he asks.

"Hot tub."

Please say no. Please say no.

As if he can hear, he turns to her with a wink, copying her earlier words. "Hell yeah."

Fuck my life.

Sam takes a long swill of margarita as he reaches over his head and pulls off his shirt in one annoyingly hot tug.

Just like when she watched him emerge from the ocean this morning, her throat runs dry at the sight of his truly glorious torso, all rippling muscle and tanned skin and rock-hard flesh. She doesn't want to look, doesn't want to rake her gaze over every inch of his bare skin, doesn't want to study each firm ridge as if she might be tested on it later, doesn't want to taste the drool pooling on her tongue, and yet...

I am a thirsty, thirsty bitch.

She swallows.

Cooper grins.

Her competitiveness rears its ugly head. *Two can play at that game, cowboy.*

Sam reaches for the hem of her shirt, fully aware of the almost physical touch of his eyes as they zero in on her. She lifts the cotton slowly, tantalizingly revealing inch after inch of her flat stomach, round curves, and perfectly respectable breasts. She kickboxes five days a week at the gym down the street. She knows what she's working with. And despite her sister's normally conservative tastes, she found a tiny electric-blue string bikini buried in the back of her closet—probably part of the wardrobe from the show. So yes, it's not exactly a surprise that when she finishes pulling her tiny shorts down her proportionally long legs, Cooper is practically panting at her. But it sure as hell feels good.

"Are you two done stripping yet?" Nina drawls from where she has already settled in the hot tub, a black one-piece with mesh panels covering her petite frame. "If I'd known I was getting a show, I would've brought popcorn."

Sam snatches her margarita from the table and climbs into the hot tub. Cooper splashes in behind her. As she's settling into the hard plastic seat, a deliciously calloused hand finds her hip. Next thing she knows, she's sidled up against his firm body, dwarfed by his sheer size. Her entire right side feels on fire, all the way down to where their ankles gently knock in the bubbling water. She takes an aggressive sip of her marvelously cold drink.

This is going to be a long afternoon.

"So," Nina says in a chatty tone, a wide smile on her lips. Something about her seems a bit too friendly, but Sam can't quite place what. "How are things going?"

She looks up at Cooper. He's already watching her. A beat of expectant silence passes before she swallows and glances back at Nina with an overly cheerful smile. "Great!"

"Yeah?" Nina responds casually before taking a sip of her drink. "It can be hard for couples to find their footing after the show. But I had a feeling you two would figure things out, especially after the proposal."

"Really?" Sam's genuinely curious. "Why?"

"There was something different about you both on the beach that day. I mean, you always had great chemistry on camera, but when we filmed that scene..." The producer shrugs. "I don't know. Your connection was palpable, not just through the rose-colored lens of the show, but here in real life. For the first time, I got the sense you could really make it."

There was something different about you both on the beach that day...

Nina has no idea how right she is.

Sam squirms in her seat. Cooper trails his fingers up and down her bicep in a soothing motion. The flurry of nerves turns to a different flurry entirely, and her breath catches in her throat.

"We have some stuff to figure out," Cooper says in that deep, confident voice. "But we're enjoying the time we have together."

"Stuff?" The producer arches a brow inquisitively.

"Where to live, when to move," he answers noncommittally. "That sort of thing."

Sam knows what he's doing. Laying the groundwork for their plan. Planting the seeds for their inevitable breakup.

Nina looks at her, that gaze far too perceptive. "You don't—"

"Dolphin!"

Sam throws her arm wildly to the left and leans forward, getting some much-needed space from Cooper's hard body and a much-needed break from this conversation. She stares intently at the brilliant blue water which is, at the moment, glassy and calm. There's not a single whitecap in sight beneath the beating sun.

Motherfucker.

"Dolphin?" Nina asks sardonically.

"I swore I saw..." Sam narrows her eyes as she trails off, pretending to study the water. Then she shrugs and settles back in her seat, leaving a bit of space between her and the cowboy. She takes a sip of her margarita and then grins at Nina. "Oh, speaking of couples from the show, I've been dying to ask about Ashleigh and Brad. Why didn't he pick her? When did he find out about the baby? Was there any behind-the-scenes drama? I need the scoop."

Nina rolls her eyes and leans back in her seat. For the next hour, Sam pesters her with questions about prior contestants and petty drama. Being a huge fan of *The Love Match* has never come so much in handy. She keeps the topics neutral, never once letting them steer into more personal territory. And just when she's about to run out of questions, Fred wakes up and joins them. The conversation switches from the show to polite chatter.

Cooper keeps his arm around her the entire time, all twinkling eyes and easy smile. She can't help but stare when he arches his head back to take a swill of his beer, his Adam's apple bobbing, the muscles of his thick neck rolling, the edge of his jaw sharpening, everything about him screaming *man*—sexy, sexy man. It becomes all too easy to lean into his touch as the alcohol permeates her blood. All too easy to catch his eyes with a knowing smile, the secret between them turning into an inside joke. All too easy to let her fingers fall on his meaty thigh beneath the water as if they're supposed to be there, gently squeezing hard muscle.

When they reach the reef to snorkel, he doesn't seem

to think twice about wrapping his large arm around her small waist to help her as she climbs out of the hot tub. He keeps it there, warm and solid and steady as they follow the others to the back of the yacht. In the water, they hold hands. And though it's too difficult to speak aloud with the goggles and the waves and the breathing tube, they meet each other's eyes, conversing without words as schools of fish dash and dart around them. *This is amazing! How beautiful! Look over here!* They point and explore. *There's a sea turtle! Do you see that stingray? Oh my god, a shark! Nemo fish!* They nudge each other with their elbows. They take turns diving deep beneath the surface. Again, and again, they find each other—to keep up the facade, of course.

All too soon, time is up.

The ride back to the resort passes in a blink of laughter and grins, the five of them now in the hot tub talking about everything they saw and how ridiculously beautiful the Maldives are, patting themselves on the back for picking such a gorgeous spot. When they make it back to the dock, Sam reluctantly slips her sandals on as the real world settles back on her shoulders.

"Want to join us for an early dinner?" Nina asks.

"I think we're just going to get room service tonight," Sam answers quickly, not letting Cooper jump in. A suggestive smile curves her lips. "I can only share him for so long."

They make their goodbyes, promising to find each other again soon. The crew turns left toward the bungalows. Sam and Cooper turn right toward the front desk. The second they're alone, the magic of the afternoon dissipates. She drops his hand. She steps a foot to the left. She marches a few steps ahead, on a mission. They don't speak more than a handful of words while Sam retrieves her laptop and phone and immediately scans her messages.

There are some from her roommate, some from her coworkers, some from her parents, and some from—

Jake.

Fear grabs hold of her heart, talons sinking too deep to dislodge. She can feel herself pale. Cooper furrows his brow, already able to read her too-familiar face.

"Is everything okay?"

"Mm-hmm."

She doesn't trust herself to speak. And she can't do this here, so she pushes past him and uses her New York power walk to book it back to the bungalow. As soon as they step through the door, rule number three goes into effect. They're back to being strangers. Even though she can tell he doesn't want to, Cooper respects the boundary and lets her retreat to the bedroom without intervening. She flinches as the door slams shut behind her, that loud *bang* revealing far too much about her emotional state.

But this is what she's been waiting days—no, weeks—for, ever since the doctor's office had called her, explaining that they couldn't get in touch with Emily and Sam was her sister's emergency contact. Retrieving the phone was never about work. She doesn't want to be fired, obviously, but she couldn't give two shits about what's waiting in her corporate inbox. This is so much more important. This is why she swapped places with her sister in the first place. It's the whole reason she's even here.

Still, Sam hesitates.

Terror leaves her rigid, unable to cross those last few millimeters. Her thumb hovers over the screen, her pulse thundering so wildly she can feel the throb against her nail. Maybe this is why she went with Cooper on the yacht. Why she didn't run straight to the lobby for the phone. Why she came all the way back to the room. Why she's still delaying. Because up until now she's been secretly telling herself it's nothing, but as soon as she reads these messages, she won't be able to avoid the truth any longer.

Stop being an idiot. Em is fine.

She's FINE.

Sam swipes the screen.

She clicks on Jake's name.

With her heart in her throat, she scans the missed texts.

Since I'm texting from his phone, you can probably guess I found Jake at the hotel like we planned. I know it's killing you a little inside to help me fly right back into his arms, but it's going to be different this time. I know it is. I promise, Sam. I love him. I love him so freaking much. And he loves me. I finally told him everything, and he said none of it matters as long as we're in it together. I'm so happy right now. Happier than I can ever remember being, and I just... Thank you. Thank you so much, sis. Not just for swapping places with me, but for giving us your blessing. It means everything. I love you.

Sorry, that was sort of an essay, wasn't it...

Oh right, you're probably still freaking out! I called Dr. Laghari and it was nothing. The sample I gave before the show got contaminated. They need me to come for another blood draw. That was it. That was everything. Totally routine. Jake and I will be on the next flight out to New York. I'll update you as soon as I can!

Landed! Can we stay at your apartment?

We're staying at your apartment.

Do you own anything with a pattern? My god. Your closet is sad. I'm actually crying.

Hey—where's that Lilly Pulitzer dress I got you for Christmas a few years ago?

You returned it, didn't you?

You did.

Without telling me?!

Angry Face

Is nothing sacred?

Okay, I forgive you. I found your stash of my jewelry. This outfit can be salvaged. Jake and I are headed to Dr. Laghari's office now!

Blood draw complete. Should have results by tomorrow.

You haven't answered, so I'm guessing you haven't had a chance to get your phone from the front desk, but in case you're still having a panic attack, I haven't heard back yet.

NORMAL!!!!!!!

All my levels are totally normal!!! WOOHOOOO!!!

I'll stop bombarding you with texts now. Call me when you get a chance and I'll fill you in! I'm on a flight back to Georgia in two days. LOVE YOU SIS!!!

Sam releases the breath she's been holding for the past five weeks, ever since she got the call from her sister's doctor.

Emily is okay.

She's healthy.

She's *okay*.

The realization rocks through her, sweeping all the strength from her limbs until all she can do is drop back against the door and slide to the floor. There's relief—so much fucking relief. And happiness. And gratitude. And every wonderful emotion under the sun. But there's also pain. A sudden, strong knot pulls on her gut. A wobbly inhale works its way down her throat. The corners of her eyes begin to sting. Suddenly, she's eighteen years old again, hearing that word for the first time.

Cancer.

She was so scared that it was back. She spent the past five weeks bracing herself for the worst. More surgeries. More chemo. More putting on a brave face. More keeping it together so her sister could fall apart. More plastering on a smile while inside she was breaking.

But it's not.

Emily is fine, she repeats. *She's fine. She's fine. She's fine.*

The words are a familiar mantra. They keep her afloat as the air seems to suction from her lungs leaving her chest tight. She heaves. The loud, ugly sound has her pushing a hand to her burning heart.

Bad news is so easy to believe.

But good news? Good news always feels impossible. Temporary. As though at any moment, it might be swept away.

She's fine. She's fine. She's fine.

Against her will, tears start to fall. Sam stumbles into the bathroom and turns on the shower so Cooper won't hear her cry.

CHAPTER EIGHT

WHEN COOPER EMERGES from the water the next morning, he's greeted by two long bare legs and one perky ass barely covered by the smallest spandex shorts he's ever seen.

He nearly crashes back into the ocean.

Honestly, he sort of wishes he had. It would have been better than what he actually does, which is hover suspended on the edge of the deck for he has no idea how long with his jaw hanging open like a deranged fish. The shaking of his strained biceps finally snaps him from the daze and he swings his feet onto the wooden planks before standing.

"Good swim?" Sam calls politely as she smoothly glides her body from downward-facing dog into upward-facing dog and looks over her shoulder with a knowing smile. Victory flashes in her warm eyes. It lights a spark in Cooper.

Well played, Samantha Peters.

Well fucking played.

After last night, he'd thought their little game was done. The moment they returned to the bungalow, Sam disappeared inside the bedroom, only emerging once to grab her plate of dinner, and even then she wouldn't meet his eyes. He'd thought maybe establishing some rules and some deadlines had ruined the entertaining rapport they'd built.

He'd be lying if he said he hadn't been disappointed by the thought.

So when he woke up to find her bedroom door still firmly shut this morning, he'd come out for a swim more to clear his head than anything else. But it seems that even without his trying, the sight of him in the water affected her enough to prompt a counterattack.

The realization leaves him grinning.

"Excellent swim," he answers and stretches his arms overhead, drawing Sam's focus. Her gaze burns a path up his deltoids, along his forearms, all the way to his fingers. He draws in a deep breath, and she zeroes in on his chest, then slides farther down to the ridge of his abdomen, and farther down still, until she distantly swallows. He folds his hands behind his neck with a smirk and flexes his biceps for extra measure.

She snaps out of the daze and finds his eyes with a heated scowl. Next thing he knows, that ass is right back in prime view as she rises hastily into downward-facing dog again. Under the guise of stretching her calves, she wiggles her hips suggestively. One leg kicks into the air before plunging forward in a deep, deep lunge that lets him know exactly how flexible her lithe body is. She lifts her torso and arches back, giving a sneak peek at those two swells hiding beneath her sports bra. Cooper suddenly finds it difficult to swallow.

"I, uh, didn't know you did yoga."

The edges of her lips twitch. "When the mood arises."

Something is definitely a-rising, and it sure as shit ain't a mood.

Dammit.

He adjusts his feet, trying to stop his body from reacting. Unfortunately, his wet bathing suit clings like a second skin, hiding nothing. A smug look crosses over Sam's face before she folds herself back over and repeats the process on her other side.

Rather than stand there and continue ogling her like a creep, he goes back inside, grabs some water, and watches from the other side of the glass like any self-respecting stalker would do. When she finishes and starts rolling up the mat, he hastily grabs a nearby book and dives onto the couch. He tucks a hand behind his head to give the illusion of comfort before she walks back inside. Sam pauses briefly in the doorway and sweeps her gaze in his direction. He keeps his face resolutely still.

"Good book?" she asks, tone far too innocent.

What's her angle? "Yup."

"Hmm. Looks a little out of your league."

"Why? Because cowboys can't read?"

"No…" She pauses for effect. He can't help but flick his gaze in her direction. She smirks the moment their eyes make contact. "Because it's upside down."

He cuts back to the book.

Well, shit.

Soft laughter trickles in her wake as she makes her way to the table where her work is already waiting. He stuffs the book beneath a pillow and watches her fill a glass with water, then take a seat. His cover is blown anyway. He might as well be honest with his interest. Sam doesn't seem to mind. Without glancing in his direction, she takes a long sip, neck arching back as her muscles work to swallow. Then she eases open her laptop. Within seconds, the quiet fills with the steady clicking of keys. She stares intently at the screen. It's admirable how quickly she sinks into whatever she's doing—or it would be, except the more focused she becomes, the more she seems to fold in on herself, shrinking, shrinking, shrinking until the beautiful, confident, challenging woman he spoke to minutes before all but disappears. It's different from simple concentration, deeper somehow. He's not sure how he knows, but he can just tell her soul is weary as her shoulders hunch and her lips bend into a slight frown. Energy that was once infectious just seeps away. Gone.

Cooper's never been one for life behind a desk. He'd rather spend the day fixing a hundred yards of barbed wire than sit for half an hour crunching numbers. Both are necessary evils, but only one allows for fresh air, sunshine, and the ache of a job well done. He can appreciate that not everyone thinks like him. But all he wants to do is shake her and say, *Look where you are! What the hell are you doing?*

He should just leave her to it.

He should walk away.

He should let it go.

He *should.*

But he can't.

"Working?" he inquires softly.

"Mm-hmm," comes the distracted reply.

"Can I ask why?"

"My boss is meeting with a client in about six hours. I need to finish inputting his changes to this deck and then double-check a few projections for the report he's presenting. It's this big acquisition we've been working on for months. He's already pissed I'm not there, but Em needed me, so..." She trails off before clearing her throat. "Anyway, I should be done by the time we need to leave for jet skiing."

"That's not what I meant."

A slight crease forms between her brows. "No?"

"I meant, why this job? What about it do you love so much that you're okay giving up all your time? Because if you can't take a break in a place like this, then I imagine when you're home, it's even worse. And I get it. When I'm home, the ranch comes first. Work comes first. I barely have time to get off the property. But I know why I do it. So why do you?"

She snorts. "Money."

"Money?" He doesn't know why he expected more. "That's it?"

"That's everything in this world, cowboy."

"You really think so?"

"I know so." She finally glances up from the screen, a bit of that spark returning. "It's what got you here, isn't it? Money to help your ranch. And my sister. Money to build her business. And probably everyone else on the show, willing to play whatever role and spill whatever secrets for a little access to some cold, hard cash. Money makes the world go round. And when you have it, you get to choose what direction everyone else has to spin. I made a promise to myself a long time ago that I'd be the one to control the merry-go-round, not ride on it."

He stares at her pensively as she refocuses on her computer. There's more to that story, he's sure, but he knows better than to push. The worst thing to do with a spooked horse is force it. A little patience works wonders.

"But why banking?" he asks instead, keeping it surface. "A lot of jobs are lucrative. Doctors. Lawyers. Agents. Techies."

"I like numbers." She shrugs, then offers a sudden grin. "I was probably the first prom queen in Georgia to also be a Mathlete."

"A Mathlete?"

"You know, on the math team? *Mean Girls* was practically my autobiography."

He arches a brow.

She shakes her head with a laugh. "We went to states,

and would have won if one of the guys on my team hadn't been so hungover he could barely see straight let alone solve a differential equation. If you think football players know how to party, you've never met a nerd on a Saturday night with access to an empty house and a fully stocked liquor cabinet."

"No, can't say that I have."

"Consider yourself lucky." Then under her breath, she adds, "His naive parents. Bless their foolish hearts."

"So math, then? Math and money?"

"And the simplicity." She chews on her bottom lip for a moment. He's mesmerized by the sight of her teeth biting into that plush pink skin. "It might not seem like it, but banking is pretty black and white when it comes down to it. I don't need to make life-or-death decisions like a doctor. I don't need to dissect every possible meaning of a single word in a contract like a lawyer, or worry about representing the wrong guy. I thought about tech for a hot second in college, but I can't code worth a damn. Businesses are relatively simple. They either make money or lose it. The math either makes sense or it doesn't. The numbers don't lie. They don't cheat. They can't leave you. Can't hurt you. They don't get sick. They're problems that can be solved. And I like that, I guess. I like knowing there's an answer."

Sam blinks and her pupils shrink as she returns from wherever it is that she went while she spoke. Her eyes widen slightly before she swallows. A hint of worry etches into the lines of her face, as if she's said too much.

She takes a deep breath before plastering on a forced smile.

He wants to know who lied to her. Who cheated her. Who hurt her. Who got sick. Every word out of her mouth is a revelation, but he knows enough about her to know that if he asks now, she'll cut and run. So he offers a little bit of himself up instead to put them on even ground.

"I can understand wanting answers. I used to search for them in all the wrong places. On the back of a wild bronco. At a bar. In a stranger's touch. Anywhere and everywhere but the one place I eventually found them— home. My mom used to say, *Not every cowboy needs to ride alone.* And I heard her. I knew what she meant. But I didn't get it, not really, until she was gone."

"Gone?"

"She passed away six years ago. Early-onset Alzheimer's."

"I'm sorry."

"I appreciate that."

"So what did she mean?"

"That I could be standing in the middle of a crowded room and still be alone. That I could be engaged, or married, or surrounded by friends, but if I didn't open up to any of them, if I kept riding alone, I'd always be that way when I didn't have to be. And my dad didn't have to be. And guess what? You don't either."

"Me?" She rears back. "I'm not."

"Numbers might not lie or cheat or leave, but they can't hold you either, Samantha. And neither can money."

A frown curves her plump lips before a sly expression overtakes her features. He watches her walls refortify in real time. "You've clearly never met any of my colleagues."

"I suppose not, but—"

"Cooper?" She stops him. "Rule four."

Nothing personal. No sharing secrets. No going deep. He shuts his mouth, respecting her wishes. But even though she gets her way, a sigh spills out. It's a reluctant, heavy sound pulled directly from the crevice he knows exists somewhere in her heart.

"I really do need to get back to work," she says, tone almost apologetic. "I'll meet you for our jet ski in a few hours, okay?"

"Whatever you say, Cuj."

She snorts and rolls her eyes before getting sucked into her screen. He watches one moment longer, then turns away. It's too painful a reminder of all the time he lost being angry, being lonely, being too wrapped up in his own feelings to pay attention to the things that really mattered. All the time his dad has wasted too, like father like son. They were so preoccupied with each other, with the ranch and his rebellion and the legacy his father was determined to fulfill, they didn't even notice his mother was sick until she was too far gone for it to matter.

Maybe if he hadn't joined the rodeo for a year, he would've seen the signs. Maybe if he hadn't moved out, and gone to college, and done anything and everything to get away, he would've noticed how odd it was that she kept forgetting the secret ingredient to Nana's raisin pie or how strange it was that the wranglers had needed to help her find her way back to the house that had been her home for nearly thirty years. And maybe if his father hadn't been so focused on trying to bring him home, he would've had time to realize it wasn't normal he had to tell her the same story three times for her to absorb it and it wasn't quirky that she kept having trouble keeping track of the date and it wasn't a simple case of growing older that made her forget her words in the middle of a conversation. These little tidbits seemed so innocuous because they weren't the focus until one day, so suddenly at the time but so painfully obvious in hindsight, the woman he thought of as his mother had all but slipped away.

He came home then, to fragments and moments and slivers of clarity—time he would treasure forever—but it wasn't enough to ease the guilt of not being there when it mattered.

Not every cowboy needs to ride alone.

She tried to tell him. Over and over again, she tried to tell him. The old Westerns didn't have it right. That romantic image of a lone man and his horse trotting off into the sunset was a sham. A lie. And even when he thought he understood, when he found a sweet girl and brought her home to meet his parents and tried to promise his mother he wouldn't be alone, she still patted his cheek and lovingly called him a fool. It wasn't until she died and he saw the utter devastation in his father's eyes that he understood. He would always be alone, in a crowded room, in a marriage, in his empty home, until he found someone who wouldn't just be on his arm, but at his side and in his heart and wrapped so tightly around his soul he didn't ever want to let go.

Cooper hasn't found her yet, but at least he gets it now. At least he knows. At least he's looking.

And he hopes one day, Sam will be too.

But it won't be today.

Today, she's too blinded by her laptop and those dollar signs and a fear he doesn't quite understand.

So he leaves her to it and retreats to the suitcase tucked into the corner of the room to retrieve the Canon EOS 5DS carefully resting near the top. It's been seven long weeks since he held the professional-grade camera in his hands. When he originally packed it, he had no idea that the "no pictures" rule on set would apply to this too. He figured his phone would be confiscated since the social media and communications bans in the contract had practically been underlined in red ink, but when Jake found the camera nestled in his things, to the vault it went. Cooper nearly had a conniption. The once state-of-the-art, now mildly outdated camera had belonged to his mother. It was one of the few pieces of her he had left, and he planned to honor her by taking pictures all around the globe the same way he still did whenever he had time at the ranch, capturing little moments she would have loved. Instead, he found himself muttering "Careful. Careful. CAREFUL!" as the producer slung it over his shoulder and carried it away.

He sent a silent prayer to the heavens to keep it safe during filming.

Cooper turns the camera over in his hands and inspects it for damage, but finds none. Relief lifts an invisible weight from his shoulders. The only thing he missed more than this camera is his horse, Nutcracker—a sorrel American quarter horse with a white stripe down her nose. To the uninformed, her bright red coat would seem the source of her name. Unfortunately, it's not. Not even close. She earned her name by completely busting his balls during the eight weeks it took to break her in. Literally, busting his balls. The wranglers used to line up along the fence to watch him hold on for dear life while she bucked like a beast possessed. The name was their idea.

God, I miss her.

He's never spent this much time away from her. He's never spent this much time away from a horse, period.

She'll probably kill me when I get back. Out of spite.

He chuckles softly to himself and dips his head beneath the camera strap. It feels good to have something familiar in his hands, a little taste of home. He's surprised how much he misses it. The ranch. The animals. The memories.

Cooper waits until he leaves the bungalow before switching the camera on. Like always, he takes a steadying breath before he lifts the viewfinder to his eye. A warm tingle spreads across his chest, equal parts pleasure and pain. He never feels closer to his mom than he does like this, with her prized possession a gentle weight against his cheekbone, and he never misses her more. Photography was her passion, her calling. When her camera is in his hands, it's as if she's alive again through his eyes, whispering in his ear to line up the composition and test the light and fiddle with the exposure. Even in her darkest days, she never lost her talent. She couldn't always remember his face. She couldn't always remember her age or their house or when and where exactly she was. But she remembered this. Right until the very end, when she stopped registering the sound of his voice and lost the ability to speak and could do little more than shuffle on unsteady feet while he kept an arm around her to keep her from falling, she could press the shutter on the camera, her whole body relaxing with that subtle...

Click.

Tension oozes from his body.

Click.

His stress melts away.

Click.

The world somehow both fades and comes into sharp focus, worries replaced by lines and shades and shapes and colors.

For you, Mom.

He presses the button.

And also for me.

sam

WHEN THEY ARRIVE at the beach for their jet ski tour, Nina is there waiting. The producer offers an overly cheerful wave. Sam does her best not to scowl.

I swear that woman is stalking us.

One afternoon. All she wanted was one afternoon without watchful eyes. One afternoon off. One afternoon with a little bit of distance from the man who is now casually threading his fingers through hers and pulling her closer. His touch is tender, but with a rough edge, his calloused palm scratching in just the right way. It's impossible not to imagine that gentle scrape against the soft skin of her stomach, those large, commanding fingers dipping low.

Aaaaaand I'm thinking about sex again...

Fuck.

She swallows and straightens her spine. This is the problem with Cooper. He's too damn hot. He walks inconspicuously into the room and—bam! Her hormones rage. Her imagination cartwheels into dangerous territory. And worse, her heart...twinges. An uncomfortable ache has pinched her chest all morning, and she's over it.

Screw you, cowboy!

Why did he have to say her name in that deep, sexy rumble that seemed to touch every sensitive part of her? She can still hear him.

They can't hold you either, Samantha.

Not Cuj.

Not Sam.

Samantha.

Even now, a shiver ripples across her skin. As if feeling it, Cooper glances over. She refuses to meet his questioning gaze. As if it's not enough for him to have six-pack abs and a jawline cut from diamonds, he's got to stand there all devilishly handsome and wax poetic about how she deserves more out of life. Then, THEN, he walks around with a camera looking all artistic and brooding and shit.

My god.

A girl can only take so much.

You cannot go there, Sam. Think of Em. Think of her business. She's depending on you not to screw this up. Well, more than you already have.

It's the kick in the ass she needs.

"Hi, Nina!" Sam waves back politely. Then she grabs Cooper's arm with her free hand and leans in to give his obnoxiously firm bicep a hug. It's the worst. Not really. But —ugh. "How are you?"

"Good. Sort of. Actually, I'm bored to death with Trish and Fred, and I was hoping you wouldn't mind if I joined you guys for the jet ski tour."

"Not at all," Cooper immediately supplies, ever the gentleman.

Asshole.

"Great!" Nina's entire face brightens. Her dark brown gaze slides to the side. "The tour guide said we only had two jet skis reserved and it was too late to change that, but you two don't mind sharing, right?"

Sam is too busy trying to shoot lasers from her eyes to answer.

Cooper squeezes her hand. "Right."

"Perfect."

The tour guide steps forward. He's middle aged and bald with the most infectious smile she's ever seen, white teeth bright against his golden-brown skin. He seems like a nice guy, the sort to jump from an airplane at the drop of a hat just for the thrill. Too bad she's too busy imagining how to rip every one of Nina's limbs from her body to pay attention to a single thing he says. A continuous stream of curse words simmers in the back of Sam's thoughts, the metaphorical current surging as they wade into the water and climb onto their jet skis. Cooper grabs her by the waist and heaves her easily into the seat as if she weighs nothing at all. Lightning strikes deep in her abdomen, a sudden flash of heat.

Kill me now.

The last thing Sam needs is the freedom to wrap her arms around Cooper's torso for the next two hours and *accidentally* feel up every inch of those rock-hard abs. Yes, they're wearing life jackets. No, that will not stop her traitorous hands.

She launches herself into the driver's seat and grips the handles.

Much better.

Except, no.

No. No. No.

Cooper settles in behind her, close enough she can feel a hefty bulge between her ass cheeks. He drops his hands to his meaty thighs for a second, then hovers them on either side of her waist, before finally reaching forward to grip the handles too, as if that's better, safer.

It's not.

His whole front presses against her whole back. His arms stretch alongside hers. His fingers mold around the outer edges of her hands. He's like her own personal cocoon. Warm breath brushes against the back of her neck. Goose bumps rise along her skin. The area burns with awareness that his lips are *right there*, and—

Abort.

ABORT.

"Got any idea what you're doing, Cuj?"

Goddamn it, why is the cockiness in his tone so attractive? And why does it go against every fiber of her DNA to let his implied challenge go? She's answering before she can stop herself. "You're not the only one who knows how to ride, cowboy."

A soft chuckle spills through his lips, puffs of air splashing against her neck like a tide. The deep rumble reverberates across his chest and down his arms, touching every part of her. Sam squirms, trying to fight the sudden tension in her core. But it has the opposite effect when she feels one very specific appendage harden in response.

"I bet you do," he murmurs, almost more to himself. Then he clears his throat. "But do you know how to ride one of these? Because I'd prefer to know exactly how close to death I'm traveling today."

She turns her face to the side. The tips of their noses graze. His eyes darken.

"No faith," she whispers, the sound huskier than she intended.

"Oh, I believe you can do anything you set your mind to. Trust me." His gaze dips to her mouth before he swallows and looks back up. "But I also believe you'd break into the gates of hell just to prove you could."

His pupils dilate, edging out the emerald. She snaps her face forward.

"I like to go fast," she warns.

"Darlin'," he murmurs, lips brushing the outer edge of her ear. Tingles cascade down her neck and across her shoulders, making her shiver. Something inside her chest swells. "I already knew that."

Sam hits the throttle, a sudden need to go, to run, to get away drowning out the rest.

They don't move.

She wrinkles her nose and holds down the throttle again. *Come on.*

Nothing.

She squeezes as hard as she can, then shakes the handles in frustration, one second from punching the stupid thing.

"Cuj?"

"I've got it," she snaps, wound way too tight.

"I know." Amusement simmers in his voice. "But it might help to turn it on first."

Oh, for fuck's sake.

She turns the key. The engine rumbles to life, which isn't really helping things *down there*, so she guns it. They jerk forward with a burst of speed. Sam flies back, saved only by the human cage wrapped around her. Cooper grips the handles, his forearms flexing so tightly his veins pop. It's a more absorbing view than the aqua waves surrounding them on all sides. Water droplets glide over muscular contours. Tan skin glistens in the sunlight. She may or may not lick her lips.

"Christ," he mutters as he snatches her hand off the throttle. The engine cuts and they slow to a stop, bobbing up and down in the water.

Cleared from her daze, Sam elbows him in the ribs and retakes control. Speed is what she needs right now. A thrill. A distraction. "Not even he can save you now, cowboy."

They're off.

"Fucking hell," Cooper grumbles as he recloses his fists around the handles and presses his legs firmly against her thighs to hold them both in place.

This time, she doesn't let it distract her.

She keeps her eyes on the water, her mind clear of everything but the wind and the waves and the electric rush.

The guide surges ahead, taking the lead. Nina shoots closer with a wide grin and revs her engine in challenge. With a sudden laugh, Sam meets it. They race, practically flying as they bump across the sea. Cooper hollers wildly, a pure burst of joy, sounding just the way she imagines a cowboy should. It's easy to picture him galloping across a field on the back of his horse, kicking his spurs, hands on the reins, a feral gleam in his eyes—too easy. She blinks the image away and goes faster, all of her concentration on controlling the machine beneath her as a turquoise world rushes by.

Twenty minutes in, a school of dolphins joins the fun, leaping alongside their jet skis, darting and diving and flipping through the waves. Forty-five minutes in, the guide cuts his engine out of nowhere and points toward a dark shadow under the surface.

"Whale shark!" he calls before leaping into the water and diving deep.

Sam doesn't even think. In a blink, she follows him in. Cooper splashes behind her. A minute later, a white-speckled mouth emerges from the endless blue, wide open, but not threatening. The gentle giant glides effortlessly by, paying them no mind. It's got to be thirty feet long. Her heart lurches into her throat as she blindly grabs for Cooper's hand. Their fingers clasp in part awe, part fear, part *I can't believe this is real!*

At the halfway mark, he takes over driving. They stop a few more times to see turtles and rays and giant schools of fish. She presses her cheek flush against his spine and wraps her arms firmly around his waist. It's all too easy to pretend the ring gleaming on her finger is real. She tells herself it's this place. The Maldives are made for romance. Bathing suits. Heat. Beauty all around. She could feign an affair with a cardboard cutout here. But deep down, she knows it's partially Cooper too. His looks, yes, but more the way he drinks life in as if it's the most satisfying cocktail he's ever been lucky enough to consume. Laughter spills freely from his lips. Joy seeps off him like the sweetest sweat. An infectious glow lives inside his eyes. He's not jaded. He's not thinking ten steps ahead. He's not dragging a deadweight. He's just...happy. Happy to be here. Happy to be present. Happy to soak it all in. It makes her want to be closer to him, as though she could get high off the residual fumes, as though maybe around him she could just be breezily, easily happy, too.

The way she used to be.

The way she wishes she could be again.

Out on the open ocean, with blue skies above and blue seas below, adrift and unmoored, no sense of place or time, it's easy for Sam to slip into this dream. But the sight of swaying palm trees and sandy shores is a harsh return to reality, a rough hand rousing her from sleep. The resort looms like a parent with watchful eyes, able to read every mischievous thought in her mind, silently demanding she behave. She suddenly realizes her hands did indeed sneak beneath the edges of Cooper's life jacket. Her fingers are spread wide over hard, hot skin, feeling muscles shift and flex as he cuts the engine. She reluctantly drops her arms.

"Wow, that was great!" Nina calls over. "Thanks for letting me tag along."

The note of farewell in the producer's voice causes a sudden ache in Sam's chest. It seems almost cruel to go from the speed and the thrill and the fun back to the room where she knows her computer is waiting with calls and spreadsheets and endless grunt work she can't afford to ignore. It's too much. She's not ready to go back yet.

"How about a drink?" Sam blurts.

Cooper swivels to look at her. His gaze touches every part of her face, seeing too much before the edges of his lips quirk. "I'm in."

"Nina?" She extends the invite not because she particularly likes the woman's company, but because in it, she has an excuse to keep touching him.

"I'm always down for a piña colada."

"I pegged you as more of a whiskey soda kind of girl."

The producer rubs a palm over the left side of her head where her black hair is cut almost to the scalp and grins. "Don't let this fool you. I'm not nearly as edgy as I seem. And piña coladas are fucking delicious, like frozen pineapple coconut crack. I make no promises you won't have to carry me back to my room."

Sam pats Cooper's bicep. "I think he can handle it."

"Rock on."

With a thanks to the guide, they ditch the jet skis and head to the beach bar. It's too easy, the way Cooper slides his arm around the back of her chair and casually runs his fingers over her shoulder and down her arm. Too natural, how quickly her own hand snakes over his lower thigh to hook under the back side of his knee. They drink and chat and joke and laugh. An hour passes in a blink. Nina begs off, walking in a zigzag back toward the bungalow, leaving the two of them in a buzzed haze.

Sam zeroes in on the shape his lips take as he wraps them around his beer bottle. The way his Adam's apple bobs as he swallows. How his red hair curls over his ears, practically begging to be pushed back.

She takes a sip of her drink.

His eyes flash as he drops his gaze to her mouth on the straw. She inhales sharply, acutely aware of her breasts and how they rise and how his attention shifts a little lower.

The heat spikes, suddenly oppressive.

"We should probably get back," she murmurs, wanting to do anything but leave this moment. The suggestion sounds weak, hollow. She clears her throat. "I have some work I need to do."

"Sure. If that's what you want..."

It is.

It is.

IT IS.

"That's what I want," she answers, voice clipped. Because, obviously, it's not. He knows it. She knows it. The bartender who's been serving them drinks for an hour probably knows it too. But the only thing she wants more than to eat Cooper's face off right here at the beach bar, then drag him back to their bungalow to have her way with him is to help her sister. And those two things are at direct odds with each other.

She quickly slurps up the last of her piña colada.

He downs the rest of his beer.

The five-minute walk back to the bungalow lasts a millennium in the taut silence stretching between them. Sam doesn't even glance his way as she fumbles with the key and pushes open the door.

He grabs her hand and stops her.

She looks then, over her shoulder, up at his too-close face and his burning gaze. His hold is gentle, yet commanding.

Don't do it, those steady eyes seem to say.

Don't cross that line.

Don't go back inside.

Don't become a stranger.

Stay here, with him.

Keep having fun. Keep laughing. Keep playing.

Keep pretending.

But that's the problem. Deep down, she can already tell that with him, on some level it's not a game. There's potential there, a popcorn kernel of it wedged so annoyingly deep no amount of pressure can dislodge it. She can't give in and let it fester. She's got to pick and prod and poke until it's gone.

He runs his thumb over the back of her hand. "Sam..."

"Rule three, Cooper."

He stills.

She takes the opening and shakes her fingers free. With her tail between her legs, she flees into the bungalow, grabs her computer from the table, and retreats into the safety of her room.

Unfortunately, work is the last thing on her mind.

Goddamn it.

Sam grabs her phone. Without thinking, she scrolls to the usual name, hovers over the call button, then —remembers.

I can't call Em.

Literally, she can't call Em. Her sister's phone is tucked away in her bag, waiting to be mailed back to Georgia the second she returns to the US.

She could call Jake.

He could pass Emily the phone.

She could come clean to them both and confess about the accidental engagement. She could beg her sister for forgiveness and promise to make it right. She could ask for her opinion...or her blessing.

She could.

Except...

They know each other too well. They once shared a

uterus, for god's sake. There's no hiding with Em. No running. It's one of the many reasons Sam stayed in New York—to keep eight hundred miles between her and those knowing eyes. Em will have questions, questions Sam definitely isn't ready to answer.

She scrolls again, dials, waits.

"Well, well, well," a familiar Texas drawl answers mirthfully. "The prodigal roomie returns."

Sam rolls her eyes. "I've been gone for like five days, Winnie."

"Five days gallivanting in paradise, not bothering to call or text. Did you even spare a thought for me, all alone in the desolate trenches of New York City?"

"We live in the Village." Sam snorts. "You're doing fine. And aren't Em and Jake with you?"

"They left for the airport this morning, about two hours ago, and let me just say, regular sex is a good look on your sister."

"Ewww." Sam slaps a hand over her face to smother her laugh. "They better not have been doing it in my bed."

"I can neither confirm nor deny hearing noises."

"Noises?"

"*Noises.*"

"I'm burning the mattress when I get back."

"Hell no, you're not. I need that deposit."

"Then I'm taking yours."

"Have at it." Winnie barks out a laugh. "Maybe the pheromones will rub off on me. Lord knows I'll take whatever help I can get in that department."

"Actually..." Sam takes a deep breath. "I could too. Use some help, I mean."

"Spill."

She falls back on the mattress and flings her free arm over her eyes as if to shield herself from the embarrassment. She can practically feel Winnie's giddiness through the phone. It's as if her roommate is there, kneeling on the bed, hazel eyes wide, black waves bouncing as she quietly claps her hands with eager delight. They've been inseparable ever since that fateful morning sophomore year when Sam sat down next to her at the start of *English 125: Studies in Literature* and muttered *fuck* as she spilled her latte completely down the front of her white tank. Winnie saved her ass by giving her a sweater, then pretty much held her hand through the rest of the semester so she didn't fail the class, then became her best friend. She was a bright light in an otherwise dark time, the definition of positivity, something Sam could use a little bit of right about now.

She groans. "I accidentally got engaged to the most attractive man on the planet, and all I want to do is rip his clothes off, but I can't."

"What?" Winnie practically screams. "Why not?"

"Because *I* didn't actually get engaged to him. Emily did. On television. For ten million people to see. Which might be a problem, considering she spent the past few days fucking one of the producers of the show. In my bed, apparently. And if that ever comes out, everyone in America would probably hate her. I mean, come on. It's juicy as hell. The tabloids would feast on her carcass. We both know it. She'd be labeled a slut and a whore, some sort of praying mantis, while the men of course got off scot free. Misogyny at its finest. No one would care that Jake was her ex. No one would believe she'd been faking it for the show. They'd see the worst. Because that's what the world always sees in a woman who makes a mistake. A villain. Her business would be ruined. And I can't—I can't do that."

"You've given this some thought."

Sam sighs. "I have."

"He must be really, *really* hot."

"So hot. You have no idea."

"Yeah… I'm going to need a visual. I need to know exactly what we're working with before I give you any advice."

"I'm not sending you a picture."

Winnie hums for a moment. "How about a celebrity comparison? I get them all the time for work."

She's an assistant designer at a publishing house. Romance covers are her bread and butter.

"Sort of like that guy from *Outlander*. What's his name?"

Winnie gasps so loudly it sounds as if she's been possessed. They're a bit of a dramatic duo. "Sam Heughan."

"Yeah, him."

"He looks like Sam Heughan?"

"Yes."

"SAM MOTHERFUCKING HEUGHAN?"

"Yes. But also sort of like Brad Pitt."

"BRAD PITT?"

"Yeah. You know that scene in *Legends of the Fall* where Tristan comes riding across the plains and meets Susannah for the first time and tips his hat with a smile and she's like, *Oh shit, I chose the wrong brother*?"

"You mean the scene that was wholly responsible for my sexual awakening at fifteen? Yes. I know the scene."

"He looks like that, but better."

"Better?" she squeals, sounding parched.

"Yeah, because he's real." Sam wets her lips, swallows. "Like how you can see an ice cream cone on a commercial and think, *Damn. I want one of those.* But if it's the middle of summer, and a hundred degrees out, and you're on the beach, and someone walks by licking a drip off the side of a fresh vanilla-chocolate swirl, it's almost a religious experience? You don't just want one. You *need* one. It's like that."

"Sleep with him."

"Winnie—"

"Sleep with him right now or I will never forgive you."

"Oh my god." Sam laughs into the crook of her elbow. "Did you not hear me? I can't. You're supposed to be talking me out of this."

"Well, I'm not."

"That's the whole reason I called!"

"Please," Winnie comments dismissively. "We both know that's not true."

Sam stills. "What do you mean?"

"You did not call me, your best friend who reads three romance novels a week, to tell me that you're fake engaged to the hottest man in the world and, now that I think of it, that there's probably only one bed because you wanted to be talked *out of it.*"

"Yes. I did."

"Sam."

She gulps. Winnie's pointed glare burns a hole in the side of her skull from across the Atlantic. "I *did.*"

"Sam."

"What?"

"Samantha Rose Peters."

"*What?*"

"Maybe you can lie to yourself, but you can't lie to me. You're calling for permission. And I'm giving it. Sleep with him. You owe it to...sex. No, not sex. Me. Your perpetually single best friend whose vagina is practically the Sahara. Do it for me."

"But...Em. And the bullying. And the misogyny. And cancel culture. And feminism. And—"

"Don't throw buzzwords at me, young lady. What's really stopping you?"

"He's a cowboy. Like an actual cowboy. From a ranch. With a hat and everything."

Winnie harrumphs. "I'm from Texas. That's pretty much a prerequisite. You could use a cowboy after all the awful finance bros you've brought home."

Sam sits up. "I do NOT date finance bros. That'd be like shitting where I eat."

"Gross," Winnie comments, no doubt wrinkling her nose. "But the point stands. They wear those vests. They have that look. Potato po*tah*to. What else you got?"

Nothing.

She has nothing.

Because Cooper pushes all her buttons yet respects every inch of her boundaries. He's way too kind to be real, but has enough edge to keep her interested. He's calloused hands with an artist's soul. A delicious dichotomy. A dangerous one. Worst of all, he's the type of guy who always has a bout of laughter simmering at the back of his throat, not because he's never faced hardship, but in spite of it. She thinks about the somber shift of his features when he mentioned his mother, the haunted shadow erupting in the corners of his eyes. To lose a loved one to a disease like that and still be able to smile? To see the joy in life? She admires him. She doesn't know how he does it. He's just...

He's perfect.

He's fucking perfect.

And that's the problem.

"You sleep with guys all the time," Winnie continues, oblivious. "What's the big— Oh."

"Oh, what?"

"Ohhhhh."

"Winnie."

"I love a good plot twist."

"This is not a romance novel."

"Actually, Sammy baby, I'm pretty sure it is."

"Sammy baby?"

"You like him."

"Sure. He's a nice guy."

"No. You *like him* like him."

"I do not."

"The lady doth protest too much, methinks."

"I protested once."

"You're afraid you can't just sleep with him. You're afraid you'll catch feelings."

"I am—"

"Not?" Winnie interrupts with a delighted giggle. "Is that another protest?"

"Okay, this conversation is officially done."

"But it just got interesting!"

"I'm going now."

"You can't run from me, Sam."

"Love you."

"I know where you live!"

"Bye."

She hangs up and lets her face fall toward the door. The soft sound of shuffling feet travels closer. He's right there, so close, so tantalizingly close, almost as though he's out there waiting, wondering, wanting in the same way she is.

Sam can't help it.

She stands up.

cooper

WHEN SHE OPENS THE DOOR, he's standing right outside of it like a fucking creeper.

Smooth, man. Real smooth.

"Done working?" he asks casually, grasping for something, anything to say.

She shrugs. "I thought I heard you pacing out here."

"I wasn't pacing."

She arches her brow.

Shit. Was I pacing? "I didn't mean to bother you."

"You didn't." She licks her lips and glances furtively up from beneath hooded brows. It's a more vulnerable glance than he's used to getting from her. "So, um, what were you pacing about?"

"Oh, just..."

He's got nothing. Unless of course he tells her the truth, which is that he can still feel her ass cheeks pressed up against him. Can still sense her auburn hair tickling at his cheeks. Can still hear her intoxicating laughter on the breeze. That every time he closes his eyes, he sees her sitting across from him in that bikini with her lips wrapped tight around her straw. Actually, he could really use a straw to grasp at right about now. Anything except the confession hovering at the tip of his tongue—that he was drawn to this spot like a moth to a flame, ready to get burned.

He clears his throat.

"Dinner."

"Dinner?" She wrinkles her nose. "It's only four thirty."

Damn. Is it really? He feels as if he's been trapped in this bungalow for hours. "I'm starving. Do you mind eating early?"

"No."

She glances to the side and stares at something deep within her room. The way she casually bites her lower lip leaves him lightheaded from the blood rush.

"I guess I could—"

"I was going to call—"

They both stop.

A slightly horrified expression takes over her face as she rushes to say, "You go. And don't give me any crap about ladies first. If I wanted to go first, I would, and I wouldn't need your permission to do it."

"I wouldn't dare, Cuj." A smile tugs at his lips. "All I was going to ask is if you wanted me to order you some room service. I'm about to call something in."

"Room service."

He eyes her uncertainly. "Yes...?"

"*Room service,*" she repeats, louder this time, her eyes bugging just a little before she shakes it off. "Right. Of course. Sure, get me the shrimp salad I had the other day. Thanks."

The door slams in his face.

He recoils as if she slapped him. *The hell?*

And then her fractured sentence registers. *I guess I could—*

Could what?

I guess I could eat. I guess I could have dinner. I guess I could stand here and look at you and talk as if I'm not affected at all.

That makes one of them.

Except he thinks about the way she briefly studied her room, the way her teeth worried over her lower lip, the way her cheeks turned a slight shade of pink. He assumed she was annoyed, but could she have actually been...embarrassed?

Shit.

He's suddenly positive about what she was going to say. *I guess I could go get dinner.*

As in go somewhere.

As in leave this room.

Together.

Shiiiit.

Well, he dropped that fucking ball, didn't he?

Cooper lifts his hand as if to knock, then lets it fall. He

knows her well enough to know that the opportunity has passed. Whatever momentary breach in her defenses occurred, it's done now. The mortar's patched. The crack is filled. That ten-foot-thick stone wall stands solid once again.

An hour later, he calls out to let her know the food is there, then he returns to the deck where he left his camera perched on a mini-tripod. The sky is just beginning to pinken, and he's itching to capture a sunset before he leaves. Dusk was always his mother's favorite time of day because it was when the ranch finally loosened its hold on her husband. Cooper spent many an evening with her on that back porch, curled against her side in the swing his father had built, watching the sky turn gold, looking for a figure on the horizon while the scent of a hearty dinner wafted on the breeze like a lure. He spent even more evenings on the back of his horse, the glow from the kitchen spilling like a beacon into an ever-darkening night, riding toward home with an ache in his gut, following his nose.

But that was before she passed.

Before the house went dark.

"Can I join you?"

He fumbles with his camera, practically jumping out of his skin as he spins. His heart is a racehorse thundering around a track. "Yeah, yeah. Of course. Yeah."

An amused smile overtakes her face. "You all right there, cowboy?"

Honestly, he's not sure. The sight of her has struck him

stupid. If he thought she was sexy in that ivory gown on the beach, or in his hat and little else, or in that barely-there bikini, he wasn't prepared for this. Her face is freshly washed and clear of any makeup. Her hair is a mess bundled high atop her head in some sort of gravity-defying bun he has no idea how she secured. Glasses he had no clue she needed rest on her nose. Black leggings cover her down to her ankles and a downy pink sweatshirt hangs off her frame, two sizes too big. He can't stop looking at the spot where it falls tantalizingly off her shoulder. He's never been so turned on by six bare inches of skin. Freckles dance along her collarbone and all he wants to do is lick them.

This is Sam.

Not the vixen or the analyst or the actress.

It's a glimpse at the real woman hiding underneath. A tease. And all it does is make him want to see how beautiful she looks when she comes completely undone.

"I'm good." Cooper forces the words up his dry throat. They come out as little more than a deep, rough rumble. Sam's eyes flutter for a moment. "I just didn't expect you. I thought you had to work."

"I'm taking a break." She shrugs and settles down on a lounger with her dinner plate. "So, Cooper. Tell me. What's the most unattractive thing about you?"

"Unattractive?" He sits across from her with a sly smile and grabs his own plate. "Why? Need a deterrent?"

She forks a cherry tomato and lobs it at his face. He

catches it smoothly and pops it into his mouth with a wink. She rolls her eyes.

"Come on, just give me something. You pick your nose and eat it. You had an STD. You have explosive diarrhea every time you drunk order a three-bean burrito from the bodega down the block, but they taste so good and the alcohol strips away every ounce of your self-preservation that you keep doing it anyway."

He arches a brow. "No to all of the above, though that last one sounded oddly specific, Cuj."

"I'm talking hypothetically."

Hypothetical my ass. "Sure you are."

"There has to be something. Anything."

"I..." He pauses to think and takes a bite of his fish. It's good, but he can't wait for a nice, juicy steak when he goes home. He was born and raised in cattle country. This seafood thing isn't for him. "Oh, here's something. I can't sing for shit."

She scrunches her face while she chews, then rocks her head from side to side as if weighing the offering. "It's not quite explosive diarrhea level, but it's a start. So, let's go. Have at it."

"I never said I'd demonstrate."

"Seriously?"

"I'll pass."

"Come on. Turn me off, Cooper Kelley. I dare you."

He offers her a flat stare. She pouts her lips in an innocent, pleading expression that's annoyingly adorable. Those doe eyes blink up at him, once, twice. And, dammit.

That's all it takes. The Devil himself would sell his soul if she asked with that face.

He clears his throat.

The opening lines of "Friends in Low Places," a classic and the first song that comes to mind, force their way up his throat. He cringes internally but keeps going at the sight of her widening smile. A twinkle lights her eyes. As soon as he makes it through the chorus, he stops and she launches into a slow clap.

He palms his face with a groan. "I can't believe I just did that."

"Fuck you," she charges with a laugh. "That was endearing."

"You need your ears checked."

"Oh, I heard it. Very...dying mountain lion."

"Shut up."

"Beyoncé ain't got nothing on you."

"Yeah, yeah." He waves her off. "Your turn."

"No way. That didn't count."

"Like hell it didn't count."

"I want something embarrassing, like really, truly, down-to-your-core embarrassing. Yours was...eh. I've been to too many Korean Karaoke bars at two a.m. Half the people I know sound worse than you."

A thought pops in.

He mentally shakes it off, but not quickly enough. She notices. Hunger fills her eyes like a wolf's on the hunt.

"Spill."

"Nah."

"Come on." She leans forward, holding his gaze. "You thought of something, I know you did. Lay it on me. It's good. I can tell."

"This will cost you."

"How much?"

"I'm not sure yet."

"I'm a betting woman, Coop."

"All right. I tell you this, and you'll owe me one honest answer to whatever question I want to ask."

"Done."

Dammit. He was hoping it would take her longer to agree. This one is...bad. This one might actually turn her off for real.

Too late now.

"When I was a kid, I had a huge thing for Shania Twain."

"Who didn't? The woman is a goddess."

"No, I mean a *huge* thing. Listened to her music. Saw all her videos. Probably would've died on the spot if I ever met her in person." He lowers his voice and stares at Sam meaningfully. "Had a box of magazine cutouts under my bed, if you catch my drift."

"I got you." She snorts. "How is this embarrassing?"

"It's not, except that, after spending the entirety of my teenage years fantasizing about the woman, I noticed a slight problem."

"Problem?"

"*Problem.*" He swallows. *I can't believe I'm admitting this out loud.* "Every time I hear her music I still, you know, down there..."

She furrows her brows, not understanding. Then her eyes widen. Her jaw drops elatedly. "You pop a woody?"

He winces and pinches the bridge of his nose. "I can't hear 'Man! I Feel Like a Woman!' without getting a very *slight* but definitely still existent hard-on."

"HA!"

He presses on, trying to explain. "It's like Pavlov's dogs. I've been conditioned. I can't stop it."

She falls back on the lounger giggling and kicks her feet up into the air. "Oh my god."

"I know."

"Oh my god."

"I know."

She whirls back up to a seated position with an evil gleam in her eye. "You do know you just handed me the key to your undoing, don't you?"

"Great power comes with great responsibility."

She hums the opening refrain of the song.

He glares at her. "Stop that."

She keeps humming.

"Don't start something you're not prepared to finish, Cuj."

That shuts her up, though the smile on her lips could still give the Cheshire cat a run for his money.

"Okay, okay. But that was so worth it. You definitely earned your one question. Shoot."

"Eh, I don't think so."

"What do you mean?"

"I think I'm going to hold on to that baby for a little while, dangle it over your head for a bit, hit you with it when you least expect it."

"Don't make me start singing again, cowboy."

"You won't."

"What makes you so sure?"

"Because, Sam," he answers honestly. She swallows at the sound of her name. "You do a good job of hiding it, but I know you well enough to know that you're afraid of going there, a helluva lot more afraid than I am, which begs the question, what's got you so interested in spilling secrets all of a sudden?"

She looks away.

Her jaw tightens.

He tilts his head to study her, aware he's drawing close to the line and unable to stop himself from testing the limits. "What happened to rule four?"

"I don't want your secrets, Cooper." She meets his gaze head-on, not backing down. A stubborn curl purses her lips as she leans forward. "I want your red flags."

Behind her, the sun starts to sink into the ocean, casting the sky in brilliant shades of orange and red. But it's not romantic. It's apocalyptic as the air between them turns taut, the conversation switching to dangerous territory as the oxygen is sucked from the sky. Tension radiates between them, a buildup they've both been trying to ignore.

He's not so sure he wants to any longer.

"For a city girl like you? That's easy. I live on a ranch in what you would call the middle of nowhere. The closest grocery store is an hour's drive and if you want to eat at any restaurant other than a steak house you'll practically need an airplane to do it. My idea of a fun night out is line dancing at the local dive, and come hell or high water I will spend every Saturday afternoon in the fall watching the Huskers kick some ass. I've broken girls' hearts. I've broken some beds too. And I've never met a rule I didn't know how to bend. But if none of that scares you, here's the real kicker."

He folds his hands between his legs and leans forward with his elbows on his knees so they're nose to nose. She doesn't back off. And damn if he doesn't like that fire.

"Over the next three months, my love story with your sister is going to play out on national television. None of it's real, but when has that ever mattered? And thanks to us both, it's going to end with a proposal. So if we don't want the entire country coming down on our heads, we'd best stick to the plan and keep our distance."

He's starting to wonder if he's talking to her, or to himself, especially as his focus drops to her lips, his eyes zeroing in on those plush pink petals. They're slightly parted and glistening with the barest hint of moisture, utterly ripe for the picking.

The ranch. Think about the ranch.

He swallows.

Think about the followers, and the money, and everything a season as the lead could bring.

But he can't.

All he can think about are those lips and where exactly he wants them.

"But like I said," Cooper murmurs, still transfixed. "Good decisions have never been my strong suit."

"This is a bad idea," she whispers, even as she leans the slightest bit closer.

"The best ones always are."

Her golden eyes flare like the flash of fire on a cold, dry night, whispering of imminent danger. Too bad for him, his innate response has always been to find his truck and drive into the flames. The risk only makes the reward that much sweeter.

"Cooper." Her gaze darts over his features as if searching for an escape hatch, a reason to turn away. Like an afterthought, she adds, "This makes no sense."

"No, it doesn't," he agrees as a new thought enters his mind, a loophole in the plan. "But just because something's fleeting doesn't mean it can't be fun. Forever isn't in the cards for us, but we still have right now. And I, for one, have never let worries about the rest of a cake keep me from enjoying my slice."

"There's just one problem with your analogy, cowboy."

"What's that?"

"This attraction between us doesn't feel like a cake. It feels like a drug." Her gaze drops to his shoulders, his arms, his legs. She looks at him the way he imagines a drunk at a bar looks at a beer growing warm on the counter, the mere act of being this close a battle of wills. "One hit might be all it takes."

"Is that what you're really afraid of, Cuj?" Is that how she sees love, like an all-consuming spiral to the bottom, a death trap? "Getting addicted?"

Her gaze flies back to meet his, lust and panic a heady mix. "Is that your question, Coop?"

"No."

She sucks in a breath and lurches away, breaking the spell. "Then I guess we'll never know."

But he doesn't need to hear it.

The answer is obvious. It's the *why* that's bugging him —and the *what*, and the *who*, and the *how come*. She's too strong, too beautiful, and too young to be so jaded.

Slow and steady, he reminds himself as he watches her gather up the rest of her dinner. *Slow and steady.*

That's how it goes with horses, and that's how it goes with women too. Don't push past their comfort levels. Don't force it. Just take what they offer when they offer it and keep plowing ahead one little step at a time.

When she retreats back inside, he returns to his camera. The sun has almost disappeared beneath the horizon but it's not gone yet, so he tests the light and snaps a couple of photographs. His mom would have loved it here, the vast, unimpeded sky so similar to the one at home, but the never-ending stretch of water reflecting it back so different from the silhouetted plains he's used to.

She would have loved Sam, too.

The thought hits him like a punch, sucking the breath from his lungs. As soon as it lands, he knows it's true. She would've loved Sam's strength...would've especially loved her ability to get him by the balls. If there was one thing his mother always bemoaned, it was the sweet, eager-to-please girls he used to bring home.

This ranch will eat you alive if you let it, she used to tell him. *Find someone who'll give you a kick in the ass when you need it, not a cavity.*

Remembering the way she gave his dad a good ass-kicking whenever he needed it brings a small smile to his lips. There were days when the man would rather face a bucking bronco than his own wife, but at the end of the night, they always found their way back to each other. He took it for granted as a boy. But now? Now he'd give anything for just one more day, one more hour, one more moment of rolling his eyes at their antics.

Maybe that's why he's still smiling when he wakes up the next day, why he keeps his boxers on for his morning swim, why he's so eager to push Sam's buttons.

He knows, without a doubt, she'll push back.

sam

SHE SHOULD BE USED to it by now, but waking up to the sight of Cooper's gorgeous, wet body gleaming in the soft morning sun isn't the sort of thing one simply *gets used to*. It's the sort of thing that causes mild heart attacks. The sort of thing that leaves her grumbling under her breath as she scrounges around for the tiniest sports bra she can find among her sister's clothes. The sort of thing that prompts one desire and one desire alone—the need to punch something.

Okay, well, *two* desires.

But the second one can go to hell. She is NOT having sexual relations with that man—not even imagined ones. Well, not anymore.

New day.

New Sam.

And yes, she could work out inside. But this is her deck too, dammit. She deserves the fresh air. She deserves the view. She deserves to have that cowboy salivating at the sight of her heaving bosom.

I have got to stop reading those historical romances Winnie keeps giving me.

Sam holds her fists in the air and ignores the man treading water twenty feet away. A punching bag would be ideal right about now, but alas, she'll have to make do. Instead, she draws up the image of Cooper's smiling face, complete with those drawn-by-the-Devil dimples, and starts swinging. It doesn't take long to lose herself in the familiar movements.

Jab. Cross. Body shot. Head shot. Rear elbow strike. Front kick. Back kick. Uppercut. Double strike roundhouse. Jump kick. Heel click. Switch.

Again.

And again.

And again.

Everything falls away. This is her favorite thing about cardio kickboxing—the ability to lose herself in the movements. Brain focused. Muscles burning. Wayward thoughts gone. It's just her and her target. Her and her body. Her and her fists and her feet smashing into every inch of that gorgeous, sculpted man she's dying to touch... but can't.

"Whoa! Watch it, killer!"

Sam snaps back to the world as his hand closes around her fist, stopping it two inches shy of his sternum. She's heaving and out of breath. Sweat drips over her arms as the sun beats down. The appreciative gleam in Cooper's eye tells her he's been watching, but there's no way to know for how long. She should feel victorious that it was his turn to ogle her. Instead, she can't help but notice how close they're standing, how broad his shoulders are, how much he towers over her, and yet how utterly safe she feels being held at his mercy.

It's terrifying.

Sam yanks her hand free. He lets go right away with an easy smile, that little pucker in his cheek practically winking at her.

"Picturing anyone specific with those punches, Cuj?"

"Yeah. You." He barks out a laugh at her unexpected honesty. She raises her arms overhead and starts stretching, feigning a nonchalance she doesn't quite feel. "I need to get my aggression out somehow."

"Aggression, huh? Is that what you're calling it?"

"Don't make me drop-kick you."

"I'd love to see you try."

"Careful what you wish for, cowboy," she warns while lifting her heels to stretch her quads. "My father is a police chief and he made sure I knew self-defense before I moved to New York. I could end you."

"Now that you mention it, I do remember one of the guys saying Em accidentally knocked him out."

She glances up while reaching for her toes. "Really?"

"Yeah. He pretended to grab her from behind and she flipped him."

Sam smirks. "Go, sis."

"The Peters girls are not to be messed with. Noted."

His eyes twinkle. "But my offer still stands. I can think of a more fun way to get out your...aggression."

Just like that, the heat notches up. She remembers what he said last night. *Just because something's fleeting doesn't mean it can't be fun.* Flings are usually her modus operandi. Keep it light. Keep it exciting. Keep it quick. But something in her gut screams it would be different with him, and things are complicated enough as it is.

"Not today, Satan."

Cooper snorts. "I like it better when you call me cowboy."

She walks backward toward the door while keeping her eyes on him as if at any moment he might pounce. If he makes a move, like *really* makes a move, she's not sure she'll be able to resist.

"I have work to do."

"You're running."

Hell yes, she's running. Has he seen himself?

Her back hits the door. "Bye, Coop."

She turns the knob and bolts inside before he has time to respond. Those eyes track her all the way to her room, burning into her skin like lasers, even through the window. A shot of espresso and a cold shower later, she can still feel them.

Sam tries to sink into work, but it's too tedious. Crunching numbers. Transferring notes. Blah. Blah. Blah. She's an analyst. She knows it's the job. She gets the brainless grunt work while all the interesting stuff goes to her bosses—corporate hierarchy and whatnot. She gets it.

This is the hazing she needs to survive in order to gain entrance to the club. But her skin still buzzes. Her heart still pounds. If she wants to oust that freaking cowboy from her brain once and for all, she needs more. So even though she has a million other things to do that she actually gets paid for, she flips over to her favorite little folder labeled *Emily Ann Designs* instead.

When her sister left for filming, she asked Sam to keep an eye on her jewelry business. So, naturally, Sam took it upon herself to completely revamp Emily's website, move her off Etsy, and launch her own shop. Her sister's social media accounts had been going bananas ever since she'd been cast as the lead, and it seemed like a waste not to set up an independent online store to keep more of the profits. Over the past few weeks, orders had been coming in like hot cakes. Not dozens. Not hundreds. *Thousands.* Emily had a mild panic attack about being able to fulfill them all when she heard the update, but Sam knew she'd figure it out. This was the dream, after all, the whole reason her sister had done the show in the first place—to build her business.

I wonder what Em thinks now.

She should be back in Georgia. The first thing she probably did when she got home, knowing Emily, was open her computer, sift through the accounts, then promptly close it again to give herself a day to freak out.

Sam's desperate to call her.

It goes against everything within her to know her sister is struggling and to not lend an ear or a hand. But if they talk, Emily will know something's up. She'll have questions Sam doesn't want to answer and opinions she doesn't want to face.

In less than forty-eight hours I'll be on my flight home, Cooper will officially be in the rear view, and this whole thing will be done.

Two days.

She can wait until then.

So instead, Sam opens Excel and starts crunching numbers—net income, projected profits, the cost of goods sold at different wholesale values, some ideas for increased markup percentages, tax estimates, various salaries Emily could take and their impact, potential salaries she could pay the employees she'll undoubtedly need, an assets-and-liabilities breakdown in case she wants to look for investors. It's nothing new, the mere basics of a startup business, the sort of thing Sam reviews for work all the time. And yet, it feels new. It feels thrilling. It feels exhilarating in a way her job never has.

She's polishing up the finishing touches on an email to Em when a knock sounds at the door.

"Come in," she calls absently.

"Are you—" The door swings open and Cooper pauses, an intrigued look flitting over his features. "What's got you so happy, Cuj?"

"Happy?" She lifts her fingers to her face, surprised by her own smile. For some reason, it leaves her feeling vulnerable, as if she's been caught in the act—what act exactly, she's not sure, but nonetheless, exposed. Her defenses rise. "Don't look so shocked. I'm a delight."

"That's one way to put it."

"Is it time for parasailing already?"

He nods. "I'll wait by the door while you get ready."

She throws on her bathing suit, cutoffs, and a loose T-shirt, then hastily twirls her auburn hair into a relatively clean topknot before sliding on her sunglasses. It'll have to do. There's no time for makeup, and it's not as if she's trying to impress Cooper anyway. She's trying to repel him.

That's my story and I'm sticking with it.

He must be partial to grunge, though, because he gives her an appreciative once-over as she approaches. It does not cause butterflies to swarm across her chest, deep into her belly, and down every one of her limbs until her entire body tingles. No it does not.

When they step out together, Cooper slides an arm around her shoulders. She settles naturally against him. They walk in sync, the adjustment innate. There's no awkward pause, no hop and skip to keep up, no taking a beat to figure out his rhythm. Her body just...knows.

"So, why were you so happy back there?"

Sam groans internally. She should have known he wouldn't drop it. "Nothing. Just work. A good project."

"Yeah..." He squints down at her. "I don't believe you."

"You don't believe me?" She pointedly raises her brow.

"Nah. Not buying it. You weren't working."

"Why do you say that?"

"Because I've seen the way you look when you're working. Bored. Blank. Empty. How I imagine that guy from Greek mythology must've looked pushing that boulder up a hill for all eternity, just waiting for it to end."

She snorts. "You're so dramatic."

"Pot, meet Kettle."

She rolls her eyes.

"When I opened the door, you seemed focused, but in a good way. And when you looked up at me, your eyes were pure fire. I liked it, is all I'm saying. You don't have to tell me what you were doing, but whatever it was, you should keep doing it."

The words burn into her skin.

She rubs her chest at the sudden pang.

"I was just, um, doing something for Em." Her voice is uncharacteristically soft, the volume low. She doesn't know why it's hard to explain, but it is. "Helping her with her business. She's always been super creative, but money management isn't her strong suit, so I was just running a few projections for her. Nothing fancy."

"It sounds pretty fancy."

"It really wasn't."

"Either way, it's sexy."

She snorts. "You got a math-nerd kink I don't know about, cowboy?"

"I'm starting to think I might." He looks down at her and winks. She swallows, fighting the sudden feeling of her heart lurching out of her chest. "I'd call it more of an impressive-woman kink. And you are, Sam. You're impressive as hell."

"It was just a couple of spreadsheets, Cooper."

"I'm not talking about the spreadsheets, though I'm sure they were far more complex than you're letting on. What you do for work? Sure, it's impressive. But I'm talking about what you're doing for Emily. Helping her with her business in the little bit of free time you seem to have? Dropping your entire life to switch places with her? Going through with this plan to help launch her dreams? Not everyone would do all that and expect nothing in return."

Sam shrugs. "She's my sister."

"I'm an only child so maybe I just don't get it, but I've seen a lot of sibling relationships and what you're doing still seems pretty amazing to me."

"Em would do it for me, too," Sam answers softly, sensing his unspoken question. *She already has.*

But now isn't the time to revisit the past.

"I think that's our boat, cowboy."

She points down the dock to where a speedboat bobs, the back half a large flat launching platform. Two employees wave them over and set them up in harnesses before helping them on board. After about ten minutes of cruising, the boat pauses and the crew hooks them up to the massive sail.

As the last clip is secured, Sam takes Cooper's hand in a white-knuckled grip. "I should probably warn you I'm a little afraid of heights."

He turns to study her as the boat lurches into motion. His brows furrow.

One blink, and they're fifty feet in the air.

Another, and it's two hundred.

Another and she forces her eyes closed, scrunches up her entire face, and starts screaming bloody murder.

"Jesus Christ, Cuj." He has the audacity to laugh—laugh! "You're going to blow my eardrums."

The shriek she absolutely cannot contain continues piercing the air at increasingly higher decibels. It's verging on inhuman. Dog whistles would be jealous. If she could bottle this up and sell it, she would. Halloween sales would be through the roof.

"For fuck's sake, woman."

She's not even sorry.

"Sam."

He squeezes her hand.

"Sam."

He wraps his arm around her waist, digs his fingers into her hip protectively—possessively—and draws her up against him.

"*Samantha.*"

It's a whisper against her skin, barely audible over the wind, more felt than heard as goose bumps spiral down the side of her neck. His rich, deep baritone penetrates the panic.

"Take a deep breath," he continues, lips brushing the outer shell of her ear. Dread and desire battle beneath her skin. "We're absolutely fine. I've got you. You're safe. And you're going to kick yourself if you miss out on this view because you're afraid."

"I'm not afraid."

He snorts.

"I'm terrified."

"One second is all I'm asking. Open your eyes for one second, and if it's too much, close them right back up and keep screaming. I'm here for you either way."

"No shit. We're four hundred feet in the air, strapped to a fucking kite. Where the hell else can you go?"

"That's not what I meant and you know it."

"Hmph."

"Come on. One second."

"No."

"One second."

"*No.*"

"I dare you."

"Do you really think that will work?"

"Yes."

"I'm not five."

"I double-dog dare you."

Fucking shit balls—

She opens her eyes. The whole world is blue—vast, impenetrable, never-ending blue. Perfect, clear sapphire above, and sparkling, simmering turquoise below, marred only by the distant white speck of their boat.

"I think I'm going to be sick." She groans.

He squeezes her abs. "Like hell you are."

Sam pulls her gaze from the speeding hull far, far

below and looks at Cooper. His face is close, too close. A wide grin splits his lips. A wild look fills his eyes.

"I hate you."

"I know."

Except the sparkle in his eyes says something different. It says he knows her secret—that she doesn't hate him at all.

Sam swallows, suddenly unsure which fear has her heart pounding—tumbling out of the sky or tumbling right into his arms.

As if sensing it's too much, Cooper lifts his face and screams, an unafraid, untamed, thrilled, excited thing, a sound she imagines he usually makes galloping at full speed on the back of his horse, full of joy and daring. He's never seemed more a cowboy than he does in that moment, staring fear in the face and hollering with reckless abandon.

"Come on, Cuj," he cajoles. "Let it out."

She shrieks. It's an absolutely pathetic attempt at copying his carefree sound. If she weren't so terrified, she'd be embarrassed.

He tosses her a look and hollers again.

She tries, and fails, to copy him.

They repeat this two more times before the knot in her chest finally loosens and a laugh breaks free. The view really is stunning. Endless sky. Endless sea. Lush tropical islands. Hints of coral beneath crystal waters and splashing wildlife. She takes it all in while squeezing Cooper's hand so tightly she's sure she's cutting off circulation but he doesn't complain. He points to one side and she points to another.

Look at this. Look at that. What's over there?

Before she remembers to be afraid, they're already lowering back to the boat, reeled in like fish on a line. As the sun sinks lower, the crew lays out a picnic dinner on the platform. She and Cooper sit facing pink-and-orange clouds. Her knee bumps against his thigh as they sip wine and dig into the meal.

"So...heights, huh?"

Sam gives him a sidelong glance. "Take it to your grave, cowboy."

"How does that work exactly? Seeing as you most likely work in a skyscraper—and hell, probably live in one, too?"

"I keep away from the windows."

"No one knows?"

"Nope." She shrugs. "I've always excelled at appearing much tougher than I am."

"Interesting."

"What does that mean?"

He keeps studying her.

She glares.

"What was it you said last night?" Mischief dances in his eyes. "*You do know you just handed me the key to your undoing?*"

She arches a brow. *You sure you want to do this?*

His smile deepens, puckering the dimple in his cheek. *Always.*

"That doesn't impress me all that much," Sam casually murmurs.

"No?"

"You have the looks, Coop. But what about the touch?"

"I know what you're doing."

Sam launches into the full version of Shania's immortal hit "That Don't Impress Me Much" and he reaches out to smash his hand over her mouth. Utilizing the traditional counterattack, she licks his palm. Cooper snatches it back with disbelief. They make eye contact for two long, challenge-fueled seconds, before they both break down.

"Truce?"

"Truce."

She's still smiling when they get back to the dock. Returned to a service area, her phone buzzes. Work, no doubt. She absentmindedly scans the message while they walk. And that quickly, all the joy from the day is sucked away like water down a drain. It's her boss.

Need you to set up an interview next week. Potential new hire. Spencer Winthrop. Make it a priority.

There's an unwritten implication at the end.

I know his father.

But that's not what makes her freeze. It's the name. The one she's tried to forget. The one she's tried to scrub out. The one that brings her right back to the darkest night and the darkest place in her life.

"Oh look, there's Nina," Cooper comments, oblivious

to how she's gone wooden by his side. He lifts his hand as if to wave and Sam grabs it.

She can't deal with Nina right now.

She can't deal with him.

With this.

With any of it.

Her breath catches in her lungs as she clutches the cowboy's hand for dear life, fighting the wave of emotions threatening to pull her under.

"Sam?" he asks, suddenly noticing her panic.

"I can't," she starts, voice breaking before she swallows and starts again. "I can't pretend right now. Please, Cooper. I need a minute. I can't talk to her right now. I can't—"

In one fluid motion she's sure she'll look back on with marvel, he wraps an arm around her waist and spins them until her back hits a nearby wall. Her arms go around his shoulders instinctively as he leans in and drops his face to the nook of her neck. His broad chest hides her, keeps her safe, gives her a moment to breathe. One of his hands goes to the wall beside her head and the other clutches her hip, grounding her. And then he repeats the same words he said while they dangled four hundred feet in the sky, his presence a lifeline.

"I've got you."

HE HAS no idea what happened. One second Sam was smiling, laughing, full of life. And the next, the blood drained from her face, leaving her paler than a ghost.

What the hell was on that phone?

The person who's sick? The person who hurt her? Both? Neither? Nothing at all?

It doesn't matter, not with Nina barreling down on them. Whatever it was, it was enough to leave her trembling, and that's all Cooper needs to know. With them out in the open like this, a lover's rendezvous was the only thing he could think of to keep the producer at bay. But she's a shark. If he's not convincing, she'll go in for the kill.

"I've got to—"

"I know."

It's all the permission he needs. Cooper slides his arm behind her back and hitches her up against his chest. One of his thighs parts her legs. A surprised gasp spills from her lips. Fisting her hair, he angles her head to the side and buries his face against her throat. It takes everything within him to keep a scant space between his mouth and her skin. But they agreed on the rules. She laid out her limits. No lips, no neck, no matter how much he wants it. So he just runs his nose up the column of her throat, breathing against her, drinking in the feel of her body pressed so tightly to his that he can feel every beat of her racing heart.

Out of the corner of his eye, he sees Nina closing in. Sam must be aware, or maybe not. He can't entirely decipher the motivation as she lifts one of her legs higher and hooks it around his hips, urging him closer. The need to taste her is almost painful. Blood rushes from his head, heading south so quickly he feels delirious. Her head falls back against the wall as if in invitation. She's heaving as her fingers twist into the front of his shirt. But he needs to hear her say it if he's going to cross her lines, so he does the only thing he can and lowers his lips to the exposed curve of her shoulder, the only place they're allowed. Her skin is salty from the ocean spray, the tang like a drug. He lets the kiss linger, then places another, and another, peppering across her collarbone because he can't physically pull himself away. His tongue darts out to lick a hot line across her flesh. She inhales sharply. Fingernails dig into his scalp.

He has no idea what happened to Nina. The producer could be right behind him for all he knows. But he's about two seconds from ravaging Sam against the wall, so it's either break their rules or break this embrace, and he's aware enough to know what he has to do.

Cooper pulls back. A few inches is the most he can manage. With their arms and legs still entangled, he rests his forehead against hers, trying his best to cool down. Her chest rises and falls against his as their panting fills the silence. They breathe hard for one long moment, then two. Her exhales brush against his mouth with the tantalizing whisper of a kiss. She licks her lips as a frustrated groan spills from his.

"You followed the rules," she says, tone breathless, skin flushed. He can't tell if it's a question or a statement. There's a hint of surprise, an edge of disappointment, and a layer of gratitude.

"I did," is all he can manage.

"Why?"

Jesus Christ, woman. He's right there at the precipice, but she just keeps on pushing. Leaning back far enough to catch her gaze, he cradles her face with his hand. Then he runs his thumb along her cheek.

"Because the first time I kissed you, it was for them. I don't plan on making that mistake again." He shifts his hold ever so slightly and moves his thumb over her puckered bottom lip. His gaze snags on that pillowy curve for a brief second before returning to her warm brown eyes. "The next time I kiss you, Sam, it won't be because of someone else. It won't be because you're upset. It won't be out of fear. It'll be because you want it. It'll be because you're begging for it. It won't be for anyone's benefit but our own."

"And if that never happens?" Her lips caress the pad of his thumb.

"It'll happen, Cuj."

"What makes you so sure, cowboy?"

"We're inevitable, darlin'." He laughs softly at the thick twang in his voice, completely beyond his control, and at the flash of desire completely beyond hers. "I'm just waiting for you to realize it too."

"We're not inevitable, Cooper. We're impossible."

She flattens her hand against his chest, then pauses, as though she can't decide if she wants to push him off or pull him closer. His lips twist with a grin.

"You're lying," he taunts.

She snaps out of her daze with a scowl and straightens her arm, forcing him to step back. A rush of cool air slices between them as she ducks under his arm and starts walking away. Laughter plays on his lips.

"It's okay. I forgive you," he calls out as she picks up her pace. Softer, he adds, "Because the only person you're lying to here is yourself."

She doesn't stop, doesn't turn around. He loses sight of her and takes a minute to collect himself before following her back to the bungalow. Her door is already closed by the time he steps inside. Another night comes and goes. The sun breaks on their final full day in paradise, and he rises with it. This time tomorrow, they'll be packed and ready to leave. He doesn't plan on wasting the time he has left.

But Sam has other ideas.

She's hiding.

She doesn't come out to exercise. She doesn't watch him swim. She doesn't emerge for breakfast. If he couldn't hear her shuffling around on the other side of the wall, he'd think she left early. When he invites her to lunch, she calls out a hasty *no, thanks* without bothering to open the door.

All day, she avoids contact.

The last item on their itinerary is a private couple's massage followed by a sunset dinner on their deck. He almost thinks she's going to chicken out, until she slinks from the bedroom right after he lies face down on his massage table, as if she was waiting with her ear pressed to the door. Her bathrobe is cinched all the way to the throat. She keeps her gaze on her slippered feet as she crosses the room. He starts clucking softly under his breath, calling her out. She levels an indignant look at him.

"Got something to say, Cooper?"

"Not at all."

Her masseuse lifts the sheet so she can undress privately. Just listening to the rustle of her robe hitting the floor is enough to tighten his throat, to get his blood pumping. It takes all his willpower to keep his mind blank as they lay side by side, in the nude, a mere foot apart. All he wants to do is kick everyone out and close the distance.

But he doesn't.

He has the worst massage of his life and then stares at her while dinner is set up on the porch, silently daring her to look back. She studiously ignores him.

Come on, Cuj. Don't let it end like this.

But she will.

She does.

The second dinner is laid out and the resort workers leave, she drops the mask and turns for her room. He won't let her go so easy.

"I didn't take you for a coward."

She stops midstride, still not turning around. "It's self-preservation, not cowardice."

"What are you so afraid of?"

"Let it go, Cooper."

"That's not in my nature."

"Let it go."

"Look at me and I will."

Her shoulders tense. She spins. An almost desperate glint lights her eyes. "Emily is my sister. She's my best friend. You don't understand. You have no idea the things she's sacrificed for me. I can't do anything that might hurt her. And if something happens between us, if it gets out, if the world turns on her... I just—I won't be responsible for tearing her dreams apart. I can't be. So let it go. Let *me* go."

She turns back around and leaves.

He lets her.

It goes against every instinct screaming out within

him, but he doesn't say a word as she crosses the room and disappears behind a closed door.

The longer he stares at that solid slab of wood, the more a voice deep inside whispers, *Wrong, wrong, wrong.* He doesn't have a sibling, so he doesn't really understand what that relationship entails, but he knows Emily. During their time together, he saw the truth in her heart. She would want her sister to be happy. And what if he could make Sam happy? What if they could make each other happy?

Thoughts of the ranch drift in and out of his mind. Yes, the extra exposure would be good. The extra followers, the extra money it might entail. But his father would rather have him home working than on another two-month joyride around the world. His mother would want him to chase happiness, no matter the cost.

And what does he want?

For starters, he wants to go home. He wants his horse, his bed, his morning view. No more cameras. No more acting.

But more than that, he wants Sam. Not thirty new women chasing after him for clout, for followers, for fame. All he wants is the one woman who keeps running away. And he's not sure he's ever felt that way before. His past is littered with quick-fading flames never made to last. He jumped from one girl to the next, always chasing a fire that felt out of reach. But now he's ready to build a pyre that will last.

And this burn for Samantha?

It doesn't feel like it's going away anytime soon.

Cooper stands. He abandons the food on the table and strides purposefully across the room. He stops outside her door. Maybe one night is all the two of them will need. One night and then they can both move on. Or maybe Sam is right to be afraid.

Maybe one night will never be enough.

He has to know. He can't live the rest of his life with unanswered questions.

Cooper knocks. Once. Twice.

"Go away."

This fucking woman. "Open the door."

"Go away."

"You owe me an answer, remember?" he calls, voice full of challenge. "You owe me one honest answer. We had a deal, Sam, and I'm coming to collect."

He hears her sigh through the wood. Soft footsteps pad closer. A moment passes. Two. She cracks open the door and peeks through with one eye, still hiding. "Fine. Ask your damn question."

"You promise you'll tell the truth?"

"I'll tell the truth."

He doesn't hesitate. His voice is strong, clear, direct, and low with seductive implication. "Do you want me to cross this line?"

Her eyes flash and she swallows, but says nothing. He pushes the door fully open. She steps back. He steps closer. Her gaze sweeps over him, pure heat. He leans forward on his toes, pressing up against the invisible barrier between them, and lifts his hands to either side of the doorframe to hold himself back. When he can't wait a second longer, he asks again.

"Do you want me to cross this line?"

"Yes."

sam

THE WORD IS out of her mouth before she can stop it. There's no time to reel it back. No time to retreat. No time to run. The moment her consent hits the air, the cowboy is on her. He crosses the threshold and takes her waist in his large hands, pushing her deeper into the room, all the way across that line. His fingers dip beneath her shirt to splay hotly across her ribs. His mouth devours her exposed shoulder, lips exploring every inch of bare skin. She's awash in feeling, unable to think of the repercussions. Every reason to stop this madness flies out the window along with her sanity as he pushes his meaty thigh between her legs, just as he did the night before, the move demanding her surrender.

And she does.

She surrenders to whatever the hell this is—lust, passion, the sexiest moment of her entire life. It feels as though there's a torch pressed up against her soul, lighting her insides on fire. His hands move to her back as he pulls her closer. She drags her fingers through his hair and grips his head as he slides his tongue across her clavicle, then runs his nose up the column of her throat.

"Permission to break rule number four?" he murmurs into her ear, his breath washing over her neck like a caress.

She can't even remember the rules. Her answer comes out half a gasp. "Permission granted."

"Thank fuck."

He grabs her by the ass and lifts her as if she weighs nothing at all. She wraps her legs around him. Her spine hits the wall. She couldn't say which one if her life depended on it. She has no sense of place. She's lost in him. Lost in the feel of his hips stretching her wide, of the hard heat pressed against her center, of the muscled arms practically ripping the shirt off her body. When he realizes she's not wearing a bra, he buries his face against her skin with a pained groan. A breathy laugh escapes her lips. He nips at her in reprimand then trails his mouth down the center of her sternum. She goes for his shirt, but he takes both her wrists in one hand and holds them above her head before circling one puckered peak with his tongue. Her head falls back as lightning zips down her spine. She's completely at his mercy, a place she loathes to be, and yet all she can do is tighten her thighs and submit to the magic of his touch. The subtle scrape of his scruff against her breast does something she can't explain. Stars work their way across her vision as he grinds against her. He fists her hair with his free hand, the gentle tug on the right side of painful as he moves her where he wants her and lifts his head. Their foreheads press together as their panting fills the air.

"Samantha." He pauses to breathe.

She speaks just to prove she can. "Cooper."

He lowers one of her arms and places a soft kiss against the inside of her wrist, just above her racing pulse. The move is too tender, too intimate. It clears the heady fog of her desire and replaces it with a sudden panic. She sobers just enough to retrieve her wits from where they'd been discarded on the floor alongside her shirt. When he looks at her with those piercing green eyes, she's ready.

"I think it's time to renegotiate the terms of our agreement, Cuj."

"What do you have in mind?"

"Let me kiss you."

He looks at her lips. His breath touches them like a promise. Tingles dance over her skin as her entire body clenches with anticipation. But it's that very need that terrifies her. "No."

"Cuj—"

It's a weak line to draw, but it's better than nothing. "Not on the lips."

"Which lips?"

She frowns at him and he barks out a laugh.

"Just checking."

"No lips and no tomorrow," she says. "This is one night, to get it out of our systems, and tomorrow we go our separate ways, like we always planned."

"No lips and no tomorrow."

"Those are the new rules."

He mulls it over for a second, two. She digs her heels into his firm ass cheeks and rolls her hips to speed him up. Heat flashes in his eyes. He resecures her hands above her head and drops his mouth to her throat. Nipping and licking, he tastes her sensitive skin like a starving man given food.

"I can agree to those terms," he murmurs between kisses.

"Are you positive, cowboy?"

"Sure, Cuj."

"That doesn't sound very convincing."

"I don't need to be convincing."

"Why not?"

"Because—" He finds a spot that brings a gasp to her lips and presses his advantage. When she's a breathless wreck of a person, her entire body tense with wanting, he finally continues, "I'm not the one you're trying to fool."

He pinches her nipple and the entire world lights up. *Goddammit.*

She moans despite herself, unable to find the words to refute his claim. But she can't let him have the last word. She just can't. "I need to know one more thing."

"Anything, Cuj." He breathes the promise into her skin.

"Did you sleep with my sister?"

"Not even a little bit."

"And the dream suite?"

"We threw some shit on the floor, and then she spent most of the night crying to me about her ex."

"Thank god."

Sam wriggles her hands free and yanks off his shirt.

Holy man chest.

There's just so much muscle. She doesn't even know where to begin. Michelangelo himself couldn't carve it better. The rippled contours. The firm, hot skin. The sinewy curves. She places her palms on his wrists, then slowly runs them up his forearms and over his biceps to his broad, sculpted shoulders. His muscles flex as she passes over them. She dips low, trailing her fingers over the ridges of his washboard abs, tracing every stacked crevice. Finally, she pauses at the deep V disappearing into his waistband. She swallows, throat dry as his muscles tense. He sucks in a soft breath as she grazes the top edge of his worn jeans. It would be so easy to dip her fingers beneath the denim. So easy to wrap them around him. So easy to fast-track to the good stuff the way she usually does.

But with him, it's all good. And if they only have one night, she wants to savor it.

Sam looks up.

He's watching her, eyes nearly black. The term *smolder* must've been created for this exact moment. His expression burns her from the inside out. He puts his hands against the wall on either side of her head, caging her in every way possible, body, mind, spirit. The intensity of his gaze overwhelms her. There's a dare buried deep inside that look, a silent challenge, as if he's giving her one last out. She flattens her tongue against his pec in response and glides it all the way up to his throat. He slides his hands beneath her shorts and tightens them around her ass.

Suddenly, Cooper swings them around.

Without the pressure of the wall against her back, she feels airborne, as though she's being launched out of the real world and into some sort of a fever dream. She tightens her arms around his neck. His mouth finds her ear.

"If you won't give me your lips, Sam, I'm going to claim every other goddamn inch of you before the night is through."

Then she actually is flying. He tosses her onto the bed and leaps after like a panther on its prey. Her shorts disappear in an instant. Then his mouth is on her stomach, his scruff deliciously rough against her soft skin. Calloused hands find their way to her panties and pull them off. True to his word, he devours every bare inch of her skin, teasing her with his lips as they drift closer and farther then closer and farther from the center of her need. He licks her hip bone, kisses her inner thigh, works his way over her knee and down her calf to pull her fuzzy socks dramatically off with his teeth, earning a laugh. She knows exactly what he's doing. Trying to drive her wild and it's working. Luckily, she's always been the sort to give as good as she gets.

As he makes another taunting pass along her lower

abdomen, Sam grabs him through his pants. He jerks with a groan. While he's distracted, she hooks her legs around his hips and flips them so she's the one on top. Then it's her turn to strip him. She works his pants slowly down his thighs, momentarily distracted by the rather impressive bulge on display beneath his boxer briefs as she runs her fingers softly over his muscled thighs. The idiot still has his cowboy boots on, so his pants bunch around his ankles. He tries to kick them off but it's a no-go. So she hops off the bed and yanks at the heels in what has got to be the least seductive pose in the history of sex, but gets the job done. He's practically cackling by the time the second *thud* sounds. Her lips curl. She's determined to make him pay. But right as she fondles elastic, he sits up and wraps his arms around her back, pulling her tight to his chest. Her arms go instinctively around his neck. He grins up at her as she arches a brow.

"I wasn't finished yet, cowboy."

"Too damn bad, darlin'."

He pulls her breast into his mouth. She grinds her hips as he works his magic, that point of pressure growing harder, wetter. The desire mounts within her. At some point he flips them so she's on her back, but she's too far gone to notice. He works her with his fingers, then his mouth. For every move of his, she mounts a counterattack. It's like a battle, each one fighting to gain more ground. The first time she cries out, it's a concession. He growls against her skin.

"Say my name."

"Cooper."

"Like you fucking mean it, Sam."

She arches her back as stars dance across her eyes. "Cooper!"

"Good girl."

He's focused, relentless, making her scream his name again and again, until it's no longer a surrender but a plea to keep going, to not stop, to give her more and more and more. When he sinks himself deep inside her, she finally understands what that look in his eyes was before. Not a dare, but a promise. To make this night count. To break down her walls. To wreck her for anyone else.

And dammit, that's exactly what he does.

CHAPTER FOURTEEN

SAM RUNS her fingers softly over his chest, tracing invisible lines along his skin. They've been quiet for a few minutes, recovering. One of her legs rests casually over his hips. Their limbs entangle. He keeps her close, holding her around the shoulders as if at any moment she might run away. Hopefully, she lacks the energy for it.

Cooper, at least, is completely spent.

When he described her as a tornado on that first day, he had no idea how accurate the choice of words would be. The woman is lethal. Two rounds with her and he's toast. He might not survive a third—but he's definitely tempted to try.

I can think of far worse ways to go.

"Hey, Coop?"

The hesitancy in her voice stirs concern. "Yeah, darlin'?"

He shifts enough to look down at her. She turns and settles her chin on her folded hands to meet his gaze.

"Our original rules are sort of null at this point, right?"

"I'd say we did a pretty thorough job of tossing them out the window."

"Right. So... Can I ask you something? Personal, I mean. Before we go our separate ways."

A heavy thud ricochets across his chest. The fact that she's lying in his arms already thinking about goodbye cuts like a knife, especially when he's been lying here marveling at how maddeningly content he feels. But he knows her well enough to know that saying any of that aloud will just trigger her flight response. She doesn't afford him many peeks behind her walls. He has to take any glimpse he can.

"Ask away."

"When your mom was sick..."

His heart seizes at the lead-in, but he keeps his face blank, trying not to let the ache show. He doesn't want to scare her off.

"Did you tell her you were scared? Or did you put on a brave face? Did you feel like no matter how upset you got or how weak you felt or how helpless you were, she could never, ever know? Like everything else was out of your control, but this one little thing as simple as smiling even when you wanted to scream was all you had to offer?"

He can tell by her tone his answer holds more meaning than she's trying to let on, so he thinks it over for a moment, choosing his words carefully.

"Yes and no," he finally tells her. "There were times when I had to be strong, had to hide my feelings. When she didn't recognize me or thought I was a nurse or she was in some other place where I couldn't follow, it helped if I stayed neutral until the episode passed. So even if it felt like it was killing me, I stayed calm and collected. I kept my emotions under control so they wouldn't confuse her or make her spiral any further. But when she was lucid, when she was present in this time and knew I was her son, then no. I didn't try to hide anything. I wouldn't have been able to even if I tried. My mother could always read me like a book. We cried together. We laughed through the tears. She gave me a good smack on the side of the head if required. I think it helped her to be the strong one sometimes, to not only be comforted but to be the one doing the comforting, to feel like even in that somewhat broken state she was still needed."

He watches her retreat inward, vision clouding until she's no longer with him but back in her memories somewhere. A shadow passes over her eyes. Frown lines etch into her brow. He brushes his thumb over her shoulder blade, drawing her back.

"Why are you asking me?"

She swallows, licks her lips.

Come on, Sam. Give me something. Give me one little piece of you.

"Who was sick?" he presses, and as soon as he says it, something clicks. Conversations with Sam. Conversations with her sister. The hints and the half-truths merge to paint a picture. It all becomes clear. "It was Emily, wasn't it? Emily got sick."

She looks at him sharply.

Fear cuts across her eyes, but there's something else playing deep in those golden depths, softening the blade —relief.

Still, she remains frozen in his arms. He pulls her closer, as if he can force all the heat beneath his skin to melt into hers.

"You can tell me," he murmurs.

"I can't."

"Why not?"

"It's not my story to tell."

"Bullshit."

"Coop—"

"Bull. Shit," he repeats, prompting a glare. But the fire igniting in her eyes only prods him on. "Of course it's your story. You think my mom dying wasn't part of my story? Sure, she was the one who was sick. But that doesn't mean I wasn't affected. It changed every facet of my life. I'm not asking what Emily had or has or what her diagnosis is. I'm asking about you. How you felt. What you went through. What you're clearly still going through."

"She asked me to keep it a secret," Sam whispers, her voice torn. "All of it."

"Well, that's a fucked-up thing to ask of another person."

"It was a small price to pay."

"For what? For her health? Because the two aren't related."

"No." Sam shakes her head sadly. "For everything she gave up for me."

Cooper frowns. He's not following, and it's frustrating as hell because for the first time since he met her, he feels so close to understanding her. So fucking close. But he just can't quite get there.

"Help me out here," he eventually pleads. "Please."

She waits a moment, licks her lips, and then sighs softly in surrender.

"Em got sick the summer before we were supposed to leave for college," Sam explains slowly, each word a revelation pulled from some deeply buried spot. The more she speaks, the more quickly the words come, an avalanche waiting god only knows how long to be unleashed. "We were supposed to move to New York together, me at NYU and her at FIT following her dream to design jewelry. But instead, she...well, she found out she had a tumor. We both still went to New York, but Em went for treatment, not school. While I was out drinking, making friends, going to classes, doing all the stuff we were supposed to be doing together, she was meeting with doctors and having surgery and getting chemo. And I felt so guilty, but she wanted me to be having fun so badly, I couldn't show her how awful I really felt. I didn't want her to think she was ruining anything for me, because I knew that was how she would see it. So every time I went to sit with her in that fucking clinic, I'd make her laugh with crazy stories of wild nights out. I didn't tell her how I cried myself to sleep every night worrying what in the world I would do without her. I didn't tell her how miserable I was. I couldn't admit how much I just wanted to quit. But then she got better, and we all went home for Christmas, and I thought maybe it would be a fresh start, but it—it wasn't."

She takes an uneven breath.

"Jake came to the house over Christmas. He wanted to see Emily. He wanted to give her some stupid note. And I wouldn't let him in the door. I was still so pissed at him for leaving her the way he did. Hell, I still am. So while she was back in the kitchen getting us ice cream, I practically shoved him off the front porch. The love of my sister's life came to make amends, and instead of getting out of his way, I lied through my teeth. I told him Em sent me out. That she didn't want to see him. That she hated him. If I'd just let him talk to her, if I'd put my own anger aside, they might have gotten back together that very night. Six years of my sister's life, wasted because I thought I knew what was better for her than she did, and that's not even the worst part."

She closes her eyes as if trying to hide from the memories. He runs his hand up her arm and to the back of her head to massage her scalp. She leans into his touch. He offers what little comfort he can, not pushing but not retreating either, giving her time to find the words to continue.

"My parents aren't rich," she explains into the silence.

Just like that, he knows where the story is going. "We took out loans even before Em got sick, and then after... Let's just say cancer treatment in the United States isn't cheap. She never explicitly told me, but I knew, when she told me she was transferring back home to a local art school, I knew. My parents couldn't afford for us to both follow our dreams. I wanted to tell her I hated New York, that I wanted to come home to Georgia too if that's where she was, but the look in her eyes, Cooper. She was acting so strong for me. I just couldn't find the words to explain that I'd been lying, that everything she thought she was doing to make me happy was slowly breaking me instead. So she moved home, and I went back to New York, and that was that. She gave up FIT. She gave up the school and the connections that could have launched her career. She gave up her dreams. She sacrificed everything for me, and I just stood there and let her because I was too afraid of hurting her feelings to be honest. I mean, how pathetic is that? How fucking weak? How—"

"Hey." He brushes away the tear cascading slowly down her cheek. "You did what you thought was right."

"No." She shakes her head sadly and takes a deep breath, sucking all her emotion back in. He watches in real time as she cuts the connection to her heart and jumps right back into the hard persona she wears as a shield. "I did what was easy. Instead of having a difficult conversation, I just went with what she said to appease her. And by the time the reality of what happened really sank in, it was too late. She'd already dropped out and transferred. She lost her dreams and the love of her life in one fell swoop all because of me, so I did the only thing I could do to earn back the loyalty I'd so deeply betrayed. I made two promises to myself. One, that Em would never know how depressed I really felt. And two, that money would never hold either of us back again. I researched lucrative careers, figured out which one fit me best, and worked my ass off to make it in a city that seemed to want to eat me alive."

"Investment banking," he states with sudden clarity. "That's why you do it."

She doesn't respond. Instead, she slides over until she's straddling him and presses her lips to the center of his chest. But his mind is spinning.

"And that's why you made our deal," he continues as she works her way up his sternum. "That's why you're so determined to help her business. You think you need to make amends."

Sam licks the tendon in his neck, then sucks gently on his skin. She glides her hands up his arms and slowly circles her hips. Heat barrels through his bloodstream. He knows exactly what she's doing. Of course he knows.

"But that's not what Emily would want."

She flinches. It's the smallest little hitch before she's right back to peppering kisses along his jawbone. But he feels it.

"She'd want you to be happy," Cooper presses, fighting the instinctual pull of her seduction as her hand drifts south. "I haven't known her very long, but I know her well enough to know that much. She wants you to be happy more than anything."

"I am happy."

Liar, he thinks, but he keeps it to himself, because he knows it'll only make her run.

She digs her teeth into his earlobe and tugs with a silent dare as she wraps her hand around him. "But I can think of something that would make me happier, cowboy."

So can I.

He keeps that to himself too. She's not ready to know the new plan coming together in his mind—the one to keep her. Now that she's in his arms, he doesn't want to let her go. Fuck the rules. Fuck the consequences. He's never met anyone who challenged him so thoroughly, who made him want to stay in one place so long. He doesn't want the morning to come. He wants to stay here in this room, in this night, wrapped up in these little revelations as long as humanly possible. Longer. Until he's seen every part of her she has to give, and even then, he's not sure it will be enough.

A salty droplet stings his tongue.

Sam buries her face against his neck, but he knows the taste of a tear. He doesn't ask. He doesn't need to. She doesn't explain, perhaps because she's hiding, but he hopes it's something else. He hopes it's because she understands that with him, she doesn't have to.

Cooper sits up.

He dips his hands beneath her thighs and stands,

taking her with him. She wraps her arms around his neck, hugging him close, in passion or for comfort he's not sure, but he'll take either one. He kicks open the bathroom door and turns on the shower, all while holding her. Her mouth finds his neck. His lips brush her shoulder. When the water warms, he steps them both beneath it then places her feet on the tiles before he drops to his knees. Her head arches back into the spray, erasing the evidence of her tears as he kisses his way down her stomach. He wants to take away her pain. He wants to ease the ache. And if he can't do that with words yet, then he'll do it the only way she'll allow. So he lifts one of her legs over his shoulder, grips her by the hips, and makes her cry in a better way, not stopping until the sounds of her pleas echo across the shower as her fingers dig into his skin and she forgets everything but the sound of his name on her lips.

When they're done and dry and back in bed, he holds her. She drifts off to sleep in his arms but he keeps his gaze on the window, his eyes peeled toward dawn. He's got this feeling as though if he relaxes for one moment, if he surrenders even for a second, she'll slip away.

And that's exactly what she does.

One moment, it's dark and she's there. One moment, she's his.

Then the sun is up and she's gone.

sam

DISHEVELED DOESN'T EVEN BEGIN to describe the state Sam is in as she walks at an aggressively fast pace through the lobby of the resort at six in the morning. She's wearing the same wrinkled clothes from the day before. Her hair is already falling out of its bun. Loose power cords dangle from her hastily assembled carry-on bag. And her overstuffed suitcase is only half-zipped because she didn't have time to sit her ass on it to force the damn thing closed. If she forgot some of Emily's clothes, so be it. She'll buy her new ones. Sam had to get out of there. Fast. Dumb luck is the only reason she was able to sneak away before the cowboy woke up, and she's not about to waste it by doing something completely idiotic like hanging around to say goodbye.

No lips. No tomorrow.

That was the agreement.

So what if it was the best sex of her life?

So what if Cooper seemed to see right into the depths of her soul?

So what if she'd never felt more at peace than when she was wrapped up tight in the warmth of his arms?

She has a job. She has a life. She has things she needs to accomplish. She can't give all of that up to run off with a cowboy. She won't make some guy her entire world. He has his ranch. She has her city. And never the two shall meet, once she gets the hell off this island and back to reality.

"I need a boat," she desperately blurts to the man working behind the front desk. "Any boat. It doesn't matter. I just need to get to the airport as soon as possible. My original transfer time isn't for a few hours, but something came up and I need to leave now."

"Of course, miss," he says amiably, obviously well-prepared for crazed patrons making demands at all hours of the day. "Let me see what I can do."

He dials a number and speaks softly to whoever is on the other end of the line. Sam drums her fingers on the countertop. She bounces her leg. She doesn't mean to be so rude, but she can't help it. Her skin is crawling with the need to get out of Dodge, because she knows the second Cooper realizes she's gone, he'll come running.

She saw it in his eyes the night before.

Mine, they whispered. *You're all mine.*

In the moment, she was euphoric.

Now, she's moving faster than a bat out of hell.

"Miss Peters, you're in luck," the clerk says jovially as

he hangs up the phone. "There's an airport transfer leaving now. The two guests on board agreed to wait for you if you—"

"Em? Is that you?"

Nina.

Fuck.

Not bothering to hear what else the clerk has to say, Sam murmurs a hasty thank-you and pushes off the desk. She dips her head and grips her bag tighter, as if she can use the leather tote as a shield. But the producer is far too astute.

"Em! Wait up!"

How 'bout no.

She hightails it through the open-air lobby and back into the soft light of dawn, then cuts a sharp left toward the docks.

"Em!"

Palm trees pass in a blur.

"Emily!"

Water shimmers up ahead.

"Samantha!"

She stumbles in pure shock but somehow manages to keep her feet. The boat bobs ten feet away. One of the employees waves her forward, already reaching for her suitcase.

"Stop right there, Sam, and give me five minutes or I'm telling the whole world the truth about you. The truth about your sister."

Everything within her comes to a screeching halt. Sam

closes her eyes for a moment, to breathe, to think. Then she plasters a smile on her face, spins around, and plays dumb.

"Nina, oh my gosh. I didn't realize that was you. A family emergency came up and I have to—"

"Cut the crap, Sam."

Deny. Deny. Deny. "I don't know what you mean? I'm not—"

"I *know*, Sam." Nina pointedly arches her brow and snorts. Shedding her friendly skin, the cutthroat Hollywood producer slithers out of hiding. "I've known since the second you two switched places. Did you really think you could fool me? I mean, obviously, yes. But it's my job to read people. To find their weaknesses. To play on their strengths. To expose the secrets they naively think they can keep hidden. And I'm good at my job, Sam. I'm very, very good. Even if I wasn't, Emily and Jake were about as subtle as a foghorn."

All the times Nina *randomly* happened upon her and Cooper in the resort run through Sam's mind. All the times the producer cajoled them into hanging out. All the times she kept their ruse going just a little bit longer.

Why?

Suddenly, Sam remembers this is the woman who stood between her and Emily while the show was filming. The woman who wouldn't let Sam get through to her sister even when she called the studio explaining there was a medical issue. The woman who tried to corner

Emily into revealing her cancer diagnosis on-screen for the whole world to see.

Fuck her.

And fuck this.

Sam cocks her hip and crosses her arms over her chest. "So why pretend you bought it?"

"I wanted to wait and see how it all played out." Nina shrugs, no hint of apology in her tone. "I wrote Jake a note after he left. I'm assuming he got it, which means he knew I knew, and so did Emily. I thought she would've told you when you got your phone back after filming wrapped, but when it became clear you and Cooper were still playing engaged, that for some reason you weren't talking to your sister, I got curious."

"Curious?"

"About what exactly was going on between you and Cooper."

Sam's throat tightens. "And?"

"And it's a masterpiece." A hungry gleam shines in the producer's eyes. "We've had a lot of crazy things on this show, but we've never had a twin swap or a not-so-fake engagement or one of the contestants running off with a producer. I really thought I'd seen it all, and so do our fans, but this is something entirely new. A rarity in my line of work. A holy grail."

Sam's heart thuds painfully against her ribs, but she forces a sharkish grin. "Then it's too bad you don't have a single minute of the truth on film."

"Who's to say I don't?"

Her blood pounds. "We would've seen the cameras."

"Would you have? Phil is pretty experienced at remaining unseen. He's been doing this for five years, after all."

"We never dropped character outside of the room."

"You mean the room Emily was staying in during filming? That room? Where we had hidden mics?"

It's a bluff.

It's got to be.

But...what if it's not?

Every single moment she spent with Cooper outside their bungalow plays through her mind. They were good. They weren't perfect. But inside that room, inside those walls...

"California is a two-party consent state," Sam says, trying a different angle. A desperate one. "That's where you're based. Those are the laws you have to follow."

"Are you willing to bet your sister's future on that?"

Sam chews on her lower lip. Nausea curls in her gut as the possibilities spin. She can't lose the upper hand. "You've got nothing."

"Maybe." Nina shrugs. Her expression is utterly inscrutable. "Or maybe I have everything I need."

"If you did, you wouldn't be chasing me down like this."

"I want to make you an offer before you leave."

"Yeah, well, you can shove it up your ass. No matter what you try to threaten me with, I'm never going to willingly risk my sister's reputation."

"I'm not trying to threaten you, Sam." Nina holds up her hands as if in truce. "I'm trying to help you."

She snorts. "Help me right over the edge of a cliff."

"I needed to get your attention. But now that I have it..." The hard lines across the producer's face soften. Her body slouches, the tension leaving her all at once as a sigh slips through her lips. Sam doesn't buy it. Nothing about this woman is real. "Jake is my friend. And Emily probably wouldn't agree, but I consider her a friend too. I don't want to hurt them. But I need ratings. I need a sound bite for a ten-second promo. I need a big reveal to cap the season off, something to draw people in. And if you don't want that to be the truth about who exactly Emily ran off with, then I need something better."

"Em will—"

"Break things off with Cooper during the live finale?" Nina finishes with a scoff. "Yeah, I figured out your big plan. And having just spent every minute of the past six weeks with your sister, I can tell you that's the opposite of what I need. We both know watching her amicably separate from Cooper will be about as interesting as watching paint dry. But you, on the other hand..."

"I what?"

"You have a natural affinity for the camera."

Sam gives her a flat stare. "Wow, what a diplomatic way to say I'm a dramatic asshole."

"I love dramatic assholes."

"Well, we don't love you."

"Come on, Sam." Nina grins. "I'm sure we could figure out a mutually beneficial agreement."

"I don't negotiate with terrorists."

The producer rolls her eyes.

Sam crosses her arms and stares at Nina hard. The boat won't wait forever. Time is ticking. And Cooper is used to waking up with the dawn. If she wants to get out of here, it needs to be now. She's done playing games. "What exactly do you want, Nina?"

"I don't know yet. But—" She cuts in before Sam can mutter the curse word playing on the tip of her tongue. "I know it involves you. I'm still working it out in my head. So for now, I just need you to keep this between us. Don't tell Emily yet. Don't get her involved. Give me a minute to parse through the options. And take my call."

"What call?"

"The one I'll make when I figure out what to do next."

Sam doesn't respond.

"Miss?" the employee behind her calls. "Are you—"

"Yes. I'm so sorry. I'm still coming," Sam rushes to answer as she spins around and pushes her suitcase toward him. Before she can take a step toward the boat, Nina's hand closes around her wrist.

"I need an answer before you leave, Sam."

She bends her elbow and wrenches her arm free. Nina lets go without a fight. Not that it matters. Her claws have already sunk deep. And from her smug expression, she knows it.

"I'll take your fucking call," Sam spits. "But leave

Cooper out of it. This is between you and me. He deserves a clean break."

"Deal." The producer doesn't hesitate. Just like that, it's done. "I hope you have a safe flight home."

"Yeah? And I hope you crawl back into the hellhole from whence you came."

"See? This is what I mean." Nina waves her hand between them. "Emily would've just mumbled a half-hearted goodbye. But you've got fire, Sam. Viewers love fire."

"You know what they say about playing with fire, Nina?"

"Bye, Sam."

She doesn't respond. Instead, she turns her back, climbs into the boat, and holds up her middle fingers until the dock, the producer, and the rest of the resort disappear from view. The first thing she does when she gets to the airport is switch her flight to the one that leaves tomorrow. She can't risk being in the airport today, not when there's any possibility of a run-in with Cooper. Leaving when he was out cold was hard enough. Leaving when he's begging her for something more? Even diamonds have their breaking points.

When the transfer is complete, she books it to the airport hotel across the street and gets a room. The sight of a bed gives her flashbacks to large, calloused hands roving over her skin and commanding lips laying claim to every inch they kissed. So she sits on the toilet. But even then her gaze pulls toward the shower and a wave of heat leaves her breathless. Eventually she ends up in the closet with her headphones on, her laptop open, and angry rock music blaring. But even that isn't strong enough to completely drown out his presence, his memory, or his deep, assured voice when he so confidently whispered, *I'm not the one you're trying to fool.*

Dammit.

cooper

"GIVE ME THE NUMBER, NINA."

It's been five days since the Maldives. And for five days, the producer's answer has been the same. "It's not mine to give."

"Nina—"

"I've got an expression for you, Cooper. Perfect for a cowboy. You can lead a horse to water, but you can't force it to drink. You get me?"

"Give me the number."

"She doesn't want you to go after her, and it won't work anyway. Trust me. I've had more experience reading people than you can even imagine and I know how she works. You've got to let her come to you."

"The hell I do."

"Then call me the Devil, because you aren't getting through me."

"Nina—"

"Goodbye, Cooper."

"Nina!"

Click.

"Fuck!"

He slams the satellite phone into the dirt and falls back on the grass, covering his face with his hat so the others around camp won't see him fume. They're settling in for another night on the open plains. But even fresh air, starry skies, and vast untapped nature isn't enough to appease him right now.

Fuck. Fuck. Fuckity fuck.

It's been five days since he woke up alone in that bungalow and he's going out of his goddamn mind. After the night they had, after the week they shared, how could she just up and leave as if it were nothing? And he knew she would. He *knew* it. The second he woke up alone, he already sensed it was too late. But he still tried. He threw some pants on and tore out of the bungalow, only to be met by Nina, sitting on the edge of the dock, kicking her feet with a coffee cup in hand, patiently waiting to burst his bubble.

"She's gone," the producer said, her tone almost bored. "Took an airport transfer about an hour ago. Probably switched herself to an earlier flight. You're too late."

"The hell I am."

She took a sip of coffee as he charged closer, not at all moved. "It won't work, cowboy."

"I have to try."

"I know." Nina shrugged. "Because you're you. The six-pack savior. The hero. But she isn't a damsel in distress, Cooper. You try to save her and she'll just keep running. You already laid the groundwork. Now you need to give Sam the space to save herself."

He stopped short. "You know?"

"I've known the whole time. It was plain on her face. Just like the way you feel is plain on yours."

"Yeah? And how's that?"

"You love her."

He reared back. "It's been five days, Nina."

"So? You've spent more time together in those five days than most of the couples do on my show."

"Ninety-five percent of the couples on your show break up."

"Five percent don't." Nina grinned. "Which group do you think you belong to, Cooper?"

He ignored her. "I need her number, Nina. I need to speak to her."

"It's not mine to give. You just spent five days sharing a suite, and it looks like you might've shared a bit more than that. If she wanted you to have her number, she would have given it to you. But don't worry, cowboy. I've got a plan."

Unsurprisingly, her *plan* did little to comfort him. He wasted a few more minutes talking in circles with the producer before running to the front desk to schedule a new transfer. Then he spent the hours before his flight canvasing the airport, waiting at the gate of every outbound plane to the United States, and searching the crowds.

He found nothing.

She had straight-up disappeared.

Then he spent his entire thirty travel hours back to Nebraska trying to formulate a plan of his own.

Switch his flight to New York and hunt her down? It was a city of eight million people and he had no idea where she lived.

Fly to Georgia and confess to Emily? He knew the name of her mother's flower shop. He could find someone in their family. But Sam would probably cut his balls off for trying, and breaking her trust didn't seem like the right way into her stubborn heart.

Sit around and wait as Nina suggested? He'd rather take a bullet to the chest. It would hurt less.

Round and round his mind spun, until he was right back where he started. The moment his feet touched American soil, he opened his phone and called the producer.

"Give me her number, Nina."

"Like I said before, Cooper. It's not mine to give."

He was ready to turn around and book a flight to New York right then and there, screw the odds, but then he called the ranch to check in. The housekeeper answered. Even before she spoke, he knew he was in deep shit. And everything she said just confirmed it. His father had started the roundup a week sooner than planned. Signs pointed toward an early winter so they needed to move the cattle to their cold-weather pastures, cull the herd, wean the calves, and prepare the ranch for snow.

Or so his father said.

A small part of Cooper couldn't help but wonder if the man had done it as punishment, a way for him to prove he'd been right that his son never should have left on some Hollywood adventure in the first place, not when he was needed at home. And he was needed. Corralling the cattle was an all-hands-on-deck situation. No matter how much he wanted to chase after Sam, he couldn't. The ranch came first—a lesson drilled in since birth.

So Cooper went home.

He found his horse and rode like a man possessed to meet up with his father, just to be greeted with a disappointed scowl. "You're late."

"You're early."

"I'm exactly on time, son. The ranch waits for no one. A lesson you'd do well to remember."

And that was it. They've been out here together for three days, and his father hasn't asked a single word about the show. No one has except Wesley, his best friend and the son of his father's foreman. They grew up together, as close as brothers. On more than one occasion he wished they were brothers, if it meant Boone could have been his father too. The first time he roped a calf, the foreman was the one to offer a proud slap on the back. His own father just told him, *Again*. That damn word. Again. Again. Even the thought of it makes Cooper writhe.

"Still moping?"

He doesn't shift his hat from where it covers his face. "Shut up, Wes."

"You gotta find this girl, Coop."

"I'm trying."

"I want to thank her."

"For making me a miserable son of a bitch?"

"Nah."

Cooper's hat is toed off by a familiar boot. He squints against the dying sun and looks up at the shit-eating grin beaming down at him. Wes's brown hair is a sweaty mop on his head, his tan cheeks are caked in dirt, and he smells to high hell after twelve hours on horseback, yet his brown eyes twinkle.

Bastard.

Wes chuckles softly and lands beside him on the grass with a *thud.* "For finally giving me a chance to get laid."

"Yeah?" Cooper snorts and eases to a seated position as he slides his hat back into place. "How's that?"

"With you taken—"

Heat spikes down his sternum. "I'm not taken."

Wes shoots him a knowing grin.

"It's not like that," he explains with a scowl. Wes's grin deepens. "It's not. We just have unfinished business."

"Unfinished business like getting hitched and having kids?"

Cooper elbows him in the gut. Wes anticipates the move and partially blocks the blow with his arm. His laughter half shifts to a groan.

"I'm just saying—"

"Well, don't."

"You've got that look, Coop."

"What look?"

"That look Beau Hardey had before he got down on one knee at graduation. The one Caleb Saunders had that night we all snuck down to the lake. Three months later, he and Haddie eloped. Six months after that he was a dad, if you catch my drift. It's the look of a man with a noose around his neck, but he likes it so much he tightens the rope all by his goddamn self. I never thought I'd see that look on your face, Coop, but it's there, plain as day, whether you want it to be or not."

Cooper lifts his hat to scrub a hand through his hair before settling it back into place. "She lives in New York."

"That's not a denial."

"It's a dead end."

"Maybe."

Wes lets the word hang there. The confirmation stings, a brand digging slowly into Cooper's skin, marking him.

"Or maybe," his friend continues, "she just needs someone to show her a better way."

Wes turns to where the sun sinks below the horizon, casting a golden hue across the plains. Clouds catch the glow, wispy edges burning like flames in the sky. Grasses rustle and sway in the wind. Crickets chirp. Cattle moo. In the soft indigo overhead, stars already sparkle. It's breathtaking. Even having grown up here, Cooper feels a hitch in his pulse. Yet his gaze shifts to somewhere over the edge of the rolling hills, not quite on the land, not quite on the sky, in that almost imperceptible in-between where the view stretches into forever, and he wonders, the way he always has, what else is out there waiting for him.

Sam?

New York?

A different life with different options and different choices?

The soil beneath him was made fertile by the blood, sweat, and tears of his ancestors. He can't be the one to let it die. He won't be. But at what cost? Will he spend the rest of his life giving everything he has to this place, always dreaming about what lies beyond?

Wes nudges him. "Get some food, Coop, before it's gone."

He does.

But the question lingers. While he sets up his sleeping bag. While he stares up at the moon. While he wakes with the dawn. While he saddles his horse. While he rounds up the cattle, spinning, circling, cutting—actions even more innate than breathing. Then he settles down at the end of the day and calls Nina one more time. She answers on the first ring.

"Don't even say it—"

"Nina."

"I'm not giving you her number."

"Nina—"

"I'm giving you something better. I'm giving you Sam, in the flesh."

His heart shudders to a halt. "What do you mean?"

"Between the end of filming and the live finale, the winning couple always gets one secret visit in a remote location, away from potential paparazzi, organized by the network. I'd say your ranch is about as remote as they come. So I need dates, Cooper. I'm going to get Sam to come to you. Trust me on this."

He does. Not because he trusts her, but because he knows their interests are currently aligned. She needs Sam to cooperate for the sake of the show. He needs one more conversation. Okay, he wants a helluva lot more than a conversation, but it's a start. Either way, he and the producer both want the same thing—Sam back in his life.

He runs a few quick calculations. "I need six weeks to get everything sorted at the ranch."

"Six weeks," Nina repeats, mulling it over. "You got it, cowboy. Six weeks. Pull that glass slipper out of storage, because your runaway bride is coming home. And this time, it'll be up to you to figure out how to keep her."

The producer hangs up.

Cooper slowly lowers his phone and fights the smile tugging at his lips as the words *Sam* and *home* and *bride* all swirl together in a heady mix. Something warm bubbles in his chest, something a little too close to hope. Nina's closing statement lingers.

It'll be up to you to figure out how to keep her.

He likes the sound of that.

He likes it a little bit too much.

sam

MOTHERFUCKER.

Sam jostles the key and yanks on the doorknob, but the lock remains stuck. So she tries again. Stuck. One more time. Stuck.

"Goddammit," she finally screams and slaps the door with her open palm. Then she kicks it. Then she slaps it again. Then she takes a long deep breath, searching for a single iota of calm in her entire body, and twists once more.

The door to her apartment swings open.

She walks straight into the living room, collapses onto the couch, covers her face with a pillow, and screams.

It's been two weeks since the Maldives.

Two longgggg weeks.

Two weeks in which the entire world has seemed out to get her.

Maybe it was too much time off. Too much time in the

sun. Too much time with a certain cowboy whispering in her ear, telling her she doesn't have to put up with this shit. She doesn't know. All she knows is that the city has never felt so oppressive. The buildings have never felt so gray. The air has never felt so polluted. Her cubicle has never felt so small, her chair so uncomfortable, or her computer so bright in the dim, environmentally friendly lighting that gets switched on at 2 a.m. for all the lemmings stuck there after hours. She had to get out of there. She had to come back to this closet-sized apartment, and this love seat masquerading as a couch, and this pillow she got for ten dollars at HomeGoods because there was a sand dollar stitched to the front and it reminded her of home.

"Rough day at the office?"

"Fuck!" Sam jumps about ten feet in the air and flings the pillow across the room before the familiarity of the voice registers. Her roommate swats the projectile away with a yelp while her heart spasms uncontrollably in her chest. She presses a palm to the spot, trying to control her racing pulse. "Winnie! What the hell? Where did you come from?"

"Where did *I* come from?" Winnie arches a perfectly plucked brow as she rests her drawing pad on her curled-up knees and turns toward Sam. Her black hair is tied up in a loose bun. Tortoiseshell glasses rest on the rim of her nose. An oversized purple NYU sweatshirt hangs lopsided off one shoulder, while the rest of her is hidden underneath a cozy sherpa blanket. She's sitting in the corner of the room on that god-awful embroidered floral chair Sam begged her not to buy—as if Winnie would ever listen. The stubborn ass. Then again...

Pot, meet kettle.

"I've been sitting here for..." Winnie pauses to check her watch. "Shit. Three hours."

"Working on a new project?" Sam asks. Her roommate usually only breaks out the pen and paper to brainstorm. Otherwise, she works digitally.

"I just got hired by a new client," Winnie explains, an excited glow livening her features as she leans forward eagerly. "She's a huge indie romance author. If I get this right, she could put my freelance career on the map. It's a small-town, rivals-to-lovers, only-one-bed billionaire romance, but she wants two covers. One a bit smutty with people, and one object-only for a discreet special-edition option. I'm trying to figure out how to make sure they go together. And I'm close. But I wanted to sketch out a few more ideas before I polish up the ones to send her."

"I got about half of that."

Winnie rolls her eyes. "One of these days, Sam, you're going to read the books I've not-so-subtly stacked up on your windowsill. Join me on the dark side. You know you want to. We have sexy men and orgasms. Lots and lots of orgasms."

Sam snorts, then unzips her pencil skirt, releases her topknot, and lets her head fall back with a sigh.

"Rough day?" Winnie asks. "You look..."

"Like a shell of my former badass self?"

"I was going to say *stressed*, but we can go with that if you want."

"It's just—" Sam pushes the heels of her palms against her eyes and groans. "It's everything. My bosses are relentless."

"Mm-hmm."

"The hours are insane."

"Sure."

"I'm so sleep deprived I need a caffeine drip."

"Don't we all."

"And it's boring. There. I said it. It's nothing but grunt work. And I know I need to pay my dues. I know I need to make my way up the corporate ladder. I know it's a good foundation for the future. But it also makes me want to gouge my own eyes out with the stupid company pens littered across every surface of the office."

"Well, that's graphic."

"Especially when I'm doing actual interesting things for my sister with her company. Real business. Real plans. Real ideas. Stuff that stimulates my brain, you know?"

"Right," Winnie agrees. "Plus, there's the whole 'accidentally fell for a cowboy who showed me I was completely wasting my life like my best friend and sister have been trying to tell me for years' thing."

"Yeah." Sam snaps up. "I mean, no. What? Winnie!"

"Don't you dare try to eliminate the Cooper of it all."

"There is no Cooper of it all."

"The Cooper of it all *is* the all."

"What are you even saying?"

"Sam."

"Winnie."

"*Sam.*"

"*Uldwyna.*"

"Don't you dare full name me, Samantha Rose Peters. Just because you're being a bullheaded ass doesn't mean I can't point out the obvious. Everything you just said is exactly how you've been living for the past three years. The only thing that's new is Cooper."

"Well, and *he who shall not be named.* He starts next week."

"Please. Spencer *wishes* he was on the same level as Voldemort. Don't give him that much credit. And you're so over him anyway. Don't even try to use that as an excuse."

"I'm not."

Winnie frowns at her pointedly.

Sam rolls her eyes. "I'm *not.*"

And she means it. This isn't about *him.* Fucking Spencer Winthrop. Of course his dad pulled some strings. Of course he got hired based on zero credentials. Of course he's starting at the same salary level as her even though he spent the past year *traveling* after getting fired from his first banking job. She knows she's better than him—at her job, at life, at being a functioning human being with actual emotions. Sure, she loathes the idea of seeing him every day, but she'll never let him get the best of her. And she'll be damned if she lets his presence affect her career. But though she hates to admit it, while she's long over him, she's not sure she'll ever fully get over the way he made her feel.

Charity case.

Pity lay.

She hasn't cried in front of a man since she walked out his door—not until Cooper. Her heart aches whenever she thinks about the way he cradled her in his arms and carried her to the shower to wash away her tears, understanding without words exactly what she needed. No derision. No shame. No judgment. Just tenderness. Just compassion. Just...

Sam blinks away the memory and rubs at her chest.

"Like I said, the Cooper of it all," Winnie comments triumphantly.

"You don't even know what I was thinking."

"I know you were thinking about him. You're like the heart-eye emoji come to life right now."

Sam throws another pillow at her head.

"Hey! Don't shoot the—"

A blaring alarm cuts through the living room. Winnie scrunches up her face, looking around for the source of the noise. Sam doesn't need to. She knows exactly what it is. Simple as that, her shit attitude disappears, replaced by an embarrassing surge of elation as she dives for her phone. Finally. *Finally.* She's been waiting two weeks for this call, this one lingering connection to the Maldives and everything that happened there, this tiny smidgen of hope whispering that maybe it isn't completely over after all.

It is.

It has to be.

But maybe, just maybe, it isn't.

Sam digs through her purse as her phone continues screeching with the unmissable ringtone she assigned a very specific number, the one labeled as a priority contact and set to override her *Do Not Disturb*. As she slides her thumb across the screen to accept the call, her stomach leaps into her throat, as if she's in a full-fledged free fall, not sitting on her couch.

She swallows once to steady her voice. "Nina."

"Sam."

"To what do I owe the pleasure?"

"I said I'd call. This is my call."

"So you figured out your next step?"

"No. I figured out yours."

Sam gives Nina the opening to elaborate. She doesn't.

Don't do it. Don't do it. Don't do it. Sam can practically hear Nina's victorious smirk in the taut silence, but she can't help it. Her nostrils flare and she practically growls, "Which is?"

"A trip."

"A trip?"

"You're going to Nebraska."

Forget butterflies. Locusts swarm across her chest like the warning of an impending apocalypse. "Nebraska."

"You do remember that's where—"

"Yes, I know that's where he lives."

"You're going to see him."

"No, I'm not," she blurts, even though her heart is

doing a happy dance as excitement brightens every crevice of her brain. "We agreed to keep Cooper out of this."

"He has no idea we made an agreement. I kept my end of the bargain. But this is out of my hands. The lead and the F1 always get one secret meetup before the live finale. Cooper said he can't leave his ranch again, so it's got to be there. Though I guess it doesn't have to be you. I could call Emily—"

"No," Sam cuts in.

Nina snorts. "Still haven't come clean, then?"

No. She hasn't. She's been dodging Em's calls for two weeks, keeping her text messages vague, and only replying to emails related to business. As far as her sister knows, everything in the Maldives went exactly according to plan and she sent Cooper packing with a gentle, mutually approved goodbye. No proposal. No engagement. No problems. Luckily for Sam, Em is far too deep in her love bubble to notice how shifty she's acting, but it's only a matter of time. She's not entirely sure why she's so adamantly against being honest with her sister, but the idea of letting Em know how much she messed this up terrifies her. Maybe because it's just one more card in the carefully built house of lies she's told her sister—her love of New York, that night with Jake, this whole crazy thing with Cooper. If she confesses once, the whole stack might come tumbling down. "None of your business."

"Actually, it's all my business. Literally. It's my job, and I'm putting myself on the line for you, Sam. So do you want to go to Nebraska or not?"

Yes.

It's exactly what she wants.

It's what she's been telling herself for two weeks she absolutely cannot do, but it's exactly what she wants. To see him again. To be near him. To be in his arms. She wants it so much it terrifies her.

But Nina doesn't need to know that.

"How long is the trip? I need to make sure it's okay with work."

"A long weekend. Three or four days. Not much."

Three or four days, Sam thinks. Just enough time to get him out of her system for good. At least, that's the lie she's going to tell herself to justify what she says next. "I think I can arrange that."

"Good. I'll email you with the details. Until next time—"

"Wait!"

"Yes?"

Shit. Shit. Shit. She isn't doing this. Yes, she is. *Fuck.* "Can I have his phone number? In case of emergency?"

"What kind of emergency?"

"A...packing emergency."

"Right. A *packing* emergency."

"Ugh, fine." Sam rubs at her neck as an uncomfortable itch forms beneath her skin. "Never mind."

"No. No. I'll give it to you."

"Forget I asked."

"God," Nina mutters. "The two of you are so annoying.

I really should be getting a bonus for all this overtime I'm putting in."

"What overtime?" Realization hits. Sam fights her grin. "Did you talk to him? Did he ask for my number?"

"Do you want him to have asked for your number?"

"No." *Yes.*

Nina snickers.

Dammit.

"I'm hanging up."

"I'm putting his number in my email."

"Goodbye, Nina."

"Good luck, Sam."

She frowns. But before she can ask what she needs luck for, the line goes dead. Sam stares at the black screen for a moment, then releases a breath. It comes out almost like a laugh as a giddy smile takes over her face. She bites her lip, trying to fight the ridiculous reaction, but it's no use. Bubbles of happiness swarm up her chest like freshly popped champagne. She covers her mouth with her hands and squeals like a fifteen-year-old who's just been asked to prom. It's embarrassing, actually. Thank god no one—

"So, Nebraska, huh?"

"Jesus Christ, Winnie!" Sam clutches at her heart. "You have *got* to stop doing that."

"Doing what?" her roommate challenges in disbelief. "I'm literally just sitting here. It's not my fault you're too in *love* to notice what's going on around you."

"I'm not in love."

"No? Care to elaborate on what the hell that sound that just came out of your mouth was if it wasn't love?"

Sam opens her mouth to retort.

She's got nothing.

"See?" Winnie grins triumphantly. "Love."

"Stop saying that."

"Love."

"I'm going to throw another pillow at you."

"Love."

Sam chucks a pillow.

Winnie dodges. "Love."

"Oh my god!"

Sam grabs another pillow and launches to her feet. Winnie leaps out of the chair and runs with Sam chasing behind. She ducks into her room for cover and slams the door closed. But a moment later, it opens.

"Wait," Winnie says, this time fully with glee. Her eyes are comically wide. She grins. "You're going to Nebraska."

"I thought we established that."

"You need boots."

Sam sneers. "No."

"You need a hat."

"Definitely not."

"You need highlights."

Sam furrows her brow. "What?"

"Can I give you a makeover?"

"Winnie."

"Oh, please. Please. Please, Sam." She jumps up and down and folds her hands into prayer mode. "What is the point in having a roommate who grew up in Texas if I can't put it to good use? I've been preparing for this moment my entire life. I can't even tell you how many cowboy romances I've read. I'll give you some. You can—"

"Absolutely not." Sam pulls the door closed.

Winnie opens it back up. "Just one. For research!"

"No," Sam stresses and turns around.

"What about a new outfit? You'd look great in fringe!"

"For the love of god."

"Sequins!"

"Good night, Winnie."

"Do you even know the hat rule?" her roommate cries right as Sam shuts the door to her bedroom, cutting her off.

The hat rule?

Sam falls onto her bed with a sigh. Nerves and anticipation and, yes, fear all swirl together beneath her skin. She rolls over and buries her face into her pillow with a groan, still unable to completely erase the smile on her lips.

What in the world have I gotten myself into?

eighteen

SAM TO COOPER: Hey, it's me! Nina gave me your number.

> *Sam:* Me as in Sam.

> *Sam:* Samantha.

> *Sam:* I just thought maybe we should connect before this whole weekend thing happens. I have questions.

> *Sam:* Mostly related to wardrobe.

> *Sam:* I know you prefer me naked but I don't want to shock the neighbors. LOL.

Sam to Winnie: OMFG you need to take away my phone.

> *Sam:* I already brought up being naked.

> *Sam:* And typed LOL. Like actually. LOL.

> *Sam:* He hasn't responded.

> *Sam:* If you don't hear from me again, it's because I've

found a nice hole in which to shrivel up and die from sheer mortification.

Winnie: You brought up being naked?!?! I need context.

Sam: Does it really matter? I must be stopped.

Winnie: It does.

Winnie: I need to know exactly how to make fun of you for this when I see you later.

Sam: I hate you.

Winnie: Love you too, boo.

Emily to Sam: YOU ARE A LIFESAVER!!

Emily: I love you. I love you. I love youuuuuu. The budget you sent is perfect. I'm trying to find an assistant to hire out in LA when I get there. Can we chat later to work on a potential base salary? I'm so out of my element here.

Emily: PS—when are you finally going to quit your job and just admit you want to run this company with me?

Emily: Please.

Emily: Pretty pretty please with a delicious maraschino cherry on top?

Sam: You can't afford me.

Sam: But I will work on the base salary with you. Add it to my bill. You're racking up some serious consulting charges here.

Emily: Exactly! That's why I want to pay you with ownership shares. 50/50? What do you say?

Sam: Em. Don't even joke about that. Your shares are the most valuable asset you have.

Emily: What if I think you're the most valuable asset I have?

Emily: I want to do this with you, officially. I want to do this together.

Emily: Sam?

Emily: SAM!

Emily: Don't you dare ghost me right now!

Sam: Relax. It's been like five minutes. And you know how affection makes me break out in hives. I had to go find some Benadryl.

Emily: Hilarious.

Sam: I know.

Sam: How's the move going, by the way? Don't think I didn't notice that casual LA name-drop back there. I can't believe it's only two months away.

Emily: I know what you're doing. This isn't over. But I'm going to let it slide, you deflection wizard, because... AHHH! Two months!!! Isn't that insane? I really can't believe it.

Emily: Jake sends me a new apartment listing almost every day. It's sort of adorable.

Sam: Excuse me while I go throw up.

Emily: Someday someone is going to sweep you off your feet and I'm just going to sit back and laugh and enjoy the show.

Sam: Until then, I'll keep enjoying your show. Dad called me last night in a panic after you made out with seven different guys in a single episode. I had to talk him off a ledge.

Emily: Oh god.

Emily: I saw him driving around in his squad car earlier and I just knew he was avoiding me. I waved from across the street and he pretended not to see, the little sneak.

Emily: I'll swing by Mom's shop at lunch to see what sort of groveling this requires. He's so fragile. Men.

Emily: Actually, I should probably go call Jake too.

Emily: Miss you!

Sam: Miss you too!

Winnie to Sam: I left a present on your pillow when you get home.

Sam: Oh my god. Stop hiding romance novels around my room. MY LIFE IS NOT A ROM-COM.

Winnie: Obviously not.

Winnie: It's a Western.

Sam to Cooper: Me again.

Sam: Just want to make sure I have the right number.

Sam: Let me know!

Jake to Sam: Nina's being weird. I met her for coffee earlier. I can tell when she's scheming. Do you know anything?

Sam: This number has been blocked. Try again later.

Jake: Sam. Come on. The phone doesn't tell you when you've been blocked.

Jake: Stop being an ass.

Sam: Payback's a bitch.

Jake: I blocked you one time!

Sam: And it was the wrong fucking time.

Sam: Em's super excited about the move, btw. It's all she can talk about. Don't mess it up.

Jake: I won't.

Jake: But do you? Know anything about Nina?

Sam: The number you have dialed is disconnected. Please hang up and try again.

Jake: Oh for fuck's sake. Forget it.

Sam to Nina: It's been over two weeks and I haven't heard from Cooper. Are you sure you gave me the right number?

Nina: I'm sure.

Sam: ...

Sam: That's it?

Nina: What else do you want me to say?

Sam: I hope you know I'm giving you the middle finger through my phone.

Nina: I hope you know I don't care.

Sam to Cooper: Hey. If you don't want me to come, I get it. Just let me know. I'll tell Nina to cancel the ticket.

· · ·

Sam to Winnie: Why is there a tan leather jacket with fringe sleeves on my bed?

Winnie: You're welcome.

Sam: Please tell me you did not actually spend money on this.

Winnie: I did. But it was five years ago and I love that jacket, so treat it like your child.

Sam: I have never seen you wear this once.

Winnie: NYC is not ready for me in fringe.

Sam: I'm bringing it back to your room. He clearly doesn't want me to come anyway.

Winnie: Shut up.

Winnie: There's a reasonable explanation. I promise. Don't give up yet.

Sam: It's been three weeks.

Winnie: We both saw the video of him saving that baby on the first episode. He's the six-pack savior. He'd never ghost you like this. I can feel it.

Sam: Social media is a lie.

Winnie: The way my ovaries exploded isn't.

Sam: I have no idea what to say to that.

Winnie: Good. Be quiet and try on my jacket.

Winnie: I'll be home in five.

Cooper to Nina: Are you fucking kidding me, Nina?

Cooper: You gave her my number and didn't tell me?

You knew I didn't have my cell phone. I've been calling you on my satellite phone every day for three weeks. What the hell are you playing at?

Nina: You're welcome.

Cooper to Sam: Shit, Sam. Hi.

Cooper: I definitely want you to come.

Cooper: Please still come.

Cooper: I've been out on the roundup without my phone. I wasn't ignoring you. I just got back this afternoon.

Cooper: If you could smell me right now, you'd know I haven't had a real shower in a month.

Cooper: Come and you'll see.

Cooper: Well, I mean, you won't. I'll be clean by then. I promise.

Cooper: Just come.

Cooper to Wes: Fuck, man. I'm practically begging her to visit and I just told her I smell like shit.

Wes: You're doing great, sweetie.

Cooper: How do I salvage this?

Wes: Taking a breath might be a good place to start.

Wes: And a shower...

Sam to Cooper: You're alive! And apparently smelly.

Cooper: I'm alive. And very sorry.

Sam: I figured there was some sort of explanation. No sweat.

Sam: Ha. Sweat. Get it?

Sam: Cause you're smelly.

Sam: Not because of any other sweat-related activities.

Sam: Anyway… What's the roundup?

Cooper: We basically move all the cattle from the summer to winter pastures. It takes a while to find them all on the open plains and drive them closer to the ranch. Now we're weaning the calves, figuring out which to sell, doing vet checks and vaccinations, fixing fences. The usual.

Sam: Sounds very unusual to me.

Cooper: You'll see it soon enough.

Sam: Speaking of… I've been doing some research, strictly for packing purposes, and I read that some cowboys still sleep in bunkhouses on big ranches. What kind of voyeuristic situation do I need to prepare myself for, Cooper?

Cooper: None.

Cooper: We have a bunkhouse. I don't sleep in it and neither will you.

Sam: Then where will I sleep?

Cooper: In my bed, with me.

Sam: You sound very sure of that fact.

Cooper: I am.

Cooper: I'm not fucking sharing you with anyone, Cuj. Got it?

Sam: Got it.

Cooper: And I'm planning for lots of sweat-related activities.

Sam: Balls feeling a little blue there, cowboy?

Cooper: You have no idea.

Sam: My rules still stand. No lips. No tomorrow.

Cooper: Whatever gets you on the plane.

Sam: I mean it, Cooper.

Cooper: Of course you do.

Winnie to Sam: Why are you sitting there with that silly-ass smile on your face?

Sam: No reason.

Winnie: If you weren't on a call right now, I'd throttle you.

Sam: I know.

Winnie: Tell me what's going on or I make no promises. Client or no client!

Sam: Cooper just texted, and I quote, "I'm not fucking sharing you with anyone."

Winnie: Damn he's good.

Winnie: There go my ovaries again.

Sam: OMFG WINNIE.

Sam: I just snorted in the middle of my boss's presentation. This is why I never work from home. Go focus on yourself and stop making that face at me.

Winnie: What face?

Winnie: Okay, I'm going. I'm going. Stop throwing

things at me.

Sam to Cooper: Did you remedy that unfortunate personal hygiene situation? I was sort of looking forward to all the fresh country air...

Cooper: Need a break from the city already?

Sam: What do you mean? I live for the smell of warm car exhaust in the morning.

Cooper: What about warm cow shit?

Sam: Damn. You really know how to turn a girl on.

Cooper: Kidding. My place is set away from the herd.

Sam: Your place? Interesting.

Sam: What sort of place are we talking? Shanty? Taj Mahal?

Cooper: I think I'd rather surprise you.

Sam: Don't make me google you.

Cooper: Like you haven't already.

Sam: Touché.

Sam: Information about the Kelley & Dunne Ranch is surprisingly sparse. I found some acreage estimates (yowzah) and some cattle industry facts, but hardly any photos. Your website could use some updating. Your Instagram too. How can I properly stalk you if you don't provide me with any material?

Cooper: My father is very private. What do you want to know?

Sam: Where does the Dunne come from?

Cooper: There were two separate ranches until 1935

when Rebecca Dunne and George Kelley eloped. Very Romeo and Juliet. Her father wouldn't honor the marriage unless his name stayed on the land. According to our family lore, there's some contract somewhere stating every firstborn son needs to have both names too. Hence, Cooper Dunne Kelley. And my father, Francis Dunne Kelley.

Sam: How very patriarchal of you.

Cooper: I wouldn't mind having a little Susie Dunne Kelley running around either.

Sam: Susie, huh?

Cooper: It's my imaginary daughter. Butt out.

Cooper: Unless, of course, you're hoping to be an active participant in this possible scenario…

Sam: Next question.

Sam: What kind of animals do you have? Aside from Nutcracker, of course.

Cooper: Aww, you remember her name? That's sweet, Cuj. She'd be touched.

Sam: No she wouldn't.

Cooper: How do you know?

Sam: Because you have a type.

Sam: Jealous assholes.

Cooper: Speaking from personal experience?

Sam: The animals, cowboy.

Cooper: Mostly cattle. But also sheep and goats. Other work horses. Some chickens and turkeys but not for commercial purposes. Barn cats. Two Australian shepherds, Harley and Scout, though they prefer to stay with my dad. We're a motley crew.

Sam: And will I meet your dad?

Cooper: You don't want to. Trust me.

Sam: What sort of activities do you have planned for me?

Cooper: I'd rather not say.

Sam: How far from the airport is the ranch?

Cooper: You'll see when you get here.

Sam: Is there a reason you're suddenly acting cagey?

Cooper: What do you think?

Sam: You're up to something.

Cooper: Me? Never.

Sam: Just tell me.

Cooper: Where's the fun in that?

Sam: Mark my words. I WILL get you back for this.

Cooper: It'll be worth it to see the look on your face.

Sam: My roommate gave me a set of cowboy boots for the trip. Maybe I'll show up wearing them with that thong you seemed to like so much...and nothing else. Might be worth it to see the look on *your* face.

Cooper: Jesus Christ, woman.

Cooper: You don't play fair.

Sam: No such thing, Cooper.

Sam: No. Such. Thing.

Emily to Sam: Have I mentioned you're a godsend recently?

Sam: Yes.

Sam: But I never get tired of hearing it.

Emily: Obviously.

Sam: Hey!

Emily: Wanna Facetime?

Sam: Sorry, can't. At the office. Things are totally insane here. Phone later?

Emily: Sure.

Emily: Have you thought any more about what I said? I meant it, you know. I want you to run this company with me. I'm totally out of my element. I can't do this without you.

Emily: I need a CFO. A real one.

Emily: Why can't it be you?

Sam: HOLY FUCKING SHIT. YOU WENT NAKED BUNGEE JUMPING AND DIDN'T TELL ME?

Emily: Oh my god, calm down.

Sam: HOW COULD YOU NOT TELL ME?

Emily: I forgot.

Emily: That episode hasn't even aired yet.

Sam: I just saw a promo.

Emily: I thought you were at the office?

Sam: I am.

Sam: Taking a quick break.

Sam: Is it wrong I can't stop staring at Ethan's ass? He's such a jerk and I hate him, but damn. He has a great ass.

Emily: That's not Ethan's ass.

Emily: It's Jake's.

Sam: OH MY GOD MY EYES

Emily: hahahaha

Sam: This is not funny.

Emily: I can't breathe.

Sam: Shut up.

Emily: You can't even hear me.

Sam: Twin telepathy.

Sam: You're still laughing.

Sam: I know you are.

Sam: Emily Ann Peters.

Emily: I wonder what Jake will think about your opinion of his ass?

Sam: You wouldn't dare.

Sam: Emily.

Sam: EMILY.

Jake to Sam: So you think I have a hot ass?

Sam: If by hot, you mean full of shit, then yes.

Jake: That's not what I heard...

Sam: She's dead to me.

Jake: Now that I have your attention, I need your help with something.

Sam: Spit it out or I'm blocking you for real.

Jake: Did you listen to any of my voicemails?

Sam: Can neither confirm nor deny.

Jake: Are you planning on being a pain in my ass for the rest of my goddamn life?

Sam: Yes.

Jake: Christ, Sam.

Sam: Call it sisterly love.

Jake: So you did listen.

Sam: Yes, Jake. Obviously, I listened. And obviously, I was making you sweat it out for a few more days before I responded because I am a petty, petty woman who can't resist a little bit of payback when it's handed to me on a silver platter.

Jake: So what do you think?

Jake: Sam.

Jake: SAM!

Sam: If someone proposed to me with a Ring Pop I would cut their balls off.

Sam: It's perfect.

Sam: She's going to love it.

Cooper to Sam: Favorite snacks? I'm going to the store this weekend.

Sam: Mixed nuts. Dried mango. If you get a jar of Atomic Fireballs, you'll be my favorite person ever.

Cooper: I thought I already was?

Sam: Well...this is awkward.

Cooper: Bite me.

Sam: I plan to.

Cooper: For fuck's sake. It's ten o'clock in the morning. I need to be able to work the rest of the day.

Sam: Good luck with that.

. . .

Sam to Cooper: Favorite color?

Cooper: Why?

Sam: I heard La Perla is having a sale. Thought I'd swing by during my lunch break.

Cooper: What the hell is La Perla?

Sam: Oh my sweet summer child. I keep forgetting you only know me with Em's wardrobe. Look it up.

Cooper: You have got to stop doing this to me in the middle of the day.

Cooper: But for those purposes...black.

Sam: Noted.

Cooper to Sam: Do you ever miss it?

Sam: Miss what? The Maldives?

Cooper: Yes. The Maldives.

Cooper: It's just, I'm sitting here on my back porch watching the sun set, and it's beautiful, don't get me wrong. But I can't stop thinking about that view off the deck and how the sun would disappear right into the ocean. I've never seen anything like it.

Sam: I don't know what you're talking about. If I lean really far over, I can almost see the bright lights of a shipping container cruising down the Hudson River through my boss's window. Is that not the same?

Cooper: I'm being serious.

Sam: Me too.

Cooper: For fuck's sake.

Sam: Yes, I miss it.

Cooper: What do you miss?

Sam: The view. The food. The weather. The room.

Cooper: And that's it?

Sam: What else is there?

Cooper: That's the question I've been asking myself, Cuj. What else could I possibly be missing this much?

Sam: I think I know the answer.

Cooper: Yeah?

Sam: It'll be there soon.

Cooper to Sam: Why is there a bag of sand leaking all over my wood floors?

Sam: You're welcome.

Cooper: No, really. Why?

Sam: It's my present. The thing you've been missing. Sand. Straight from the Maldives.

Cooper: There is no way this is from the Maldives.

Sam: Take your shoes off. Dig your toes in.

Cooper: And risk the plague?

Sam: I never thought someone who just spent a month without running water would be so squeamish.

Cooper: I'm a cattle rancher, not a cretin.

Sam: Are we sure those are mutually exclusive?

Cooper: I'm saving this until you get here.

Sam: Good. Please do. Then I can show you how to properly react to such a thoughtful gift.

Cooper: From anyone else, it would be. But I know you.

Sam: I resent that.

Cooper: I will give you an honest answer to any question right now if you can send me one selfie in which you don't have a shit-eating grin. Just one.

Cooper: Five.

Cooper: Four.

Cooper: Three.

Cooper: Two.

Sam: All right. ALL RIGHT! Maybe it wasn't completely benevolent...

Sam: [Picture message]

Cooper: You're a devil woman.

Cooper: I think I just saw the sand move.

Cooper: Oh man. It definitely moved.

Sam: Throw it out!

Sam: Cooper?

Sam: Cooper!

Cooper: Gotcha.

Sam: Oh my god, my heart is pounding. You can't do that to me!

Cooper: I'm pretty sure I just did.

Sam: That bag better be gone by the time I get there.

Cooper: You don't want to take your shoes off? Dig your toes in?

Sam: You've ruined sand for me.

Cooper: What the hell did you think it was?

Sam: I don't fucking know, but I'm pretty sure I saw your life flash before my eyes.

Cooper: Aww. You do care.

Sam: Well I don't anymore, you jerk.

Cooper: Good night, Sam.
Sam: Night.

Cooper to Sam: What are you up to?
Sam: Nothing really. Work. You?
Cooper: Just got in. Can I call you?
Sam: Why?
Cooper: No reason.
Sam: Is that a good idea?
Cooper: Is it a bad one?
Sam: I don't know. Maybe?
Sam: I thought we were keeping things casual. Extending the rules for one last weekend. Sticking to the plan.
Cooper: And the sound of my voice might, what? Lure you to the altar? We're already engaged, Cuj.
Sam: Phone calls aren't casual, cowboy.
Sam: I'm not answering that.
Cooper: Answer the fucking phone.
Sam: I'm not.
Sam: I'm not.
Sam: Stop calling.
Sam: Oh my god, fine. But I draw the line at Facetiming.

Cooper to Sam: That was fun last night.

Cooper: You know what? Don't answer. I have a lot to do today and I don't need any distractions.

Cooper: Screw it. I'm already picturing it again.

Cooper: What time do you get home tonight?

Sam: Not sure. Work is kicking my ass.

Cooper: Call me.

Sam: It might not be until late.

Cooper: Call me.

Sam to Cooper: I just faceplanted into my keyboard. I'm so tired. I blame you.

Cooper: It wasn't my idea to stay up until four talking.

Sam: Well, it sure as hell wasn't mine.

Cooper: At least you got to sleep in. My alarm goes off at dawn, remember? I can't ride for shit right now.

Sam: Same time tonight?

Cooper: Done.

Cooper to Sam: You free?

Sam: Give me twenty minutes.

Sam to Cooper: You back from dinner with your dad yet? I snuck out early.

Cooper: Thank fuck. I've been waiting for your text.

• • •

Cooper to Sam: You around?

Cooper: You know what? I'm just going to call you. Pick up if you can. If not, call me later.

Cooper to Sam: You sounded stressed last night. Everything okay?

Sam: I'm not stressed anymore. Wink wink.

Cooper: I'm serious, Sam.

Sam: So am I. It's nothing. Don't worry about it. I'll call you later.

Cooper: I'll answer.

Sam to Cooper: Shit, sorry! I can't believe I fucking fell asleep.

Cooper: You don't need to apologize. It was worth it to me just to hear you breathe.

Sam: Cooper.

Cooper: Yes?

Sam: That's not casual.

Cooper: It's the truth.

Sam to Winnie: Shit. Shit. Shit.

Winnie: I'm going to assume this has something to do with the cowboy?

Sam: I cannot be falling for him, Winnie.

Sam: I can't.

Winnie: Why the hell not?

Sam: I just...

Winnie: Did you just scream? And not in the fun way?

Winnie: That's it. Phone sex or no phone sex, I'll be in your room in ten minutes with margaritas.

Sam: It's 11 a.m. on a Sunday, Win.

Winnie: Exactly.

Sam to Cooper: What are the five things you hate most about me?

Cooper: What the hell kind of question is that?

Sam: Just answer it.

Cooper: 1. I hate that you ask stupid questions.

Sam: That doesn't count.

Cooper: 2. I hate that you won't let me kiss you.

Sam: You know that's not what I mean, Cooper.

Cooper: 3. I hate that you're not even here and you're already putting one foot out the door.

Sam: Ugh. Never mind.

Cooper: 4. I hate that you're a secret.

Cooper: 5. I hate that you live in New York.

Cooper: You know what? Scratch that last one. Because if I'm being honest, you live rent free in my goddamn mind. Every free second I get, you're the first thing I think about and it would actually be really fucking annoying if I didn't like it so much. So you better not be backing out on me, Cuj.

Sam: Are we sure this visit is a good idea?

Cooper: Yes.

Sam: Because I've been lying here for an hour, unable to sleep, staring at my packed bags, trying to come up with five things I hate about you, Cooper. It's this little game I play. And for the first time in my life, I can only come up with one thing.

Cooper: Dammit, Sam. Pick up the phone.

Sam: The only thing I hate about you is that I'm pretty sure I don't hate anything at all.

Cooper: Get on the plane, Sam.

Cooper: That's all you have to do.

Cooper: Get on the plane.

Cooper: When you land, I'll be there waiting. And it'll all make sense. I can't tell you how I know but I do. Just get on the plane. Just get here. Just come.

Sam: Good night, Cooper.

Cooper: Sam.

Sam: I'll see you tomorrow.

CHAPTER NINETEEN

Sam

OH GOD. *This is a bad idea.*

The thought has plagued Sam all morning. On the subway. At her office. In the meeting she couldn't afford to skip. In the taxi. At the airport. On her flight. During her layover. On the second flight she almost—*almost*—didn't board. And now here, with nothing but metal doors standing between them.

This is a bad idea.

She stops in the middle of the hallway. The other passengers on her flight flow around her like a river to a rock. She puts a hand to her stomach, as if she can somehow feel the knot that's twisting and tightening her insides. Her fear has been festering for days, just waiting for the perfect moment to strike.

Apparently, now is that moment.

She can't move. She can't breathe.

Panic swells her throat.

This is a really bad fucking idea.

What is she doing here? She doesn't belong here. She's wearing three-inch pumps and a black suit that probably cost more than her plane ticket. The airport is hardly bigger than her apartment. There's not even a baggage claim. They just unloaded the plane right on the runway and set up shop.

She should've left everything that happened with Cooper in the Maldives. A vacation fling. A blip on the radar. A fun memory to look back on with a smile. Not... whatever the hell it is now.

She should've told Nina to go screw herself.

Really, she should've told Emily the truth as soon as she had the chance. Except that would've involved a phone call—which would have been difficult enough before but now seems completely impossible with Em begging her to become CFO of the business. Turning the offer down via text was hard enough. If she actually hears her sister say the words, she won't have the strength to say no. And she has to say no. She has a plan. If she sticks with her job, she'll be earning millions by the time she's in her midthirties. Practically guaranteed. Who is she to pass that up on a startup whim that may very well fail before it even begins? When she told herself no one in her family would ever want for money again, she meant it. She still does.

And that plan does not include falling for a cowboy from

the middle of nowhere either. Get a grip. Sam swallows and squares her shoulders. She's built this up too much in her head. She's built *him* up too much. *He's not as hot as you remember. It wasn't as good as you remember. You will not let a man unravel all the goals you set for yourself, all the promises you made. You—*

"If you're planning on running, I'd reconsider. The next flight out doesn't leave until tomorrow, and there's nowhere you can go in this town where I won't find you."

A shiver works its way down her spine as that deep rumble punctures through every one of her defenses to settle in her bones. All at once, everything becomes clear.

He is that hot.

It was that good.

And she just might.

Fuck.

Sam lifts her chin and turns around. "Cooper."

"Samantha."

He arches a brow in question even as his eyes sparkle. One of those damn dimples digs into his cheeks. He might not be making a sound, but he's laughing at her clear as day, amused as ever by her futile attempt to keep a little distance between them.

"Oh, shut up."

"I didn't say a word, Cuj."

"You didn't have to. What are you even doing here? I thought I'd find you waiting outside in a pickup truck."

"And I thought I'd find you in cowboy boots and a

thong, so I guess we were both wrong." He leans in close, the tip of his nose like a brand against her cheek. His warm breath brushes over her skin. Tingles cascade down her back. "Though that tight little skirt is sexy as hell."

She rolls her eyes. "It's a suit, Cooper. For work."

"It's begging to be bunched up around your hips is what it is."

"Well, I *am* wearing that thong you can't seem to stop thinking about."

"Don't tempt me with a good time, Cuj," he murmurs as he slips his hand through the slit in her jacket and slides his warm palm around her waist to toy with the zipper. In a sudden rush, he pulls her flush against him and nips at her earlobe. "I have the home team advantage here, and I plan to play dirty."

Her heart leaps like a professional gymnast going for gold. After so many hours on the phone with nothing but his voice and her imagination, she's overwhelmed by his presence, by his proximity, by the feel of his hands on her and the memory of exactly how skilled they were. But there's one little question nagging at her through the lusty haze, the only thing keeping her from jumping on him in the middle of this airport. "How'd you get on the other side of security, cowboy?"

"I have my ways," he says distractedly as he drags his fingers down her spine and over the curve of her ass as if he just can't stop himself.

"Cooper."

"Come on." He chuckles softly and pulls back. "You'll see soon enough."

"See what?"

He steps around her without bothering to answer and starts wheeling her suitcase in the opposite direction to the exit.

"See what, Cooper?"

He keeps ignoring her.

"What aren't you telling me?" she asks, racing to keep up as he leads her across the one-room terminal. "What are you hiding? Why are you smirking? And why—"

He bursts through a set of metal double doors, and everything within her comes to a screeching halt. Gleaming in the fiery sunset like a harbinger of doom sits a forest-green four-person helicopter with the words *Kelley & Dunne* painted on the side.

"Oh, fuck no."

She starts to wheel around, but he stops her. "I have a pilot's license."

"Good for you."

"We'll be home in twenty minutes compared to the hour and a half it takes to drive there."

"Not happening."

"You'll get an amazing view of the ranch."

"Not if I pass out."

"You don't have to be afraid with me."

"No, apparently I need to be afraid *of* you."

He steps close and cups her face, then arches her head

back until she meets his eyes. "Remember what I told you on the parasail? Same thing applies here. I've got you. You're safe. And you're going to kick yourself if you miss out—"

"Because I'm afraid," she finishes softly, teetering.

"Because you're afraid," he agrees and brushes his thumb across her cheekbone.

"I'm not just afraid, Cooper. I'm terrified."

"I know." He presses a soft kiss to her forehead. She's not sure if they're still talking about the helicopter or something else, something deeper. "Don't make me double-dog dare you again, Cuj. Get your pretty little ass in the copilot's chair. Now."

She snorts. "Order me around again, cowboy, and you'll be kissing my pretty little ass instead."

"You say that like it's a threat."

"Isn't it?"

"How can it be when it's all I've wanted to do for the past seven weeks?"

The hungry gleam in his eye makes her heart skip a beat. A flush creeps up her neck as she goes hot all over. "Twenty minutes you said?"

"Twenty minutes."

She squeezes her eyes shut, utterly torn.

This is insane.

It's a death trap.

You're not doing this.

You're not actually thinking about doing this.

No.

No.

No.

A flashback to their last night in the Maldives permeates her denial, all stars and sighs and feeling.

Screw it.

She can survive anything for twenty minutes.

Sam squares her shoulders and marches toward the helicopter. Cooper seems to sense this is his one shot because he throws her suitcase into the back seat and then hops in without a word. Buttons are pushed. Seat belts are secured. He flicks switches, spins knobs, and says something into the comms that her anxiety-ridden mind isn't able to process. A heavy set of headphones slides over her ears, canceling out the roar of the blades spinning faster and faster overhead. The sense of weightlessness grows, until suddenly, the ground slips away and they're floating. It all feels surprisingly peaceful as they rise higher and higher, like a balloon cast adrift.

Then the wind shifts.

They drop.

And the brutal reality of being hundreds of feet in the air without a safety net comes careening back into focus.

Sam screams.

Cooper laughs.

Bastard.

Another gust of wind slams into them from the side and the helicopter tilts left. She presses her palm against the window as if that might do anything and searches desperately for a handhold while all her organs shove themselves up her throat.

And now I'm coughing. Great.

She finds a handle and grabs on, needing to feel grounded.

"I wouldn't hold that if I were you," Cooper says through his mic.

"Why not?" Sam practically squeaks.

"It's the emergency exit."

"Shit!"

She lets go as if burned. Her heart pounds. Spots start to invade her view as she squeezes the seat cushion, needing something firmer, sturdier—

Strong fingers suddenly thread through hers in an iron grip.

She looks up at Cooper, surprised. "Don't you need it to fly?"

"I'll tell you if I do."

"Are you sure?"

"Just hold my damn hand, Cuj."

She doesn't ask again—not because of his tone, but because the moment he touched her, the panic subsided. Not entirely, but enough. Enough for her to catch her breath and look past the fear to the beauty waiting on the other side of the glass. Like always on the plane, the first thing she did when she sat down was close the window. But now, there's nowhere to look but out at the pink-and-purple-stained sky, the clouds gilded by the dying sun, the stars already starting to pierce through the soft glow. To the far left, the cliffs of a majestic plateau gleam. To the right, rolling hills stretch endlessly into the mounting darkness. It's awe-inspiring.

Honestly, it's not at all what she pictured.

"You look confused," Cooper comments wryly.

"I thought it would be...flatter?"

"Flatter?"

"And full of corn?"

"Ahh." He nods. "You're thinking of Eastern Nebraska. This is cattle country. It's a whole different landscape."

"It looks kind of like...home, actually. Like the dunes we walk through to get to the beach. Only here, there's no beach. They just go on and on."

"That's a pretty good description, actually. They *are* dunes."

She scrunches up her face. "What? But there's no ocean."

"Nope. Just sand hills. Lots and lots of sand hills held in place by grass." He pauses, then turns to her with a grin. "You know what cows like to eat, Cuj?"

"Grass."

"Ding ding ding."

She snorts. "Well, whatever it is, it's beautiful."

"I've always thought so."

"You say that like you— Wait." She perks up and turns to look at him. "Are we on the ranch already?"

"You've been on the ranch since you landed. We lease the land to the local airport because it's at the far edge of the property, too close to town for the cattle."

"So all of this..." She trails off, turning her gaze to the

view, the distant horizon, the endless wilds seemingly untouched by man.

"Home sweet home, as far as the eye can see."

"It's..." She swallows, not sure what to say, her tiny little concrete box of an apartment suddenly seeming ridiculous in comparison. "Wow."

"Speechless? I didn't think that was possible."

She squeezes his fingers. "Not speechless, just soaking it all in. I might have read on your website that the ranch consisted of about two hundred thousand acres, but reading it and seeing it are two different things. Especially when most of my life fits in an eight-by-eight cubicle without windows."

"Don't feel too bad. We're land rich and money poor out here."

"You've got your own helicopter, cowboy. I think you're doing just fine."

He barks out a laugh and shakes his head, then juts his chin forward. "That white farmhouse over there? That's the main house where my dad lives. Then the stables are just ahead, and those are the hay barns. You can see some of the cattle in that pasture over there."

"And the bunkhouse?" she asks in a teasing voice.

"None of your damn business."

"Worried I might find someone to replace you?"

The helicopter takes a sudden dip and she yelps as her free hand goes to the ceiling, as if bracing would somehow make a crash any less fatal.

"Cooper!"

"My hand slipped."

She glares at him as he folds his lips between his teeth, trying to hide a smile.

"What were you saying, Cuj?"

"That I'm definitely finding the bunkhouse later."

They drop again.

"COOPER!"

She squeezes his hand so tightly she's afraid her nails might draw blood...not that he deserves any less.

The asshole laughs outright.

"Sorry. Slipped again. You were saying?"

"Where's your damn house?" she growls. "I'm ready to get the hell off this thing."

"Just over that ridge."

A brilliant shimmer like liquid gold catches her eye first, the sunset reflecting off a small lake nestled in the hills. But as they fly closer, a long black roof appears, the top of what looks like a large rectangular barn and— Sam narrows her eyes, not sure if she's seeing it right. But she is. Glass. Walls and walls of glass, punctuated by charred wood siding and portions of natural stone. It's nothing like she expected. Modern yet cozy. Masculine yet soft. Blending into the landscape yet living in stark contrast with it. It looks like him. She's not sure if that even makes sense, but it's true. If someone had asked her five minutes ago what Cooper looked like in house form, she would have had no clue. But it's this. It's him. They haven't even landed and she's already itching to explore because she just knows walking through that door will feel like a warm hug, like stepping inside a piece of him, maybe even like going...

Home.

"My buddy helped me build it a few years back," Cooper explains, not noticing how still she's gone in the wake of that single word sending tremors through her soul. "He's an architect out in Denver, but he flew out a bunch to oversee the project. I know, *I know*, it's a little funky, but it's—"

"Perfect."

He turns to her with a pleasantly surprised expression. "You think so?"

"I wouldn't say it if I didn't." She squeezes his hand. "Now, stop fishing for compliments and land this fucking thing. Your twenty minutes are up."

He slides his hand free and flips some switches. They start to descend.

"Cooper!"

"What?" He turns to her. "You said to land this fucking thing."

"I didn't mean right here," she says, looking around in panic as they sink below his roofline. "Isn't this— I mean, don't you—" They touch down. "We're in your front yard."

"So?"

"You can't just land a helicopter in your front yard."

"Why not?" He shrugs and unclips his seat belt. "It's my house, and my helicopter, and my yard. I can do what I damn well please. And right now, what I damn well please is getting you inside that house as quickly as I can. I'll take it back to the landing pad tomorrow."

With that, he hops out of the side. She's still frozen with shock as he rounds the helicopter and opens her door.

"You coming? Or do I have to haul you out?"

"I don't—"

He takes her hand and pulls her through the door so she lands over his shoulder. With a little shuffle he wraps an arm across the backs of her legs, braces her weight, and spins them toward the house. It's possibly the least romantic carrying style ever, yet butterflies swarm across her stomach as he marches confidently for the door.

"Oh my god, I can walk."

"Not fast enough for my liking."

"This is not how I envisioned you carrying me over the threshold."

He smacks her ass. "Tough shit."

"I've got to hand it to you, cowboy. You really know how to seduce a woman."

"I got you out here, didn't I?"

"I'm pretty sure Nina and a hefty dose of blackmail got me out here."

"Keep telling yourself that. I like a challenge."

He swings open the door and steps inside. She arches around, trying to get a look at the place, then finally pinches the small of his back. He jumps and puts her down, grumbling something she doesn't quite hear, but it doesn't matter. All of her attention is immediately snagged by the view waiting on the other side. A wall of glass spills onto a sweeping stone veranda, and beyond that is a scene of brilliant, bursting color. The sun has just started to drop beneath the hills, the sky like a painting as the dying rays scatter through the clouds. The lake, though small from above, seems to stretch as far as the eye can see from this vantage inside the house, the still surface reflecting everything above.

Sam's breath literally catches in her throat.

"I chose this spot for its sunsets," Cooper explains, his voice drifting in from behind. Soft footsteps thud as he walks closer. "I used to ride out here as a kid just to watch them from the hill. It's always been my favorite view."

"I can see why," she says, awed.

"It's never looked as beautiful as it does right now."

She glances over her shoulder, already aware he's watching her, but it does nothing to lessen the blow. Those green eyes pierce like a blade right to her heart, pleasure and pain a heady mix as her desire and her fear flare. He closes the last foot between them, molding his front to her back, and gently takes her by the hands. But he doesn't swing her around as she expects. Instead, he takes three steps forward, forcing her to go with him, until her hips hit the edge of the kitchen island. His lips find her neck as he reaches for her lapels and slides her jacket off. He loosens the first button on her blouse, then another, and another, working his mouth over to her shoulder as her shirt falls open. Between the silk and his hands, her skin turns to flame. A sudden brush of cool air only fans the inferno as her shirt drops away.

"Fuck, Sam," he groans against her spine.

She smirks. "You said black."

Calloused fingers toy with the edges of her lace bra. No space between them, she can feel his passion growing, but he takes his time, pulling one strap over her shoulder, then the other, kissing along the path his fingers create, as if every inch of her deserves to be touched, caressed, worshipped. It's overwhelming. It's maddening. It's driving her insane.

But right as she's about to turn herself around, he braces her hands on the counter and orders, "Not yet."

He slides his hands down her sides, over her hips, to the edges of her skirt. Then he sinks, dragging his mouth down her spine as he goes. She stands there, exposed, waiting, already on the edge. He takes it slow, torturously slow, as he lifts the hem, inch by inch, over her hips, and kisses his way up the backs of her thighs until her legs tremble.

"Tell me you missed me," he murmurs as he stands and slides his palm down her front, so close to the place she desperately needs it.

"No."

"Say it."

He traces the scalloped edge of her thong, again, and again, and again, each pass making her pulse flutter a little more. He's deliberate, patient, and calm. She's practically panting when she finally relents.

"Fine. I missed you."

"Good."

He moves suddenly then, kicking her legs apart, gripping her around the waist with one arm while sliding the other home. With a gasp, she arches against him.

"Because I fucking missed you, too."

cooper

"I KNEW we wouldn't make it to the bedroom," Sam comments as she takes the wine from his outstretched hand. Their fingers brush. Even though he just had her, that single touch is a burning ember landing on an arid autumn plain—enough to spark a fire. "But I have to admit, I thought we'd make it more than ten feet inside the door."

She's perched on his kitchen counter wearing nothing but his dark blue flannel with two buttons strategically fastened for coverage. It would almost be easier if she were naked, because he can't stop staring into those tauntingly deep shadows, fully aware of the bare skin waiting within if he just slipped his hand between the folds.

"What are you talking about?" Cooper forces his gaze away and glances over his shoulder. "It's at least fifteen feet to the door."

"Smart-ass." She slaps him playfully on the bicep. "Are you going to let me go explore?"

He slides his palms up her exposed thighs, unable to keep away. "What exactly are you hoping to find?"

"Your hidden stash of Shania Twain paraphernalia, obviously."

"Then you're definitely not leaving." He digs his fingers into her ass cheeks and pulls her against him. Putting his jeans back on was a stupid idea. It's been five minutes and he's already straining against them.

"Hey." Sam puts her palms to his chest. "You promised me food."

He leans down to nuzzle her neck. "I know."

"And Wi-Fi."

"I know."

"And a shower."

"That can be arranged." He strokes her throat with his tongue.

"Cooper," she says with a laugh as she pushes him. "I actually do need to pee so at least point me to a bathroom, and then I'm all yours."

He steps back with a groan and grabs her around the waist to lower her off the counter, taking any excuse to keep touching her. "Second door on the right. I'll get started on dinner. Steak okay?"

"It's better than the Easy Mac you'd be getting from me."

"You don't like to cook?"

"It's not that I don't like to cook as a concept. I just

don't like to cook in my kitchen. It's the size of a closet. Literally. There are two folding doors to close it off and everything." She shrugs and runs her hand along his granite countertop, eying his kitchen island with a sigh. "It's just easier to get takeout, especially since the company pays for it if I'm in the office past nine. Which I am. Every night." She looks up at him suddenly. "Do *you* cook a lot?"

"If I want to eat."

He laughs at the confused expression on her face, then leans back against the fridge and crosses his arms. They spent almost every night for two weeks on the phone with each other. How did this never come up? Actually, he's sort of happy it didn't, because now he gets to see the real-time, unfiltered reaction written all over her face.

"The closest restaurant to me is an hour and a half away, Cuj."

"An hour and a half?"

"Twenty minutes by helicopter."

"That's—that's—" She short-circuits, eyes twitching as her words fail her. Her jaw drops to the floor.

He lifts it gently with his finger. "I mean, my old man has a cook, but then I'd have to go over there and eat with him, so it's just easier to make it myself. Frozen pizza only gets you so far."

"Frozen..." She blinks rapidly. "You don't even have a pizza place?"

"None that deliver."

"Tacos?"

"In town."

"Sushi?"

"Never tried it."

"Ramen?"

He furrows his brow. "Like Cup Noodles?"

"Oh dear god." She digs her fingers into his arm. "Please tell me there's at least a Starbucks."

"About two hours in the other direction."

She gasps like a dying fish sucking air.

"You all right there, Cuj?"

"Yeah." She wheezes, then coughs to clear her throat. Before she meets his eyes, she takes a big swill of wine. "I don't think I'm cut out for this life, Cooper."

"I can make you a latte, Sam."

"What about dim sum? Can you make that?"

"Sure." He shrugs. "As soon as you tell me what the hell it is."

"Cooper—"

He takes her by the shoulders to spin her toward the bathroom. "Get out of here."

"But, Cooper—"

"Go."

She stumbles forward and he shakes his head in amusement as he watches her leave. It's only as he opens the fridge that what she said registers—*I don't think I'm cut out for this life*—with those words and that phrasing, as if there'd been an earlier point in time when she'd thought, even for a moment, that maybe she was.

He grins and grabs the steaks.

By the time she returns from the bathroom, both are seasoned, the potatoes are in the oven, and he's just about done chopping the vegetables for the salad. "For a second, I was worried you fell in."

"Ha. Ha," she replies as she jumps back onto the countertop and plucks a cherry tomato from the bowl. "I got distracted."

"By...?"

"Everything."

He rolls his eyes while she tries to hide that mischievous grin behind a sip of wine. "What?"

"Nothing."

"What?"

"Nothing. It's just—" She half laughs, half sighs. "You are such a cowboy."

"You say that like you didn't know."

"I didn't. Not really. I mean, sure, I knew about the hat and the boots and the whole Midwestern drawl. But you're not just a cowboy, Cooper." She leans in and lowers her voice. "You're a *cowboy.*"

"You lost me, Cuj."

"There are horns mounted on your wall. There's a picture on the bookshelf of you wearing chaps at five years old. There's a rope hanging by the door and it's too dirty to be decorative. Every piece of upholstery in your house is leather. I mean, you are *such* a cowboy."

"I have no idea what to say to that."

She laughs outright and glances around again. "Were all these photographs taken on the ranch?"

"Yup."

"I especially love the one over your fireplace."

"Yeah?" He glances toward the mantel, finding the photograph in question as a lump forms at the back of his throat. "Me too. It's a bit hard to tell with all of the fog, but that's actually this view before the house was here. We got an early cold front before the water temperatures dropped. My mom always loved those misty mornings, so I woke her up at dawn and drove out here with her. She was pretty far gone at that point so she mainly stayed in the car. Then right as we were about to leave, she put her hand on my arm and said, *The sun's about to break through.* I'm not really sure if she knew who I was at that point. Until she said that, I honestly didn't even think she knew where she was. I just liked having her there. But then she pointed to the sky with this perfect moment of clarity and gave me a little shove. So I hopped out and, well, she was right, as you can see. I'm not really sure if I believe in God or all that, but for a moment, it really felt like more than the sun was shining down on us out there. I guess that's why I put that one on the mantel. I like to think she might be that thing shining down on me now." He clears his throat as his eyes start to sting, suddenly aware he might have said too much. "Anyway—"

"Don't."

He cuts his gaze to Sam. "Don't what?"

"Don't minimize it." She takes his hand and threads their fingers together. "Did you take all of these?"

"Some are mine. Some are my mom's. Why? Who'd you think took them?"

"I don't know. A professional or something."

"You saw me walking around with my camera in the Maldives, Cuj. What'd you think I was doing?"

"Taking the same terrible photos as everyone else. But these, Cooper? They're incredible."

He's not a shy person, so he's not sure why he has to fight the sudden urge to look away from the intensity in her eyes, only that he does. Ants crawl beneath his skin as a spot deep inside his chest reverberates with a resounding pang. It's pain and heartache, but something else too, something that almost feels like pride. It's actually sort of nice, until she has to go and ruin it by getting an idea. He's not sure what the idea is, but he's positive he won't like it as a frenetic sort of energy builds behind her growing smile. The cogs practically spin in her eyes.

"No."

"You don't even know what I'm thinking."

"I don't have to. No."

"Hear me out."

"Sam—"

"This is how you save your ranch."

He winces. *My dad would just love that.*

"I know that sounds crazy," she barrels on. "But it's not. The people who end up the most successful after doing one of these shows are the ones who can use their fifteen minutes not just for fame, but to launch a sustainable business. You've got that fame right now, Cooper. Everyone is talking about you online. I literally get daily alerts from my mom whenever Emily is mentioned on *Wake Up, America!* But it won't last. It never does. Not unless you can convert it into something more. *This* is that something more."

"They're just a couple of landscape shots, Sam."

"They're not. They're evocative and moody and captivating, Cooper. Honestly. I'm not even your target audience and something in these photographs made me want to keep looking. But more importantly than all of that, they're a way for the people at home to connect with you, to get a little piece of you to keep for themselves. Set up a shop on your website. Sell prints. Sell canvases. See if you can partner with a frame manufacturer. Post your photographs online for people to see. Add stories in the captions like the one you just told me. And yes, slip a few thirst traps in there to keep people's attention. Lose the shirt if you're okay with it. Because a business like that? If you do it right? It can lead to so much more. Book deals. Licensing. Longevity. Not just for you, but for this place you love."

"I'm not a businessman, Sam. I'm a cowboy."

"Who said you can't be both?"

"My dad won't even let me open us up for horseback riding tours."

"So?"

"It's his ranch."

She rears back in confusion, then cocks her head to the side. "But isn't that the whole point?"

"What?" he asks, clueless to what she's implying.

"It'll be yours," she says, as if that's the most obvious thing in the world. And maybe it is. But it feels brand new. Not the idea that he'll inherit the ranch one day. He knows that. He's always known it. But that when he does, it won't be his father's ranch anymore, or his father's, or his father's before him.

It'll be mine.

"Someday, hopefully in the very distant future, it *will* be yours, Cooper," she says, as if she can read on his face how her words are resonating. "Your father won't always be the one making the decisions, and an opportunity like this might not come around again. There's a saying my old boss used to like. Sometimes it's better to ask for forgiveness than permission. If you start bringing in money, if you show him your way can work, he won't be able to say no."

Isn't that why he went on the show in the first place?

Isn't that why he risked so much?

To make something of himself.

To make something *for* himself.

To prove his father wrong.

Or had his father been right all along? Had he just wanted an excuse to run away again, to gallivant around the world instead of putting in the real work here?

"You can do it, Cooper." She slides her palm over his

cheek to stroke his skin, drawing him out of himself and back to her. "You can make it yours."

All he wants to do is taste the confidence on her lips, as if her kiss might be able to infuse that belief into his soul.

But he can't.

So he does the next best thing and fists her hair. As he lays her back on the counter, he tugs her head to the side, gaining access to her throat.

"The food—"

"Can wait." He undoes those two taunting buttons. "I want an appetizer first."

Lips pressed against her skin, he feels her pulse pound as he spreads her knees wide. With a grin, he sinks lower.

Eventually, they make it to the food.

And after that, the bedroom.

At some point, they must fall asleep, because when he opens his eyes the first strains of daylight filter through the window. And this time, Sam is still there with him, nuzzled against his side with their legs entwined. It's heaven, just pure bliss, to wake with her warmth still seeping into his skin, to feel the gentle brush of her breath on his chest, to know she didn't vanish in the middle of the night. The absolute last thing he wants to do is extricate himself.

But the ranch waits for no one.

So he's careful not to jostle her as he gently rolls free. He's quiet as he grabs a set of clothes from the closet and brushes his teeth in the bathroom before slipping away. He puts a pot of coffee on, lays out one of the croissants he picked up from the bakery in town, and pens a quick note to let her know he should be back after lunch.

An odd feeling washes over him as he fires up his truck and eases down the dirt driveway toward the main house. His gaze keeps drifting to the rearview mirror as the house grows smaller and smaller, a sinking feeling in his chest at the thought of Sam being farther and farther away. It's only when he slams on the brakes after having almost run into a deer that the truth smacks him in the face.

For the first time in his life, he's looking back.

Not ahead.

Not at the horizon.

Not at whatever waits beyond.

But behind.

At his house.

At her.

In a sudden rush, he finally understands why his father constantly used to look over his shoulder, why he always went to the main house first instead of the stables, even if it added an extra twenty minutes to his day, why he now seems so lost. It's the same reason his mother sat out on the porch every night waiting for her husband to return. Cooper gets it in a way he never has before. He gets it the way his mother always said he would.

She was right.

He *was* searching for all the wrong things in all the wrong places. Looking for an escape, for a thrill, for another life, for anything and everything that would free him from the binds of his birthright for even a moment.

But he sees the truth with perfect clarity now. It was never freedom that he needed.

It was an anchor.

A person.

Someone who would turn this place from a jail cell into a home.

sam

THE BED FEELS cold without him. It's an unwelcome realization—both that he's gone, and that she cares.

A taste of my own damn medicine.

She frowns and scrubs the sleep from her eyes. Bright sun streaks through the windows. She knows his days start early, but it's Saturday, and she's in town. She'd thought maybe...

Maybe he'd rearrange his entire life for me?

She snorts.

No tomorrow. That's her rule, not his. This weekend is a glorified booty call to stave off Nina's machinations for a little while longer. Nothing more. Nothing less.

So why does her heart start to flutter as if she's a fourteen-year-old on Valentine's Day when she sees a note on the kitchen island held in place by a single blue iris?

She lifts the bloom to her nose and inhales the sweet, earthy scent.

Iris spuria, she thinks, drawing on a childhood spent surrounded by the flowers at her mother's store. *Represents faith, devotion, and trust.*

There's no way Cooper knows that. There's no way he'd think she does either. Just as he couldn't possibly know it's one of her favorite flowers—complex, underutilized, able to stand completely on its own, and not nearly as cliché as a rose. Still, she can't help but wonder what, if anything, it means.

Sam flips open the note.

The vet is coming this morning to check the last of the herd. I couldn't skip it, but I should be back by midday. Make yourself at home. There's a milk frother by the coffee machine. Your fireballs are next to the fridge. And in case you were wondering, no, I don't have a second truck. You're stuck with me, Cuj. Unless of course you want to try your luck with the chopper...

She rolls her eyes and locates the coffeepot, surprised to see it's already on. The milk frother rests beside it, shiny and seemingly brand new. And right next to that, there's an unopened box of sugar. Now that her curiosity is piqued, Sam can't help but scan the rest of the kitchen as she plucks a fresh carton of almond milk from his refrigerator. There's the massive plastic tub of Atomic Fireballs, the two bags of dried mango beside them, the four canisters of nuts and an empty bowl sitting next to them, presumably for mixing—all things she asked for—but some other choice items catch her eye as well. The fresh vase of irises in the window. The two suspiciously clean dish towels hanging from the oven. The completely full bottle of hand soap by the sink. The dozen lemons sitting in a bowl. When she glances at the living room and notices the two mismatched pillows plus a cozy throw with the tag still on, a warm sensation spreads across her chest. She lifts her fingers to her lips as if covering them could erase her silly grin as she pictures Cooper stalking down the aisles of a Walmart, feverishly throwing half the store into his cart just to make sure she's comfortable in his home.

It's sweet—so sweet it's almost painful as this feeling she refuses to acknowledge thrums beneath her skin, all heat and goodness and joy, as if her blood has turned to warm honey.

That's enough of that.

Sam swipes the croissant from the kitchen island and marches toward the patio with her computer and coffee in tow. At the last second, she grabs the blanket. When she wraps it around her shoulders, she's unable to wipe the smile from her lips, imagining it's his arms instead.

Work.

Focus on work.

She slides open her laptop, in dire need of a sobering distraction, but it's impossible to focus on her emails with this view. The lake water glitters with the late-morning sun, a diamond with infinite facets. Rolling hills stretch into the distance, not another building or object or soul in sight. A crisp breeze blows across the patio, sending sparkling ripples through the water and swirling her hair. Sam pulls her knees into her chest, drops her head back, and breathes in, practically groaning at the sweet grassy scent. She's become frighteningly accustomed to the smell of a stranger's BO on the subway every morning. She's forgotten what fresh air smells like, how the cool touch of clean oxygen makes her lungs swell with pleasure.

I could get used to this.

Isolation has its upsides. And honestly, the coffee isn't that bad. It's actually pretty good, she thinks as she takes another sip—

Then practically spits it out as the door behind her slams open.

"I knew it!" an unfamiliar deep voice shouts. "I fucking knew it!"

She barely has time to put down her coffee cup before she's yanked to her feet. Two rather large hands grip her upper arms. She looks up into a completely unfamiliar, though not totally unwelcome and rather handsome, face. Dark brown curls spill out around the edges of his cowboy hat. His tan, sunkissed-skin is caked in dirt, making his teeth shine even brighter. Mostly, she notices the joyous wrinkles around his eyes, which are kind and ooze with humor.

What the hell is in the water in Nebraska?

If women knew what kind of men lived here, the last thing it'd be called is a flyover state.

"You're real," he says.

"I'm real."

"You're here."

"I'm here."

"You're coming with me."

"Wait. Whaaa—aaahh!"

He grabs her by the waist and throws her over his shoulder. She knows enough self-defense thanks to her dad to get out of this if she needs to, but honestly, she's a little curious to see where it goes.

"I'm getting shockingly used to being manhandled by cowboys," she says as he starts hauling her across the patio, "but can I at least get a name to go with the pretty face?"

"I'm hurt you haven't already guessed. I'm—"

"Wes!"

Three voices say it at the exact same time—one with humor, one with realization, and one with unadulterated fury. Sam snaps her head to the side just as Cooper barges through the door. If she hadn't heard him talk about Wes so much on the phone, she'd be a bit freaked out by the murderous gleam in his eye. Alas, she has a sister, so she gets it.

Sometimes, you just want to kill them.

"Put her down," Cooper thunders.

"No can do."

"Put. Her. Down."

"So you can lock her away in some other tower? I can't believe you weren't going to tell me she was here."

"The network—"

"Fuck the network."

"It's supposed to be a secret visit. No one's supposed to know."

"Who am I going to tell?"

"How about the whole damn town? Or did you forget about blabbing to Kelly Michaels after the senior prank and almost landing my ass in jail?"

"Honest mistake."

"Or telling everyone that Haddie was knocked up after we heard she and Caleb ran off to Vegas?"

"It was obvious!"

"Or that time you told my dad I took Caroline to the Peak? He showed up in the chopper!"

"Okay." Wes winces. "That was bad."

"I can keep going."

"What's the Peak?" Sam interrupts, unable to stop herself. *And who the hell is Caroline?*

They both look at her.

Then at each other.

Then at her again.

Then—

"Cooper! Wesley! Why'd you—" The new voice stops short.

Sam snaps her head up.

An older man fills the doorway, tall and broad. His jawline is surprisingly chiseled for his age, and there appears to be a permanent furrow etched into his brow. It doesn't take a genius to figure out who he is, especially when those hard green eyes, so like his son's, yet so different, zero in on her.

Sam sighs.

Ass-up in worn leggings is definitely not how she planned to meet Cooper's father, but there's no hiding now. She waves once from her perch over Wes's shoulder, completely forgetting about the ring she casually slipped back onto her finger before leaving for the airport the day before—to keep up appearances, obviously. Not because she'd missed it. Or because her finger felt oddly bare without it. Or because it meant anything.

Because it doesn't.

Except it must, because the second Frank Kelley sets eyes on it, he goes stiff.

"What the hell is going on here, boys?" he bellows as his gaze darts between the three of them. "And who does she belong to?"

"Excuse me?" Indignation burns like a stick of dynamite up Sam's chest. "My own damn self, thank you very much."

"Don't get your panties in a twist."

"My panties are just fine. Ask your son."

His eyes narrow as his gaze flicks toward Cooper. "So she's yours then?"

"Dad." Cooper pinches the bridge of his nose. "You can't—"

"Then what's she doing with him?"

"I'm stealing her away," Wes says with a grin, seemingly amused by the entire exchange.

Well, that makes one of us.

"No, you're not," Cooper interjects. "Put her down, Wes."

"I have questions."

"What questions could you possibly have? You're the number-one fan of the show. You won't shut up about it."

"The show?" his father says, something clicking behind his eyes.

"Here's a question," Wes says, oblivious to the shift. "Is your sister single? Because they keep teasing her in the promos, and I gotta say, I'm kind of into this boss-bitch vibe she's giving off. Now, I know you're identical twins, so don't take this the wrong way, but she's hot. And if she's open to it, I wouldn't mind being handcuffed to a few bedposts by her if you know what I mean…"

Sam snorts.

Cooper, on the other hand, sees red. "I'm going to kill you, Wes."

"What'd I say?" Wes mutters as he takes a proactive step back.

But before Cooper can close the distance, his father grabs him by the arm. "She's the girl from the show?"

"Not now, Dad."

"I told you I didn't want any of them on my ranch."

"It's my ranch too."

"Not yet. Not until you've earned it."

"Dad—"

"After everything your mother told you? After everything you put her through? You gave this girl a ring for some goddamn television show?"

"It's not like that."

"You didn't propose?"

"Dad."

"You're not engaged?"

"Dad."

"Are you trying to leave again?"

"What?"

"You leave again, boy, and I won't let you come back."

"Are you serious right now?"

They both fall silent, chests heaving as they stare at each other across the distance, one a mirror to the future and one a reflection of the past.

"Psst," Sam whispers, nudging Wes. "Can you put me down now?"

"I'm not sure that's a good idea."

"I didn't ask if it was a good idea. I said put me down."

"You don't know them like I do," Wes continues, keeping his eyes on the duo across the patio. "We may still need to make a quick getaway."

She has half a mind to pinch him on the ass right here right now and see how he likes being manhandled. But instead, using her sweetest voice, she says, "I'm getting off your shoulder in the next five seconds. So either you can put me down, or I can do it my way, and my way involves breaking your nose. Five. Four. Th—"

Wes slides her off his shoulder faster than a man on fire and places his hand to her hip to help steady her. Those thick brows furrow as a realization sparks in his brown eyes. "You're not Emily, are you?"

"No," Sam says. "And to answer your earlier offer, I'm very much taken."

Wes whistles softly as an elated smile breaks out across his lips. "Now I definitely have questions."

Sam ignores him and turns toward the father and son still very much locked in a stubborn, bullheaded, clearly familiar argument.

"He's not going anywhere, Mr. Kelley."

"I didn't ask you," the man sneers, not bothering to even glance in her direction.

He's Cooper's father.

Be cool. Be calm.

WWED—what would Emily do?

Definitely not say what Sam is about to say, but who is she trying to kid?

"Then it's a good thing I'm a grown-ass woman who doesn't need your permission to speak, isn't it?"

The man rears back in surprise.

Sam steps closer and cocks a brow. She's just getting started.

"Whether you asked me or not, the answer is the same. Your son isn't going anywhere. And if you pulled your head out of your ass long enough to take a good, hard look at him, you'd know that for yourself. You might call him a boy, but he isn't. He's a man. A man who could have left a long time ago if he wanted to, but he didn't. Because he loves this place. He loves this work. He loves this legacy. And despite whatever grudge you're still holding for choices he made when he was a teenager, he loves you. So no, he's not *going* anywhere. He's actually doing anything and everything he possibly can to make sure he stays right here."

"Is that so?" Frank Kelley answers calmly...a bit *too* calmly.

Sam gets the distinct impression she's running headfirst into a trap, but she's already gained too much speed to stop now. "It is."

"And you're what?" The man gives her a once-over, his gaze snagging on her ring, her manicured nails, her matching two-piece athleisure set, and her four-hundred-dollar faux-fur slippers that were *yes* a lot bit indulgent but are so damn comfortable she couldn't resist. There's no way he surmised their price tag, but the look in his eyes is clear. They and she don't belong. "Going to stay here with him?"

No.

Obviously not.

But she's in too deep to admit defeat now. Her only choice is to keep digging. "Yes."

He snorts—snorts! The audacity. "You're going to give up the fame?"

"Easily." It's not hers anyway.

"You're going to leave the big city?"

"I grew up in a small town." Not two-hours-to-the-closest-Starbucks small, but he doesn't need to know that.

"You're going to quit your job?"

"I don't have to." The answer rolls off her tongue before she can stop it, as if it's been simmering there all this time, just waiting to wriggle its way free. "My sister and I co-own a jewelry design business, and thanks to the show it's finally taking off. Last I checked, this place has a phone and the internet. I have everything I need right here."

Frank offers an intelligible grunt.

Ha! Take that, she thinks haughtily, the taste of victory already sweet—until she flicks her gaze to Cooper. All at once it turns bitter. A soft smile plays at the edges of his lips. The corners of his eyes crinkle. Heat simmers in his gaze. Suddenly everything she just said hits her like an eighteen-wheeler to the face. *Shit!*

But it's too late to take it all back.

"Clear this up quick." Cooper's father motions between the younger men. "The vet leaves in two hours and I'm not paying her to come out here again. And you —" He looks at Sam. "You're having dinner at the main house. Six o'clock. Don't be—"

"No can do, Mr. Kelley," Wes interrupts. "We're taking her to the Barn tonight."

Cooper's head whips sharply to the side. His tone fills with warning as he says, "Wes."

"Tomorrow, then," Frank says, ignoring his son.

"Dad."

Sam has the distinct impression she should be helping him out somehow, but she's got nothing as Frank Kelley tips his hat and walks away.

Cooper glares at his friend. "We're not going to the fucking Barn."

"Yes." Wes grins. "We are."

"Hold up," Sam interjects, looking between them. "If this is some weird initiation thing where I need to stick my hand up a cow's asshole, you can count me out."

"Not the barn," Cooper says with a sigh as he rubs at the wrinkle in his brow. "*The Barn.*"

"It's a bar," Wes adds.

"Ohhhhh." A sudden spark of anticipation flares at the prospect of booze and music and Cooper's arms wrapped around her as they slow dance in the center of a crowded dance floor. "I'm in."

cooper

THIS IS A BAD IDEA, Cooper thinks for the hundredth time today. He and Wes are waiting for Sam in the foyer. *The fucking Barn.*

He sighs again, then scrubs a hand through his hair before resettling his hat on his head.

"Relax." Wes nudges him with an elbow. The asshole hasn't been able to wipe that shit-eating grin off his lips all day. "Everything is going to be fine."

"You need to call her Emily."

"I know."

"I mean it, Wes."

"I know."

"And tell everyone no pictures."

"Will do, boss."

"If the truth gets out…"

"Breathe, man," Wes says with a laugh. "I've never

seen you wound so tight. You've got a stick the size of Nebraska up your ass right now."

Cooper rolls his shoulders. "I know. I just—"

"Answer me this," Wes interrupts as he glances around the corner toward the bedroom door to make sure it's still closed. "You love this girl, right?"

"I think I might."

"You want her to move here?"

"I think I do."

"So what does it matter if the truth gets out? Don't you want it out?"

"*I* do." He resists the urge to run a hand through his hair again. "But she doesn't. Not yet. And until she does, I can't break her trust like that."

"Okay." Wes nods, then leans closer. "But between you and me, I don't think she'll care all that much. In fact, I think she might want the truth out just as much as you do."

Cooper's heart skips a beat as he cuts his gaze to the still-closed bedroom door, imagining the woman on the other side. He hears her voice again. *I have everything I need right here.* Fuck if hearing that didn't make his entire damn year. He's been playing that little piece of audio on repeat in the back of his mind all day, trying to decipher just how much of it was true and how much was Sam needing to beat his father. She's competitive as hell. He knows she'll say and do whatever it takes to win an argument. But if there was even a small part of her that meant it, a sliver he could work with...he has to know.

He looks at Wes. "What do you mean?"

"It's a hunch." Wes shrugs.

Cooper's mood plummets. "A hunch?"

"Yeah. Plus when I talked to her earlier today, she said she was *very much taken*. And that sure as shit doesn't sound casual to me."

Talk about burying the lede. Cooper's pulse rockets. "She said that?"

"Yeah, and—"

Wes cuts off as the *click* of a door reverberates down the hall.

And what? Cooper thinks. *AND WHAT?*

But the moment Sam walks into the hallway, every thought in his head disappears. She's wearing a sinfully low-cut black tank top tucked into a pair of skintight black jeans. He runs his gaze over her curves, drinking in every swell, already imagining himself peeling the garments off to reveal inch after inch of that milky skin.

Black, he thinks. *I had to tell her black.*

His weakness.

When his gaze finally reaches her feet, a small smile plays over his lips. She's wearing a pair of scuffed tan cowboy boots that couldn't possibly have been purchased just for this trip. They look lived in, as if she's been wearing them every day of her life...as if she belongs in them.

As she takes a step closer, completely unaware of the effect she's having on him, she shrugs into a tan leather jacket with fringe sleeves and sighs.

"Be honest. Is the jacket too much? Winnie is obsessed with it and I promised her I'd bring it, but it feels like, I don't know, like I'm trying too hard or something."

"Definitely not too much," Wes murmurs.

Cooper knows him well enough to recognize that tone. Without even looking he shoves his hand in his friend's face. "Eyes off."

The bastard chuckles. "I'll wait in the car."

"You know," Sam says after he's gone, "you won't be able to cover everyone's eyes at the bar."

"Is that a challenge?"

She grins and slides her hands up his chest. His heart pounds like hooves on the plains as she hooks her fingers behind his neck and meets his eyes, her mouth so close he can't think of anything but taking it. "So it's good, then?"

"You look..." He trails off, not sure how to finish.

Like a fucking dream.

Like everything I never knew I needed come to life.

Like you were made for me.

"That good, huh?" she teases.

"Sam—"

She puts a finger to his lips, shutting him up, as if she knows, by the look in his eyes or the sound of his voice, that he's about to say too much. "Save it, cowboy."

For when? he desperately thinks, searching those honey eyes for an answer. *I've only got thirty-six hours left with you. When will you be ready? When will you finally let me in?*

"Besides, you should be happy if everyone is looking."

"Yeah?" he relents. "Why?"

"Because." She leans in close and stretches onto her tippy toes, pressing completely against him as her lips brush his ear, sending a spike of heat deep into his lower abs. "No matter how much they look, or how much they pine, or how much they try, I'll be coming home with you, Cooper. Only you."

She pushes past him while he melts into a goddamn puddle on the floor.

This is a really bad idea.

Her.

Him.

Them.

The bar.

Everything.

And yet, he follows her out the door like the sad little puppy he's somehow become, trailing at her heels. Wes already has the truck fired up when he hops in.

"To the Barn?" his friend asks.

Cooper slips his arm around Sam's shoulders and pulls her into his side. She curls easily into the spot and settles her head against his chest. He lifts one foot onto the dash, drops his head back, and surrenders to just how right this feels. "To the Barn."

They peel off down the gravel road.

For the first half of the drive, Wes peppers them with an endless stream of questions about everything that happened on the show and in the Maldives to get them to this point. He's half superfan and half needling-best-friend. By the time he's done, Cooper is exhausted. But Sam is apparently just getting started because she then spends the second half of the ride demanding to hear every embarrassing story of his youth, starting with, *Okay, I've been thinking about this all day. What's the Peak? And who the hell is Caroline?* He grins at that one, noting the jealousy in her tone. But the smug attitude is quickly wiped away when Wes abandons all loyalty and tells her everything she wants to hear—that the Peak is a well-known makeout spot at the top of a bluff about forty-five minutes outside of town, that Caroline is the daughter of his father's best friend, and that a thousand-watt spotlight hit them right about the same time his zipper came undone. Apparently, history means nothing in the face of Sam's mischievous eyes. By the time they pull into a parking spot, all his dirty laundry from age five to now has been aired.

But he doesn't mind.

He likes that she keeps asking for more. He wants her to know everything about him.

He wants to know everything about her, too.

"Is that Cooper Fucking Kelley?" a voice shouts the second he steps out of the truck.

"*The* Cooper Kelley?" another taunts.

"The six-pack savior?"

He lifts his middle finger high into the air and turns to offer Sam his hand. The moment her auburn hair slips into view, a true murmur rises.

"Is that her?"

"Is that Emily?"

"Why is she here?"

"Do you see that ring?"

"Are they engaged?"

So much for keeping a low profile. Sam looks up at him and grins, the same thought clearly running through her mind. *I should have told her to take off the ring.*

Except he didn't want to.

If he's being honest, he likes seeing it there. He likes knowing there's some little piece of her that belongs to him, even if it's fake.

Because he wants it to be real.

Besides, this is a small town with small-town loyalties. No one will blab to the press. He's more worried about being indoctrinated into the local lore for the rest of his goddamn life. Though, really, it's already too late for that.

Cooper pulls Sam against his side and mutters into her hair, "You ready for this, Cuj?"

"Honestly?" She laughs, the sound warming him up like a shot of whiskey. "I have no idea. Let's go."

They close the distance and step inside the bar to open stares. He's known practically everyone in this place since birth, so he's not the one they're looking at. Sam either doesn't notice or doesn't care. She gasps and points at a sign on the wall just inside the door that reads *Bull Riding Arena*.

"Bull riding?" She squeals. "Like actual bull riding?"

"They don't call it *the Barn* for nothing."

"We have to go."

"Whatever you say."

This riding is nothing compared to some of the rodeo riders he's seen, but Sam is mesmerized as they step through the double doors into the arena. It's Saturday night so the entertainment is already in full swing. The bleachers are full to the brim with half-drunk patrons but he squeezes them into a good spot near the middle.

"I can't believe there's actual bull riding in a bar!" She squeezes his hand so hard he just about loses circulation. Before he can answer, the announcer comes on the loudspeaker welcoming the next rider.

Her eyes are glued to the ring.

His eyes are glued to her.

Every gasp, every flinch, every grin—he drinks them in. They watch five, maybe six, riders. He loses count.

"That was incredible!" she says when the show is over.

Yeah, he thinks. *You are.*

But he doesn't want to push too hard, doesn't want to spook her, so he just says, "Drink?"

They head to the main bar. He points out the pool tables, the live music, the line dancing, the mechanical bulls. Sam wants to see it all. They pull Wes and the girl he's chatting up in for a game of pool. Then she tugs him into the throng of line dancers, diving in headfirst as she stumbles over her feet, laughter spilling through her lips. He loves her enthusiasm. He loves how she doesn't care that she has no idea what the hell she's doing. He loves the joy bright in her eyes.

He loves...her.

Cooper grabs Sam by the hand and spins her into his arms as he leads them to a different area closer to the music. This is all he wants. Her head on his chest. Her fingers playing with the curls at the base of his neck. Her body swaying in time with his. The two of them perfectly in sync, as if alone, despite the looks that have been following them all night.

It could be like this, he realizes. *It could be like this for the rest of our lives and I'd never, ever get tired of it. I'd never want to leave.*

"Emily, you're almost up!"

The words don't register until Wes puts his hand on Cooper's shoulder. Sam looks up, her lids heavy, her gaze heady. They're both in a daze, caught in the same spell, until his friend says it again.

"*Emily.* You're next on the bull."

Sam jolts. "Oh, right! I totally forgot."

"You don't—"

"Hold this, will you?" She cuts Wes off and shimmies out of her jacket, carefully avoiding Cooper's eyes. "Winnie will have my head if anything happens to it."

He knows her well enough to know exactly what's happening. She's running. But it doesn't make him mad. Quite the opposite, in fact, because her reaction just means that everything he's feeling, she is too.

Cooper fights a grin as she hands him the jacket. It must be a losing battle because she eyes him strangely.

"You okay there, cowboy?"

"Never better."

She frowns. "You think I'm going to fall."

"I never said that."

"Look at that smug expression on your face. You totally think I'm going to fall. Don't you?"

No. I know you already have. He keeps that sentiment to himself even as his lips curl higher.

As expected, Sam fumes. "I can't believe you!"

"I didn't do anything." He chuckles.

The operator calls her name. Cooper recognizes him—Ben or Ken, he can't remember. But he doesn't have to know the guy's name to understand the appreciative look in his eyes as Sam steps forward. Cooper's hackles immediately rise...then rise again when she steps up onto the inflatable ring and half a dozen more heads whip around to watch.

For fuck's sake. Don't they see the diamond?

Sam turns around with a smirk. "I think I'll be needing this."

She plucks the hat from his head, and he can tell by her expression it's supposed to be a jibe, but all he can think is, *Damn straight she's got my hat on her head. Back off, assholes.*

Cooper's too distracted by the growing crowd to hear what exactly she's saying to Ben or Ken or whatever his name is as he helps her onto the bull. The wicked gleam in her eyes as she tosses a quick glance over her shoulder should terrify him, but he's too focused on the way that jerk's fingers are lingering to really notice. The music shifts and he still doesn't understand what's happening, too absorbed by the slow roll of her body as the bull eases into motion. It's not until he feels himself twitch against the seam of his pants that reality sets in, and by then it's too late.

"Man! I Feel Like a Woman!" blasts from the loudspeakers. Sam gyrates beneath a spotlight, hips circling, hair whipping, breasts bouncing in that low, low top, as she fights to keep her seat. The speed ramps up as the crowd hollers. But she keeps going. And the song keeps playing. And though he knows the whole thing can't last more than twenty-five seconds, thirty tops, by the time she flies off, he feels like a middle schooler with a raging hard-on in the middle of biology class.

Three guys rush to offer her a hand, but Cooper shoves them aside. At the sight of his glower, Sam smirks. He takes her by the hips as she swings her legs over the side of the inflatable wall, but instead of lowering her to the ground, he keeps her perched there and steps between her open thighs. She bites her lips to swallow a gleeful laugh as that almost painful source of heat nudges against her. Cooper arches a brow.

"Was that really necessary?"

"No," she chirps and drapes her arms around his shoulders, looking up at him with a victorious expression. "But it was fun."

"Remember what I said in the Maldives, Cuj?"

"Great power comes with great responsibility?"

He drops his lips to her ear and whispers, "Don't start something you're not prepared to finish."

"Oh, that," she teases, then leans back to meet his eyes. "Winnie told me something interesting."

"To be honest, I don't really give a damn what Winnie told you right now."

"She reads a lot of Westerns," Sam continues, ignoring him. "And she told me about this rule."

"Rule?"

"Yeah." She hooks her ankles behind his back, and his pulse jumps so fast he's afraid he's having a heart attack. "Whoever wears the hat, rides the cowboy."

"You know what? I've always liked Winnie."

Sam barks out a laugh. "You've never even met her."

"Remind me to thank her when I do."

Cooper slides his hands beneath her ass cheeks and lifts her against him. He steps back from the inflatable ring, taking her with him.

"Wes!" he shouts, not breaking contact with Sam and the heat simmering in those gorgeous, glowing eyes. "Find your own ride home!"

sam

FOR THE FIRST time in longer than Sam cares to remember, when the sun peeks up over the horizon, she isn't alone. Warm arms hold her against a solid chest. Red hair tickles her cheeks. Soft breath cascades over her shoulder, in, then out, then in, then out. He seems asleep, which means there may still be time to make a run for it, time to sneak down to the kitchen under the guise of needing coffee, time to slip away.

But she doesn't want to.

All she wants is to stay right here in the safety of Cooper's embrace for a few more minutes, before the soft golden light sifting through the curtains turns to the harsh light of day and reality comes crashing in.

Because this can't last.

It's a fairy tale.

A dream.

They're from two different worlds. Ten million people think he's engaged to her sister. Emily's entire career hangs in the balance—a career Sam already destroyed once before. Not to mention, she has plans of her own, which don't include running off to Nebraska to live on some ranch in the middle of nowhere, even if said ranch belongs to the sexiest cowboy she's ever seen, with a body cut from marble, a touch savvy enough to unravel her every seam, and a gaze so coveting it snatches the very breath from her lungs.

Try telling that to her heart, which thunders like a Kentucky Derby hopeful on the final stretch of the track as the man in question stirs and pulls her farther into his chest.

"Morning," comes Cooper's deep, raspy voice.

She wants to trap the sound in a little jar so any time she's sad or depressed she can open it back up and listen, because it's impossible to do anything but beam when she hears it. That's how she feels, like a glow stick that's been cracked alight by deft hands, no way to stop the chemical reaction or turn it off or go back to the way things were before.

It's too much to face before caffeine.

"What are you still doing here?" She turns over so they're nose to nose. "Don't you have a cow to rope or something?"

"I do." Cooper grins. "And so do you."

"What?"

"You heard me, Cuj." He smacks her playfully on the

ass as he rolls off the bed. "It's time for you to earn your keep."

"I'm pretty sure I already did. Three times last night."

"That was just for fun."

"Cooper." She whines and pulls the blankets up over her head.

"The ranch waits for no one."

"Well, the ranch can kiss my New York City ass."

He yanks the covers off in one fell swoop and leans over to bite one round cheek.

"Hey!" she squeals. "I said *kiss*!"

"I know."

An hour later, Sam finds herself ankle deep in what she really hopes is mud. Based on the smell, there's a hefty dose of cow shit mixed in as well, but she's trying not to focus on that as Cooper leads her through the muck. They're surrounded by fences and cows and cowboys doing Lord only knows what. She's sure it's important, but it also happens to be completely beyond her understanding. Cooper, though, is unperturbed.

"Wait here for a minute," he says as he hops a fence. "I'll get a horse saddled up for you."

"A what now?"

He lands with a *splat* on the other side, ignoring her as he calls something out to one of the other guys. She leans a hip against the fence and crosses her arms. The sky is blue overhead. A crisp breeze fluffs her hair. Aside from the obnoxious smell and the loud din of mooing, it *is* sort of peaceful in a way. Still, if someone had told her three months ago that she'd be standing in cowboy boots going eye to eye with a heifer, she would've laughed in their face.

What do you want?

She narrows her eyes at the beast as it twitches its tail.

That's what I thought.

Said tail lifts and a huge wad of fresh dung plops out.

Oh god. Sam steps back with a grimace, her boots squelching in the mud. *I am so not cut out for this life.*

"A little different from New York?" Wes comes up from behind her and leans his elbows on the fence.

She keeps her attention on Cooper and shrugs, remembering the fresh feces she nearly stepped on while running down the subway platform last Monday. "Surprisingly, no."

Wes snorts.

A yearning twinge fills her chest as Cooper tips his head back, laughing at something one of the guys said. He's got that rare gift of seeming at ease no matter what he's doing. Jet skiing in the Maldives. Running his hand down a cow's spine. If she put him in a suit and plopped him in the middle of her office, she bets he'd fit right in. Not like her. Sam hasn't felt at peace in a long time.

She flashes back to waking up in bed this morning.

The comfort of his deep breathing.

The security in his touch.

The promise of what could be if she'd only just let it.

Maybe it hasn't been so long, after all.

"Whatever you're thinking, don't," Wes says, dissecting her with his eyes. She's too afraid to meet them.

"He's got a good heart, and it's already been broken once before. Don't do it to him again, Sam. Please. I'm begging you. Don't do it again."

Something in his tone makes her turn. Those brown eyes probe and plead, protective in a way she understands.

"His mom?" she asks softly.

"Everything about this place changed when she got sick. Coop. His old man. Even the very air we're breathing right now felt different, like the land itself was in mourning. She was the glue, and that's what they both need right now. More glue. Not a wrecking ball with a pretty face."

"I don't want to hurt him."

"Then don't."

Wes pushes off the fence before she can answer. A few minutes later, Cooper comes back with two horses—a light brown one with black hair who looks boredly ahead, and a reddish one with a white stripe down its nose who's giving her the stink eye.

"Let me guess," she comments dryly. "The infamous Nutcracker?"

"How'd you guess?" Cooper answers with a snort, though the pride in his voice is clear. The horse in question neighs in protest, then nudges Cooper with her nose. He laughs softly and wraps his arm under her head to pull her in for a hug. A scratch here, a pet there, and the animal becomes putty in his hands. His skills with women clearly extend to the equine species. Cooper leans up to whisper in Nutcracker's ear. Sam can't hear what he's saying, but she's guessing it's something to the tune of *You'll always be my number-one girl* if the victorious side-eye coming her way is anything to go by.

"I hope you're not expecting me to ride her, because I can recognize when a woman is marking her territory, even if that woman is a horse."

Nutcracker bares her teeth. He tuts at her and starts stroking her neck. "Her bark is worse than her bite."

"Wes told me you had to ice your balls for weeks."

"For fuck's sake." He rolls his eyes, then grabs her hand. "Get your ass over here."

"What—"

"Relax," he interrupts, seeing her panic. "You're not riding her, but you've got to introduce yourself. I happen to know from experience the only ways to get past her defenses are constant, stubborn exposure and good old-fashioned bribery. Take these."

He drops three white sugar cubes into her palm. There's a ten percent chance Nutcracker is going to bite her hand off, but Sam extends her arm anyway. A wet tongue quickly laps the treats from her fingers. The horse snorts, as if to say, *That's all you got?* Sam arches a brow, fighting fire with fire. They stare at each other for a second, a sense of mutual understanding seeming to pass between them.

"Good," Cooper mutters. "Now, hold your hand like this. Fingers closed. Yup. And lift here." He guides her palm steadily down Nutcracker's smooth, muscular neck twice before letting go with a soft, "Keep going."

Sam repeats the stroke again and again, noticing how the horse's tension begins to melt away. Her own, too. After about fifteen times, Cooper gently catches her wrist to stop her.

"Good, now repeat that again, but with your horse for the day—the friendly, lovable Duchess, who's been working here longer than some of the ranch hands have. You've got nothing to worry about."

"Hi, Duchess. I'm Samantha," she announces into an intent ear while she runs her fingers down a long caramel neck. Then she leans closer and whispers, "Please, please don't throw me."

"That's enough of that," Cooper interjects. Suddenly, large commanding hands grip her around the waist and she's airborne as if she weighs nothing at all. He plops her into the saddle, letting his fingers linger a little longer than necessary, before turning back to Nutcracker.

Sam can't help but smile as he glides smooth as butter into his own saddle. There's something unabashedly sexy about a man who looks perfectly at home on top of a nine-hundred-pound animal who can just as easily kill him as carry him across the plains. And he does look at home as he gives the horse a few strong pats, then motions to the other men mounted up behind them. With a click of his tongue, the group launches into motion.

He guides Nutcracker without the reins, using just the pressure of his thighs, oozing a quiet confidence that heats Sam's blood. They move past the paddocks and into the open grasslands, the backdrop of rolling hills just heightening this wild, rugged air he's giving off. She's never experienced anything like it before—a man so in his element, so commanding over nature. He cuts and gallops, the movements like a coordinated dance between horse and man, bodies and minds perfectly in sync. One moment he's laughing with the group and the next he's staring broodingly off into the distance, studying some unseen sign, all while constantly turning back to check on her, to make sure she's comfortable and safe, to make sure she's having fun. The juxtaposition of such raw masculinity set against such tender care leaves her absolutely entranced.

Sam can't look away.

"So you really love him, then?"

The voice startles her so much she nearly loses her seat. A firm hand grasps her around the upper arm, holding her secure. Sam looks up into Frank Kelley's inscrutable face. She didn't even hear his horse close in while she stopped to gawk under the guise of a water break.

"I—" She stutters and shakes her head. "I'm sorry. What?"

"I wasn't sure, yesterday," the man continues, in that stern, indecipherable tone. "But I see it now. I recognize that look."

"Mr. Kelley, I—"

"Save it. I don't need any explanations. I don't want any either. Whatever's going on between you and my son, keep it that way. I just wanted to say that for the first time since that boy could walk, he seems content to stay right where he is. Those two feet aren't itching to carry him away. And if I have you to thank for that, then thank you. I didn't understand why he wanted to go do that show. Hell, I still don't. But if it's what he needed to find his way home, then I'm glad he did. Because make no mistake, Ms. Peters, this *is* his home. And I won't let anyone stand in the way of that."

"I'm not trying to."

He turns his eyes on the horizon and draws in a deep, heavy breath before releasing it slowly. "It's not for the faint of heart, ranching. It's not an easy life. It takes grit, Ms. Peters. From what little I know about you, that seems like something you've got. But that's not enough on its own. You have to love it. You have to want it, too. You have to want it just as much as he does."

Sam doesn't know what to say, so she just keeps her mouth shut. The silence still speaks volumes. Her gaze slides back to Cooper, on horseback a little ways down the hill. He's finally noticed the two of them talking. Even from this distance, she can read the worry in his brow.

Frank turns back to her. "I hear you're leaving in the morning."

It's a statement, not a question. She answers anyway, more to remind herself. "I am."

"Don't worry about dinner at the big house tonight then. You don't need an old man getting in the middle of things. We'll save it for the next time you come visit."

Cooper starts riding over. She forces a swallow. Frank's

horse neighs with restless energy, though deep down, she wonders if maybe it's just picking up on the tension rapidly filling the air.

The older man leans in, his voice low. "You *are* planning on coming back, aren't you?"

Sam gulps. Her palms grow slick on the reins. Suddenly, it feels as if every inch of her is sweating beneath the blistering sun, despite the cold autumn air.

"Yes, sir," she whispers, not sure if it's the truth, or a lie, or just some desperate attempt to end this conversation.

Sir? she thinks, pulse thumping. *I haven't unironically called anyone* sir *since the seventh grade.*

"Good." He stares at her a moment longer. "She would have liked you, I reckon. She would have liked seeing him so settled."

Sam doesn't need to ask who. Her voice is hoarse when she murmurs, "Thank you."

"Don't thank me yet, Ms. Peters. My wife and I hardly agreed on anything, especially when it came to our boy."

With that, he rides away, nodding at his son as he flies past.

"What'd he want?" Cooper asks, eyes on his father for a second too long, clearly suspicious.

"Nothing really." Sam clears her throat and offers him a wide smile. "Word of our antics last night must've reached him. He said he was canceling dinner tonight because we, and I quote, *don't need an old man getting in the middle of things.*"

"He called himself an old man?" Cooper snorts and stares after his father. "That's a first."

"I don't know," she quips. "Another minute on this horse and I might start referring to myself as a senior citizen too. How do you do this all day? My ass and my back are killing me."

"Practice. Years and years of practice." He reaches across the distance, slides an arm around her waist, and drags her into his lap. Nutcracker offers surprisingly little protest. "Come on, city girl. I'm taking you home."

He pats Duchess on the rear and the horse takes off running toward a whistle in the distance. Wes, she suspects, but Sam doesn't have the energy to look. It's too comfy being snuggled up against Cooper's chest while that word rings in her ears.

Home.

Why does it sound so right?

Cooper drops her off at the house to shower before he brings Nutcracker back to the stables. By the time she hears his truck pull up out front, she's wrapped up in one of the flannels from his closet, scouring the kitchen for ingredients. The front door creaks open. Boots thud. He leans against the doorway and crosses his arms over his chest as a dimple slowly digs into his cheek. When it becomes clear he's not going to say anything, she finally turns to stare back.

"What, cowboy?"

"Nothing." His grin deepens. "I just like watching you, here in my kitchen, wearing my shirt, making my dinner."

"Who said I'm making your dinner?"

"That's a lot of food for just one."

"All right," she relents with a laugh. "Maybe I am making you dinner. But I have a confession."

"Shoot."

"I've never cooked a steak in my life."

He puts a hand to his chest as if he's been shot. She throws a towel at his face.

"Shut up."

"I'll show you how. Just give me twenty minutes to get cleaned up."

He disappears down the hallway. Her gaze follows him, lingering on the empty air even after he's gone. Pressure builds in her chest. It's too normal, too domestic, too much of a view into the future she knows they can't have, even if she wants it.

And she does want it.

She can admit that much.

She wants it more than she ever thought possible.

So she decides right then and there that for tonight, she'll let herself have it.

By the time Cooper comes back, her guard has disintegrated into nothing. They cook together, then eat together, all the while touching and talking and sharing meaningful glances that say so much more than words ever could. If he can sense the change in her, he doesn't mention it. He doesn't ask about the future. He doesn't question what the morning will bring. It's as if he understands on some level that stepping outside the here and now will ruin everything. They watch in comfortable silence as the sun sinks below the horizon, the official start of their last night together, even if for the first time it feels like the beginning of something else. Cooper holds her against him as they cuddle beneath a warm blanket on a lounge chair, his chin resting on her hair. Dusk settles, bright yellows, reds, and pinks replaced by a soft mauve sky. As the stars brighten, his promise from the Maldives comes simmering back.

The next time I kiss you, Sam, it won't be because of someone else. It won't be because you're upset. It won't be out of fear. It'll be because you want it. It'll be because you're begging for it. It won't be for anyone's benefit but our own.

She can't help but think, *Damn it. He was right,* as she spins in his arms and places her palm over his cheek. He glances down at her curiously. She wets her lips and says the only thing on her mind.

"Kiss me."

He furrows his brow, as if concerned he heard wrong. She slides her leg over his thighs until she straddles him, the blanket still around them like a safe cocoon. His hands settle on her hips as though they belong there. She runs her fingers through his hair. He closes his eyes for a moment, a pleasured sigh rumbling through his chest. When he reopens them, it's as if the stars fell down to earth just to live in his gaze. It's not just heat, not just fire. It's that same brilliance she felt when she woke up this morning, purer, more peaceful, not raging but radiant.

Everything within her screams to give the feeling life,

to just say the words, but it's the one line she won't let herself cross.

"Kiss me," she whispers instead. "Please, Cooper. I need you to—"

He doesn't give her time to finish.

He arches up, closing the distance, and takes her mouth with his. Wrapping one arm around her waist, he holds her in place and grips the back of her head with his other hand, tilting it the way he wants, opening her up. He moves with slow, deliberate purpose, claiming her with his fingers, his lips, his tongue. It's everything she knew it would be, everything she was afraid of, the sort of kiss that rewrites the timeline. Her life shifts on an axis right here in his arms. What came before no longer matters. What comes after is too painful to bear. She wants to live in this moment forever, live in his touch and his kiss and the feelings he stirs deep inside her soul.

She can't say how long they stay on the lounger, making out beneath the blanket like a couple of teenagers with no responsibilities, no concerns, no place to be except lost in each other. Eventually, the cool air turns biting and Cooper carries her inside, keeping her legs wrapped around him, their mouths connected, their bodies close. He moves them seamlessly down the hall to the bedroom, not breaking the kiss, then lowers her down onto the bed with tender ease. Piece by piece, their clothes fall away. Each time, their lips find their way back, two magnets unable to fight the pull. Even after they're finished and she lies wrapped in his arms, she brings his fingers to her mouth, needing to taste him. When he kisses her shoulder, her eyes grow heavy with absolute repose.

Just before she falls asleep, cocooned against his chest, his mouth beside her ear, she hears four little words that shatter her heart into a million little pieces.

"Let me keep you."

He tightens his arms around her, every inch of them molded together as if made to be, and presses one final kiss to the base of her neck.

"Please, Sam. Let me keep you."

CHAPTER TWENTY-FOUR

cooper

HE FEELS the change before he even opens his eyes. It's in the rigid set of her shoulders, the slight quiver to her breathing, the pulse pounding beneath her skin, the heaviness of her stare—a weight he can feel behind his closed eyelids.

Kiss me, he hears her voice again.

Was it a dream?

Was any of it real?

Love me, he wants to tell her back. *Sam, I need you to love me.*

For once, he's the one who's too afraid to ask. So he waits. All morning, he waits. While they get out of bed. While they get dressed. While they eat breakfast. While they step out the door with her suitcase in tow and she snorts at the sight of his truck.

"What?" she says. "No chopper?"

"I'm not interested in making time move faster today."

The words are a soft volley just itching to be smacked out of the park.

She swallows and looks away.

He keeps waiting, trying not to push, trying not to press. They hold hands and make small talk for the entire hour-and-a-half drive. All the while he waits for her to offer some sort of an explanation for why, after the weekend they just had, she's still planning on saying goodbye. It's not until she grips the strap of her purse and gives him a fake-as-fuck smile in the parking lot of the airport that he realizes the truth.

She's not planning on saying a goddamn thing.

"Well," she mutters with an uneven sigh. "That was—"

"If you say the word *fun* right now, Cuj, so help me god," he snaps, all patience and poise vanishing in a blink as that cold, hard reality sets in. "You were really going to leave, just like that? I can't believe you."

"Well, how do you want me to leave, Cooper?" she snaps right back. "No tomorrow. That was the rule."

"The rule." He grinds his teeth.

"Yes." She lifts her chin and offers him a look so high-and-mighty he's amazed she hasn't passed out from a lack of oxygen. "The rule *you* agreed to."

"We agreed to a lot of fucking rules, Sam, and we broke every single one of them."

"Not that one."

"Why?"

She turns her face away. He locks the doors in a desperate attempt to keep her close.

"You're not getting out of the car until you tell me why."

"You know why."

"Enlighten me."

"I already told you. I ruined Emily's life once, and I can't do it again."

"Bullshit."

"Excuse me?"

He stares her in the eye and says it again, nice and slow. "Bull. Shit."

"Look, you might not like the explanation, but—"

"It's not the explanation."

"Then why don't you enlighten *me*, Cooper? You seem to know everything."

"I don't, Sam. I don't know a fucking thing, because you won't tell me. But I talked to Emily enough to know this isn't about her. That's an excuse. Your sister was prepared to leave the show without a proposal. She didn't care what America thought. She wanted to be true to herself. I mean, for Christ's sake, she's moving in with one of the producers two days after the live finale. She clearly gives fuck all for what the gossip rags might say. So if you called her up right now and told her what's been going on between us, I know what she'd say."

"It's not about what she'd say," Sam cuts in. "It's about not putting her in the position where she has to say anything at all. Do you think I don't know that she would do anything for me? *I* won't do that to *her*. I know she would choose me over her career. That's why I refuse to give her the chance. It's not about her choosing me, Cooper. It's about me choosing her. After all these years, it's about me finally choosing her."

"I hear what you're saying. But I don't believe you."

"Too bad."

"You're making the easy choice again."

She scoffs. "You think this is easy?"

"Easier than staying and fighting."

She tugs on the handle, but the door doesn't open. All she needs to do is pull the knob to release the lock, but he's not about to remind her of the workaround.

"You're running," he presses.

She keeps yanking, the need to flee seemingly compulsive, like a caged animal longing for the wilds.

"You're running to New York the same way you did back then."

She smacks the window with her palm and practically snarls with frustration. "Let me out of the car, Cooper."

"You're afraid."

"Let me out of the fucking car!"

"Tell me what you're so afraid of, and I will."

She digs through her purse and pulls out her phone. "I'm calling the cops. You can't hold me hostage like this."

"Go ahead." He crosses his arms over his chest and readjusts in his seat as if hunkering down for the wait. "It'll take them ten minutes to get here and this conversation is worth going to jail over. What are you so afraid of?"

She shoves the phone away and looks around in desperation.

"Just tell me, Sam. What are you so—"

"WHY AREN'T YOU AFRAID?" she finally screams.

He reaches for her hand but she snatches it away.

"NO!" She takes a deep breath to recenter herself and runs her palms over her thighs. Her fingers tremble. She finally whispers, "Why aren't you afraid, Cooper? I didn't even lose Emily and I'm scared absolutely shitless. But you, you..."

"You're right. I know exactly what it's like to lose someone I love." He reaches across the center console and takes her hand. "That's why I'm not letting you go."

She looks away with a wince. "Don't say that."

"Why not? It's true. I—"

"Don't, Cooper." Even as she tells him to stop, she grips his fingers as if they're a lifeline. "You don't know the whole story."

"Baby, please." He strokes her with his thumb, desperate to understand what's going on in that beautiful mind. "Just tell me."

She lifts her head and stares through the windshield. Those normally shining eyes are clouded over and glassy, clearly looking at something only she can see. The grip on his hand tightens again as she takes a deep, shuddering breath.

A second passes.

Two.

Then—

"I told you how I went to NYU without Emily. How much I hated it. How much I lied to her. How much I hid. But there's more. Stuff I'm ashamed to admit. Even Winnie doesn't know all of it, though she's the only person I ever came close to telling. And before I get started, no, this is not about a boy, not really. But in order to make you understand, I have to tell you about my ex. We met the first week of freshman year, and his name is Spencer Winthrop."

I hate him already.

The disgust must be written on his face, because Sam half snorts, half laughs as she drops her head back against the seat, still looking straight ahead. "I know. I know. I should've known by the name he'd be an absolute douche, but I was eighteen, without my sister for the first time in my life, scared out of my mind for her, and—yes, I'll admit it—intimidated as hell by New York. He was a rich upperclassman from the suburbs who seemed to know everyone and everything, and he still chose me. And at the time, it felt good. It wasn't like I hadn't dated people before. I had my pick in high school. I went out with the class president, the quarterback, half of his teammates, and just about anyone else I wanted. But I never treated any of those guys seriously. I always had my eye on New York, on getting out, and then I was suddenly there. All my reasons for holding back were gone. And I was in this emotional turmoil I never expected. Spencer became more than a warm body. In a very short time, he became... everything. My tour guide. My therapist. My social calendar. My safe place. I was too preoccupied with school and with Emily to even think about figuring anything else out on my own. His friends became my friends. His favorite spots became my favorite spots. I changed what I wore, what I ate, how I acted, all to fit this mold I thought he wanted. God, it's so embarrassing, looking back on it now. I can't believe the hold I let him have over me. It's just so..."

She trails off with a sigh. He studies her profile, the auburn hair slipping out from where she tucked it behind her ear, the graceful arch of her neck, the freckles painted across her cheeks, that smart-ass mouth he can't get enough of. It's difficult to imagine her any other way than the confident woman she is now, but he understands. He was a helluva lot different at eighteen, that's for damn sure. And it's not a time he likes to relive either.

"Anyway—" She cuts sharply back into the story, the pain in her voice evident. "About a week after Christmas break ended, I got the call from Emily to tell me she was dropping out of FIT and moving home. I knew it was coming, but I'd been holding out hope that she would change her mind or talk to me or that we'd, I don't know, win the lottery or something. We didn't. And by the time she called, she had already dropped out. It was done. I'd waited too long to talk to her. There was nothing I could do. So I did what I always did—I went to Spencer. He was the only person who knew the truth about my sister, about what I was going through. All fall, he'd been there every time I cried. He'd held me. He'd wiped away the tears. He'd told me everything would be all right. And I needed that. I needed him." She grits her teeth as her nostrils flare. "But that night, after he did all the things he'd always done—listened, dried my tears, kissed away the pain—I saw a text on his phone while he was in the bathroom. It said, *Are you done with that depressed bitch yet?*"

Cooper sucks in a shocked breath, silently seething. But Sam grows eerily calm, face blank, voice turning detached as she continues.

"I unlocked his phone and scrolled up to read more of the conversation. His friends had texted, *Where the hell are you, man?*, while I was walking over to his place. He'd responded with, *Just got a call from Sam. She's fucking crying again. I'm so over this shit. At least she's an easy lay. Let me hit it and then I'll get rid of her. See you in an hour.*"

An anger more intense than anything he's felt in his life explodes beneath his skin. Every muscle in his body tenses with rage. He's never understood the term *seeing red*, but he does right now, as the blue sky pulses to an angry crimson for a beat while his heart thunders inside his chest.

I'm going to kill him.

If I ever see him, I'm going to fucking murder him.

"It's okay," Sam says gently and brushes her lips against his knuckles, her kiss a balm to his raw fury. When she drops her head to the side, the rest of his anger melts away. It's impossible to be mad when she's looking at him with those bedroom eyes. "Don't waste your energy on him. I'm over it now, I promise. But at the time, it felt like my entire world was falling apart. I confronted him when he came out of the bathroom. He didn't even try to deny it. He called me a charity case, and a pity lay, told me I wasn't even worth breaking up with because I was never his girlfriend in the first place. I left his room in a daze, not sure where to go or what to do or who to call. All my friends were his friends. They wouldn't care. All the bars I knew of were the ones he showed me and I was too afraid to run into him. I couldn't call Emily or my parents because they thought I was having the time of my life at NYU. I had no one, nothing. I wanted to go back to my room and bawl my eyes out, but I heard those words as if he'd whispered them right in my ear, *She's fucking crying again*, and I just thought, *No. No, I won't cry. Not over him.* I walked back to my dorm without shedding a single tear, and I lay in my bed all night staring at the ceiling, and I decided right then and there that I would never put myself in that position again. I would never let myself get so consumed by someone else I forgot who I was. I would never need someone so much I couldn't stand on my own two feet. It was easier said than done, of course. I got drunk a lot. I cried a lot. I almost flunked out of my classes. I went so insane the first time I saw him with another girl that I snuck into his room, cut the crotch out of every single pair of his boxers, and left a note that said *This should make it easier to swing your little dick.*" She snorts and shakes her head. "If I hadn't found Winnie at the start of my sophomore year, I have no idea what would've happened to me. But I did. And eventually, we figured out how to conquer New York together. Now, here I am."

"Here you are, what?" he asks, frowning at the prideful tilt of her chin.

"Winning."

"This is winning?"

She shrugs.

"Working yourself to the bone, closing yourself off from everyone, lying to your own sister all because some asshole broke your heart six years ago, that's winning? I don't follow, Cuj."

"It's not about Spencer. It's about me, Cooper. I won't be weak like that again. I won't need someone so much that losing them leaves me crippled."

"It's not weak to need someone, Sam. You just have to pick the right person to need—someone who needs you too. And I do. I need you."

"For now."

"What the hell does that mean?"

She untangles their fingers. An ice-cold drop of dread slips down his spine the second his skin loses contact with hers. The walls he worked so hard to disassemble stand to attention as she crosses her arms over her chest, jaw set, gaze hard. He's terrified he just touched her for the last time.

"People fall out of love every day, Cooper. For little

reasons. For big reasons. Sometimes for no reason at all. So yeah, maybe you think you need me now, but one day, that feeling might just—*poof!*—vanish. And where would that leave me? If I moved here, to the middle of nowhere, to your land and your house, to live with your family and your friends, where the hell would that leave me when it all fell apart? This ranch is one of the most stunningly beautiful places I've ever been, but it is also my worst nightmare come to life. It's everything I told myself I would never be again."

"I won't stop."

"You don't know that. You can't."

"Look at me, Sam." He cradles her face in his palm and stares into her stricken eyes, willing her to believe him. "I won't stop needing you."

"It doesn't matter."

"I'll give it up." She sucks in a sharp breath. For a moment, he thinks he has her. "I'll go to you. I'll surround myself with your friends and your family. I'll live wherever you want to live. I'll do whatever it takes."

The brief light in her eyes burns out. "I won't let you throw away your life for me. Just like I won't let Em do it either. I'm not worth it."

You are.

He wants to shake her and scream.

YOU'RE WORTH EVERYTHING!

But he can already tell it won't get through. So he slides his hand to the back of her neck, holding her there with him for just a few seconds longer, fully aware of the desperation that must be written all over his face but lacking any care to hide it.

"I'm not the type of man who likes to live with regrets. And if I let you leave now, I already know I'll regret it for the rest of my life."

She places her warm palm over his and closes her eyes, melting into his touch for the barest instant. Then she slowly peels his hand away. "It's not your decision to make."

I know.

Nina's proverb from all those weeks ago comes back to haunt. *You can lead a horse to water, but you can't force it to drink.*

He can't make her stay. He can't make her fight. He can't make her want him. And even if he could, he doesn't want to spend the rest of his life convincing someone to believe in him. So he leans over and pulls the knob on her door to release the lock, willing her to understand that the only prison she's in is the one of her own making.

She doesn't even look at him as she pushes open the door.

He should let her go.

He knows this. He understands it.

But he just can't.

Cooper takes hold of her hand. Sam pauses with one foot on the ground and glances slowly over her shoulder, eyes already wet with unshed tears.

"Tell me you don't love me," Cooper rasps.

She tenses.

"Tell me you don't love me, and I'll let you go."

"Cooper, I—" She takes a deep breath. He holds his, everything about him suddenly still, waiting. She licks her lips and opens her mouth. "I—I can't."

He tightens his grip. "Then *I* can't stop fighting. I won't."

She sighs. For the first time since he's known her, defeat flashes in her eyes. It worries him more than a single word she's ever said.

"Get your shop set up, Cooper." She changes the topic, her tone flat. "There are still three weeks before the live finale. You need to capitalize on your popularity while you still can. I know you think your dad won't go for it, but he will. He'll agree to anything that keeps you here and keeps you happy. It's not about the ranch. You're his connection to your mom, just like photography is for you. That's why he's holding on so tight. That's why he's so afraid. You're his tether. He needs you."

Cooper doesn't want to talk about his photography or his father, but it doesn't matter what he wants. The door slams shut and she walks away.

CHAPTER TWENTY-FIVE

sam

THE WORDS on Sam's computer screen blur. She grits her teeth and pauses typing long enough to curl her fingers into fists.

You have got to be kidding me. She hasn't cried over a guy in six years, and now she can't stop. *Again?*

It keeps happening like this, too quick to mount a defense. One second, she's fine. And the next, pain radiates across her chest. Tears collect in her eyes. A knot forms in the back of her throat, making it difficult to breathe. Suddenly, she's paralyzed as a bottomless well of dread yawns like a fissure down the center of her being.

Sam blinks rapidly to keep the quickly pooling water in her eyes at bay as her boss drones on. The meeting will be over in five minutes. She just needs to keep it together until then.

I can do this.

Focus.

The second they adjourn, she slams her laptop shut and jumps to her feet, racing for the bathroom. When she turns the corner, Spencer's there like the shock reveal at the end of a horror movie. Sam claws at her chest as an embarrassingly loud gasp escapes.

"Jesus. You scared me."

He smiles. "I have that effect on women."

What does that even mean? Sam furrows her brow. "Excuse me. I have to pee."

"Sam, wait." He circles her wrist with his hand. Nausea curls in her gut the moment his skin comes in contact with hers. To think she once swooned at his touch. *Kill me now.* He's repulsive. "I've been meaning to talk to you."

"That's funny, because I've been actively avoiding you."

His nostrils flare. She fights the urge to grin.

"Come on. It was a million years ago."

"And yet I still hate you with the fiery passion of a thousand burning suns. It's almost like the anger you feel after someone takes advantage of the fact that your sibling might be dying in order to sleep with you, and then laughs about it with his friends behind your back for three months, is the sort of rage that only festers with time."

"Shh," he admonishes and then looks around. "Someone might hear you."

She snorts. "And what? Figure out what an asshole you are? They don't need me for that. I have full confidence you'll screw this job up all on your own."

"You're impossible."

"Thank you."

"I just want—"

"Save it. I couldn't give two shits what you want. Now take your hand off me."

He rolls his eyes, but lets her go.

Sam eyes the sharp cut of his lapel and the custom silk interior visible near the neckline of his jacket. "Nice suit."

"I had it made."

"I can tell."

She leans in closer than would be considered appropriate for an office setting. The asshole can't hide the intrigue in his eyes, but this isn't foreplay.

"Touch me again," she whispers, her voice as sharp as the scissors she really freaking wishes she were holding, because the effect would be epic, "and it's snip snip, motherfucker."

He whips back. His eyes go wide.

"I knew that was you! I fucking knew it!"

Sam lifts her middle finger and brushes by him on her way to the bathroom. The second the stall door closes, the tears fall. Cooper's words swirl through her thoughts like a mocking breeze.

This is winning?

Sitting on a toilet at the office of the job she hates, bawling her eyes out over the guy she stupidly let get away, in a four-hundred-dollar suit she doesn't even like but had to buy in order to keep up appearances while she saves every cent she possibly can in case an illness that all medical knowledge says is unlikely to return somehow does, and—worst of all—fooling herself into believing she's being strong.

But what's the alternative—quitting? Telling Emily the truth? Accepting the job as her official CFO? Running off to Nebraska to live happily ever after on a ranch with the sexiest man she's ever seen?

Sam can envision it so clearly, like pictures from a future she's already lived. Late nights on the phone with Em. Flights to Los Angeles. Presentations with investors, tours of factories, interviews with new employees. Cooper picking her up in that fucking chopper just to see her stew every time she gets home. Mornings curled up on the deck to watch the sunrise. Evenings snuggled up by the fire. Afternoons spent poring over spreadsheets while she sits at the desk he set up in front of the window so she'll see that lone silhouette of a cowboy on horseback long before he officially makes it home. He'll say it's because he likes the thought of her watching him, but really it's because he likes the sight of her greeting him at the door with nothing on but that old shirt of his she still uses to keep warm.

In her daydreams, there's no possibility they'll break up, no chance the company won't make it, no future that would leave her destitute and desolate beyond repair.

But that doesn't mean it's not there.

How do people do it—make that leap of faith, face those fears, overcome them?

She would give anything to understand.

Buzz.

The vibration against her hip pulls her back to reality. Sam sucks in a ragged breath and wipes the wetness from her cheeks. The name on the caller ID is the last one she expects to see.

Your better half.

Em.

Sam silences the call. She's been avoiding her sister for weeks, and mid-cry in a bathroom stall over the fake engagement that might destroy Emily's life isn't really the ideal time to change course.

A text comes through.

I know you're at work. Sorry!! But I'm having a panic attack. I need you.

The phone rings again.

Sam slides her finger across the screen.

"What?" she asks, her heart in her throat. There's absolutely nothing in Emily's text to imply it's something serious or health related, but that doesn't matter. It's where her mind goes with her sister. Every time. Even after six years of good news. She doesn't know how to stop. "What's wrong?"

"I need to go to LA," Emily says in a rush.

"When?" Sam asks, trying to catch up. "Why?"

"Logically, I knew this was coming. The season always ends with a live finale, but I don't know, I've been blocking it out or something. I completely forgot. But Nina just called with my flight info. It's real. It's happening. I'm going to sit on that stage and talk to the thirty men I broke up with in front of the whole freaking world, and I need to somehow not let it slip that I got with their producer instead. How am I going to do this, Sam? How am I going to face them?"

That's what this is about? Sam exhales as the tension in her body lets out. "Em, half those guys were assholes and the other half were there for Instagram followers. None of them are going to give a shit that you're with Jake. And none of them have to know, either. Just be the sweet Southern belle I know and love, and you'll be fine."

"I'm a terrible liar, Sam. You know I am. I'm going to let something slip—"

"You won't."

"I will. On live TV. I'm going to let something slip and it's going to ruin everything."

"It won't."

"You need to help me."

Her heart shudders to a stop as she slaps her palm against the stall for support. "Em."

"You break up with guys all the time. You know how to deal with exes. I clearly don't since the one and only time I've had to face an ex, I jumped almost immediately back into bed with him."

"Em."

"Oh god. Do you think they'll be mad? Are they going to be mad?"

"I just told you they won't be."

"But what if they are? Maybe I should just be honest. What's the worst that could happen? Everyone in America turns on me? Okay. That would be bad. But Mom has a nice flower shop. I can work there forever. And Cooper! He wasn't mad when I told him. Maybe people would understand. Maybe they—"

"Jesus Christ, Emily. GET A GRIP!"

A shocked beat of silence passes. "Is everything okay, Sam?"

Is everything okay?

IS EVERYTHING OKAY!?

No. It's not okay. Because for a moment there, Sam thought Emily was about to ask her to do the live show in LA, and the very idea that she might have reason to see Cooper again left her so excited she couldn't breathe, and now she's the one having a panic attack. Fear claws up her throat like a creature from the deep.

"Sam?"

"I need to tell you something." The words are out before she can suck them back in.

No. No. No. No.

"What?"

"I—"

The confession lodges in her larynx.

I didn't turn down Cooper's proposal.

The engagement ring is on my nightstand, and I put it on every night before I go to bed.

I'm the one who's lying to everyone.

I'm the one who's going to let something slip.

I'm the one who's ruining everything.

"What, Sam? What is it?"

She's keeping far too many secrets. It's no surprise when one finally breaks free. "I'm the reason it took so long for you and Jake to get back together."

There's a pause, then a cautious, "What do you mean?"

"That Christmas when we came home after all your treatments, Jake came to the house. You were in the kitchen getting us ice cream. I met him at the door and I told him to fuck off. He had some stupid note he wanted to leave on the doorstep. I don't know if it was to apologize or win you back or explain, and I never will, because I ripped it to pieces and threw it in his face. And, god, I'm so sorry, Emily. I should have told you. Years ago, right when it happened, before he left, I should've told you. But I was afraid. I felt like we finally had some good news as a family and I didn't want to ruin it. I—" She stops to lick her lips, the truth sitting heavy on her tongue. But it's now or never. How does someone find the bravery to take that leap? They just do. "I just got you back, and I didn't want to lose you again. Not to cancer. Not to Jake. Not to anything. And I know I was being a selfish asshole. I knew it then, but I just couldn't stop."

The other end of the line is silent except for the soft *creak* of a chair, as if Emily has fallen back into her seat with the shock. Sam feels unexpectedly lighter though. Even in the face of losing her sister forever, the heavy burden of the lie has fallen away. And it would be in Emily's right not to forgive her. It's what she deserves.

"You guys probably would've gotten back together

that winter if not for me," she continues softly, ripping the veil over the hideous truth clean off. "You wouldn't have spent seven years unhappy and alone. You would've had the love of your life. You wouldn't be freaking out about facing your thirty exes on national TV because they wouldn't exist. It's me, Em. I'm the reason for everything. If I'd just let him through the door, your whole life might be different, and—"

"No."

The word is so quiet, barely more than air. Sam holds her breath, unable to tell if that whisper was infused with horror or heartache.

"No," Emily says again, stronger, louder, and this time Sam hears the last thing she ever expected. Beneath the sadness and the anger and the hurt, at the base of it all, there's love. "That's not on you, Sam. You did a shitty thing. And yes, I'm pissed. It's going to take me a minute to process this. But you're not the reason it took so long for Jake and me to find our way back to each other. You don't need to carry that burden. He could've fought his way past you. He could've come back the next day. I could've called him. I could've gone to LA. There are a million things the two of us could have done differently, but we weren't ready. Back then, we weren't prepared to fight for each other, but we are now. And that's what made the difference."

Sam can't quite believe her ears. "You're not going to yell at me?"

"What would it accomplish?"

"Hate me?"

"I could never."

"Set a plague on both my houses?"

"We're from the same house, idiot."

"Huh." Sam relaxes on the toilet and drops her chin into her palm. "I guess you really are the nice one."

"Maybe." Em snorts. "Or I could just tell Mom you said you're finally ready to settle down and get married."

"You devious little bitch!" Sam gasps in mock horror, then grins despite herself. "It's brilliant."

"Yeah. Let's see how you like it when she shows up on *Wake Up, America!* demanding you get a boyfriend too."

Maybe it's finally time to come clean. About the engagement. About Cooper. About all of it.

"Hey, Em?"

"Yeah?"

I am completely head-over-heels in love with Cooper Kelley.

The truth sits there like a weight on her heart. She already knows what Emily will say. *Go after him. Come clean. I don't care.* But just as Em won't let Sam bear her burdens, Sam won't let Em bear hers either. She's got to figure her own way out of the mess she made.

"I love you."

"Love you too, sis."

In the ringing silence that follows, Sam thinks about how easy those three words are to say to her sister. *I love you.* As simple as breathing. As innate as her heartbeat.

It could be like that with Cooper.

If she lets it.

Emily's explanation turns over in her mind, again and again, as though if she keeps flipping it and twisting it and dissecting it, the truth will emerge. *We weren't prepared to fight for each other, but we are now. And that's what made the difference.*

Cooper's been fighting. For every step she took away, he took one closer, keeping them connected, keeping them bound. Wasn't that his parting promise?

I can't stop fighting. I won't.

She's the weak link.

She's the missing piece.

She's the only thing keeping both of them from living happily ever after. And maybe *ever after* won't be forever. Maybe it will. There's no way to know. But there's suddenly something that scares Sam a hell of a lot more than Cooper leaving her—the thought of never having him in the first place. Never seeing him again. Never wiping that stupid smirk from his face. Never slipping that hat over her head and kissing him against the backdrop of the fading sun. The idea is so suffocating, the bathroom walls cave in, the ceiling drops, the floor lifts. She's Alice in the shrinking house, the pressure so immense she can't breathe.

One moment of courage is all it'll take to get everything she wants.

One brief, beautiful moment of wild abandon.

A switch flips in the back of her mind. An idea comes to her, the same way all her best ones always have, like a bomb exploding in reverse, the messy debris fusing back together to form the perfect picture. There's a way to save Emily's business. To help Cooper keep his. To get her dream job and her dream man and her dream life. There's a way to fix everything, if she's brave enough to reach out and take it.

Sam lifts her phone. She pulls up her messages. She taps Nina's name. A series of unanswered texts flood the screen. The ones she's been ignoring ever since she got back from Nebraska, a silence that must've prompted the producer to take action by calling Emily in the first place. Because somehow that terrible, conniving, brilliant woman always seems to know exactly what Sam needs, and what she needed this time was a push.

She briefly wonders if she should run it by Cooper first, maybe tell Em, but the impulse fades. There are too many factors to work out, too many things that could go wrong. The last thing she wants to do is give either of them false hope. And as she told Cooper over the weekend, it's better to ask forgiveness than permission.

Sam types her message to Nina—*I figured out our final step*—and hits send.

The reply is immediate. *About damn time.*

CHAPTER TWENTY-SIX

COOPER STALKS across the small dressing room like a caged lion yearning for the hunt. It's been three weeks since Sam walked away without so much as a single glance back, three weeks since he last saw that sly little look cross her face, three weeks since her laugh has sent goose bumps down the back of his neck. And somewhere on the other side of this door, Emily is waiting like his last ray of hope shining in the black. He can't stand it.

He tries the door again.

Locked.

Goddammit!

Is this part of the producers' plan? To make him go completely insane before sending him out onto the stage for the live finale being watched by ten million people? Because it's working.

"Nina?" he calls.

Nothing.

"Fred?"

Silence.

"Trish?"

Nada.

"Fucking hell!" he shouts and kicks the door. He just needs to talk to Emily. He needs to find out what Sam told her. He needs to fill in the gaps. He needs to explain everything before they go on air and there's no turning back. "Can someone please open the door?"

The knob suddenly turns.

Cooper isn't used to feeling like the small one of the group, but a guy with at least two inches and probably fifty pounds of muscle on him slips through the crack. He's amazingly quick for his size, nothing but a blur of blond hair and tan skin in the dull fluorescent lights. For a moment, Cooper wonders if the network sent someone in to subdue him. Then he remembers this isn't the Mafia —*Idiot!*—and he jumps forward.

"Wait, don't—"

The guy spins in surprise. Behind him, the door closes with a definitive *bang*.

"No!" Cooper lunges for the knob. It doesn't budge. "Shit! It must have an automatic lock or something."

"You trying to get out?" a deep voice asks.

Cooper looks up at his new cellmate, then does a double take. "Are you—"

"Tyler Briggs." He stretches his hand forward for a

shake, offering the sort of smile that makes it clear this isn't the first time he's been met with shock and awe. "Nice to meet you."

Cooper's jaw just about hits the floor. This guy is one of the most famous pro hockey players in the country. He just signed an eight-year, ninety-million-dollar contract with the Los Angeles Royals. What in the world is he doing here dressed in a suit and tie?

"So, you want out?" Tyler asks again. "Because I can probably help you with that."

Cooper frowns. "How?"

"I'll pick it."

"Pick it?" he asks, wondering if he heard correctly.

His companion just shrugs. "Why not?"

Cooper looks around, wondering if a film crew is about to pop out of a secret panel in the wall because surely he must be getting punk'd. Either that, or the solitary confinement has really gone to his head. Because seriously. Tyler Briggs? The guy is worth a fortune. What does he know about picking locks?

Enough, apparently.

The hockey player crouches down, retrieves a credit card from his wallet, and gets to work. The soft scrape of plastic on metal fills the silence.

"I gotta ask," Tyler says after a few moments, his focus remaining on the lock. A concentrated wrinkle forms in the center of his brow. "Why do you want out so badly?"

"I'm trying to win back my fiancée," Cooper says

carefully, still not entirely convinced this isn't some hoax Nina set up to catch him in a lie. He's starstruck, yes, but not stupid. "Why did you want in?"

"I'm hiding from my agent." The man tilts his head to the side, then adjusts the angle of the card. A little bit of venom leaks into his tone. "He thinks I'm risking my carefully cultivated image by going on the show. He's convinced I'm going to do or say something that'll get me into trouble, but contrary to popular belief, I'm not a total idiot."

If Cooper had a drink, it would be all over the right winger's back right now. "You're going on *this* show? On *The Love Match*? The dating show?"

"You're looking at next season's lead." Tyler pauses to offer him a thousand-watt grin that Cooper knows will make half the female viewers combust at first sight. Then the man's eyes go wide. "Oh shit. I don't think anyone is supposed to know that. Keep it between us, okay?"

"Sure," Cooper says automatically, and then because he can't help it, he adds, "How the hell did they get you to sign up for the show?"

Tyler clenches his jaw. His entire demeanor shifts, the light seeping out so fast it's as if a curtain has been thrown closed to block out the sun. Nina's grubby little hands are written all over this reaction.

"Sorry, I didn't—"

"Don't worry about it."

They fall into an awkward silence. Cooper swallows

and shifts his weight uncomfortably, hoping he didn't totally mess up his one chance to get out of here and find Emily. But the guy is still doing, well, whatever it is he's doing.

"So how does a professional hockey player learn to pick locks?"

"Let's just say you can take the boy out of the trailer park, but you can't take the trailer park out of the boy. Now…" Tyler stands and pulls up with one arm while he twists with the other. The door pops open. Cooper takes a step forward, but the right winger keeps ahold of the knob, blocking his path. "One question."

"Fair trade."

"Filming the show. How bad was it?"

"The dates are hokey. The reshoots can be painful. The cameras definitely get annoying after a while. And there's a cutthroat undercurrent that at times made me feel like livestock just waiting for the slaughter," Cooper answers truthfully, thinking about where that strange and windy road has led him, "but it's the best decision I ever made in my entire life."

"Huh," Tyler grunts in surprise and releases the door. "Then, good luck with that fiancée, I guess."

"And good luck finding yours."

Cooper charges into the hallway without looking back. At some point when he has time, he's sure he'll reflect on just how ridiculously bizarre the past five minutes of his life have been, but right now he has one thought and one alone—Emily.

As luck would have it, she's two doors down from him and the hallway is miraculously absent of any production crew he recognizes. They must all be busy getting things ready onstage, a fact for which he is eternally grateful as he opens the door and slips inside, holding a hand over his eyes, just in case.

"Sorry to barge in like this, Em, but I need to talk to you. Are you dressed?"

She sucks in a breath so sharp it sounds as though she's been possessed by the antichrist, which he takes to mean he caught her in a bad spot.

"Let me just turn around," he says hastily, giving her privacy but not time as he races on. "I have no idea what Sam told you, but I'm guessing most of it was complete horseshit if I know her as well as I think I do. And, trust me, I do. You must know that we accidentally got engaged in the Maldives. And I'm sure she said the plan was to break up on air tonight with some lame excuse like we realized we just weren't right for each other or the long-distance relationship was too much to overcome. But the most important thing you need to know—the part I'm absolutely positive she left out—is that I am so fucking in love with her I can't even breathe right when she's not around. You probably don't know that she came to visit me in Nebraska, but ever since she left, it's like I've been walking around with a piece of myself missing. There's this knot in the back of my throat I just can't shake. I can't draw air. I can't think. I can't do a goddamn thing except miss her."

He sucks in a ragged breath, that ache pulsing steady beneath his skin as his lungs burn. He waits a moment for Em to say anything. When she doesn't, he just plows onward.

"Look, I know I sound insane. We've only known each other for three months. We only spent a little bit of that in the same place. You probably think I've lost my mind. But I haven't. I actually think I've finally found it. There's this settled feeling deep inside me I've never felt, like for the first time in my life, I'm in the right place doing exactly the right thing at exactly the right time. And I've never had that before, that sense like I'm exactly where I'm supposed to be. But I do with Sam. Lord help me, I do. She drives me nuts, don't get me wrong. You know how she is. She pushes every one of my buttons and takes a perverse sense of glee in doing it, but fuck if it doesn't turn me on every time. I don't want an easy life if she's not in it. I'll pick her competitive ass every time, and shit, I'll even let her win if it puts that satisfied little smile on her face, that's how gone I am. I want her face to be the first thing I see in the morning, and the last thing I see at night. I want to spend the day knowing she's waiting for me back at home, not in some misogynistic way, I promise. I want her to take over the world if that's what she wants. She's smart as hell and it only makes me want her more. I just mean, I want to know that she's out there keeping me in her heart the same way I'll be keeping her in mine. Because she's there, whether I want her to be or not. Even if she doesn't want me back, she'll still be there, like a goddamn tattoo I don't want to erase. And here's the real kicker, Em. Even though she left me, even though she hasn't reached out, I'm pretty sure she loves me too, which is where you come in."

He pauses to run a hand through his hair before settling his hat back into place, hoping for a word of encouragement, hating that he's saying all of this to an ugly white wall devoid of any character. But Emily is utterly silent.

"I know this is a lot." He cuts into the quiet. "And I'm sorry for ambushing you like this. I'm not asking you to come clean out there. Hell, Sam will kill me if you do, so please, let's make a pact to lie through our fucking teeth. All I really need, if you're willing to provide it, is her address. My flight to New York leaves as soon as the show wraps. I just want to see her. I just want to talk to her, face-to-face, without the pressure of tonight hanging over our shoulders. We can keep it quiet for a while if that's better for your business, wait until all this publicity blows over. Or you can let the tabloids run wild and go with the scorned woman angle. I don't care if the rest of the world calls me a sleazebag for breaking up with you tonight and going out with her tomorrow. I just want her, any way I can get her. I know she thinks it's weak to need someone, but it doesn't scare me. I need her like I need air, and I'm not afraid to admit it. I'm drowning without her. So please, Emily, help me go get her."

Cooper waits for her to say something, anything. He

tries to give her space to process, but in the back of his mind, all he can hear is the tick of a clock winding down. The show is supposed to start any minute. Someone is going to come get her. Someone is going to find him. It's only a matter of rapidly diminishing time. And he needs that address. He needs it more than he's ever needed anything in his entire life.

"Emily, I—"

"*Cooper.*"

He spins around so fast the world wobbles off kilter. But he knows that voice. He hears it every night in his dreams. And there she is like some sort of mirage, sitting at the vanity in a black silk dress that looks like glorified lingerie with her red hair pulled up into a knot above her head and brilliant emerald jewels that have her sister's name written all over them dangling from her ears. The look in her firelight eyes matches the whisper of her voice, steeped in love and longing and undeniable anguish.

He doesn't think. Doesn't hesitate. He marches across the room with so much conviction the Devil himself would be hard pressed to stop him.

Unfortunately, Nina Chen made a deal with that douchebag a long time ago.

The door slams open behind him.

The producer shouts for help.

Before he makes it halfway to Sam, two men grab him by the arms. Apparently, they do have security guards on this show, and yes, they're more than willing to use them.

"Sam! Get the fuck off me. Sam!"

Fight as he might, Cooper can't get loose. Inch by inch, he's dragged backward, holding Sam's gaze the entire time. And all he can think as the door shuts in his face is that she didn't say a word, not a single goddamn word, to stop them.

sam

"ARE YOU KIDDING ME, NINA?" Sam snaps the second the door closes, the pleading in Cooper's brilliant eyes almost more than she can bear. "This isn't the fucking CIA. What the hell was that?"

"Please." Nina snorts. "The CIA *wishes* they had me."

That's probably accurate. "You didn't have to drag him out of here like that."

"You promised me a finale to remember. That means no talking before we're live."

"I wasn't going to—"

"Save it. You were about two seconds from mounting each other and we both know it. Now, I just got word from Trish."

Sam's heart lurches so hard she needs to steady herself against the vanity. Her throat suddenly runs dry. She has to swallow before she speaks. "And?"

"We're a go."

"Really?" The word comes out as an embarrassing squeal as her hope balloons so rapidly she almost can't breathe. "They said yes?"

"They said yes."

"You have it in writing?"

"I've got the updated contract right here."

"Give me a pen."

As any good businesswoman would, Sam takes a moment to review the changes from the last draft. They're exactly as requested. Granted, she should probably have her friend from legal give it a final once-over, but there's no time. She glances at the clock. The show starts any minute. If she wants to win Cooper back and secure her sister's business, it's now or never. So she flips to the last page and signs on the dotted line.

It's happening.

It's really happening.

Sam catches her reflection. The energetic buzz beneath her skin matches the rosy flush of her cheeks and the brilliant shine in her eyes. Behind her, the room is brighter, no longer a drab and dull gray but a vivacious and crisp white. It's like looking through the window on those rare snow days from her youth, the world sparkling with a thousand possibilities as each hopeful flake falls. She feels like a kid again, full to the brim with the buoyant, naive idea that somehow everything's going to be okay—a sense time and puberty and life ground out of her, now suddenly returned.

This must be what optimism feels like.

"Keith just went live," Nina says, one hand pressed to her headphones while the other clutches her clipboard. She finds Sam's eyes in the mirror. "They're leading the guys out now. A clip reel is playing. You'll be on in five. You ready?"

"To put Ethan, Chad, and every other fame-hungry asshole who played with my sister's heart in their place while simultaneously getting everything I've ever wanted?" She spins around on the stool and straightens her shoulders with a defiant tilt of her chin. "I was born ready."

"You know, I think I actually feel a little bad for those guys. The poor bastards have no idea what's coming."

Sam stands and brushes the lint off her dress. "Nina?"

"Yeah?"

"Fuck off."

The producer laughs and holds out her arm. "Come with me."

Walking out onto the stage is surprisingly easy. Waving to the adoring audience. Sitting beneath the blinding spotlights. Talking to Keith about the season. Telling off the jerks. Giving all the sweet guys their due. She takes it all in stride. The first two-thirds of the show pass in a blink. It's not until her conversation with the runner-up starts to wind down that Sam's palms grow sweaty. Doubts tunnel like worms beneath her skin, wiggling and writhing, carving closer and closer to her heart.

What if this doesn't work?

What if the audience turns on me?

What if he says no?

There are a million ways this could go wrong. But there's one possibility she cups between her palms like a wounded bird waiting to take flight.

What if it all goes right?

Keith Holson looks at the audience as the runner-up walks off. Sam's ears ring so loudly she doesn't hear a word he says, but deep down she knows what's coming. The cameras shift at the same instant, all pointed somewhere offstage. Her gaze follows instinctively.

And there he is.

Cooper stands in the shadows, just outside the spotlight, his hat riding low over his brow, those red curls sneaking out behind his ears. His green eyes smolder in the darkness, bright as fire on a starless night. The sight of him in a suit hits her even harder than it did that day on the beach now that she knows the man beneath the body. A cowboy with an artist's soul. A son who loved his mother more than anything in the world. A restless spirit who said in her he finally found a home.

Love slams into her like a tidal wave, stirring up every fear, every doubt, every memory of everything that ever came before him. She thinks of what he said back in the dressing room. *I need her like I need air. I'm drowning without her.* The words hang there while she flips in the current, spinning, churning, lost in the rush. Her chest burns.

And then he's there.

He sits next to her and takes her hand. Just like that, she's saved. The second his fingers wrap around hers, warm and solid and sturdy, she draws in that first fresh breath of air since she stepped out of his car and the slate wipes clean. Nothing matters, nothing except the here and now.

"So, Emily and Cooper," Keith says in that warm yet hollow hosting voice. "Where do things stand since we last left you with that beautiful proposal in the Maldives? Still happily engaged?"

Cooper keeps his eyes glued to her, dissecting every curve of her face, every iridescent shimmer of her eyes in the spotlights, searching for the right answer. But it's not his answer to give.

Sam turns to Keith. "Actually, Keith, before we get to that, there's something I need to confess."

The hand threaded through hers tightens. Despite the murmur of the studio audience, it's the soft hiss of Cooper's sharp inhale that grabs her full attention, the sound balanced on the edge of hope and hurt, two sides of the same blade.

"Confess?" Keith asks with a put-on laugh. He turns to the audience with a wide grin, but it pulls at the corners. She's going off-script and he has no idea what to expect, which is good. Nina said it would play better if he was just as confused as the audience. "What do you think? Should we hear what she has to say?"

"Yes! Yes!" come the shouts.

"Well, Emily. Take it away."

"That's just the thing." Sam swallows. She turns to Cooper, lifts his hand to her lips, and presses a soft kiss against his fingers. His gaze darts rapidly back and forth from one of her pupils to the other, as if he's unsure he can trust the message he's reading there. But he can. This is real. This is happening. "I'm not Emily."

The gears in the backs of Cooper's eyes shudder to a stop. Sam tightens her fingers reassuringly and turns back to Keith, who is watching her with an unsure expression.

"Don't tell me," he suddenly blurts with a nervous laugh as he glances quickly off camera. "You're Mrs. Kelley already?"

"Nope," Sam answers, letting the *p* really pop off her tongue. Then she grins. "I'm Sam. Well, Samantha Rose Peters if you want to be exact. But everyone calls me Sam."

The audience gasps.

"Sam?" Keith says slowly, the panic rising in his eyes.

"That's me," she chirps, turning back to Cooper, pulled toward him by some inner instinct she doesn't want to temper. The crinkles at the corners of his eyes tell her everything she needs to know. He leans back in his seat and drapes his arm around her, then hugs her against his side as his chest swells with what she knows is his first full breath in three weeks. "Though someday, maybe, I might be Mrs. Kelley, too. I haven't decided if I'm really the taking-my-husband's-last-name type, but it does have a nice ring to it."

Keith stares at her, then at Cooper, then somewhere offstage. If downtown Los Angeles had crickets, they'd be chirping up a storm in the silence that follows. It's probably no more than a second or two, but beneath the blinking red lights of a dozen cameras, she feels as though it goes on for a year. Suddenly, the host snaps out of his daze and looks directly into the lens.

"We'll be right back."

The *on air* sign blinks off.

"What the FUCK," he explodes, jumping to his feet. Nina runs onstage and starts talking to him too softly for anyone else to hear. Every member of the studio audience launches into conversation all at once. In the center of the storm, Sam watches Cooper, and he watches her, each wearing a silly, stupid smile across their lips.

"Couldn't have given me a little heads-up?" Cooper comments, arching a brow. "I've been out of my goddamn mind, Cuj."

"Yeah? Just wait until you hear what's next."

"What?"

"Hey." Nina snaps her fingers, drawing their attention. "Thing One and Thing Two, save it for the show."

Sam rolls her eyes.

Cooper grunts.

"I am *not* going to miss her," he says under his breath.

No, you definitely won't. Sam laughs softly. A ten-second countdown begins as the producers scramble to quiet everyone down. She leans up until her mouth hovers beside his ear, needing to give Cooper one moment that's just for him.

"I was out of my goddamn mind, too, cowboy," she whispers. "I love you."

He whips toward her.

The countdown hits one.

They're live.

"So, *Sam*," Keith says, the easygoing laugh back as he keeps his cool, collected mask firmly in place. "You sort of dropped a bomb on us there. Care to explain?"

"There's not much to explain." She shrugs, trying to keep as calm as possible as nervous bolts snap down her spine. *This is it. They have to believe me. They* will *believe me.* Everything—her heart, Cooper's ranch, Emily's business—it's all riding on this moment and this one little white lie she absolutely needs to get right. "I've been Sam the whole time. When my mom went on *Wake Up, America!* asking for help finding my sister a boyfriend, she didn't realize that Emily had recently gotten back together with her high-school sweetheart. No one except for me knew about it. Things were still fresh. My sister never imagined that the clip would blow up. She never dreamed the producers of our favorite show, *The Love Match*, would come calling asking her to be the new lead. But when they did, she couldn't accept. She was already in love. It wouldn't have been right to lead thirty men on when her heart belonged to someone else. But we both knew what this kind of exposure could be for her jewelry business, a dream she's been chasing her entire life, a dream I want more than anything for her to achieve, especially since I'm also the CFO of the company. So I suggested we pull a trick out of our old identical-twin playbook and switch places."

"Switch places?" Keith asks.

"I told her I would come on the show and pretend to be her. No one would know the difference. I was single at the time. We could still give America exactly what they wanted. I thought I would come out here, date a bunch of cute guys, wear my sister's fabulous jewelry, and then go back to my life, simple as that."

Keith glances between her and Cooper, then drops his gaze to their intertwined hands. "And then you met Cooper?"

"And then I met Cooper." She laughs and shakes her head. "What was I supposed to do? Let a little thing like my name come in between us? I mean, look at him, ladies." Sam gestures at him, grinning as the audience hoots and hollers their approval. She looks up at the man in question, hoping he sees the complete honesty shining in her eyes. "I knew falling for him would break every single one of my rules, and I tried not to. Lord, how I tried. But when have rules ever mattered when it comes to love? I knew being with him would risk everything. I knew there was a chance that all of you amazing people watching the show would never forgive me or my sister for lying to you like this. I knew my actions could destroy her dreams. I knew all of that, but when he looked at me, none of it mattered."

The audience swoons.

She has them in the palm of her hand, and yet, just as

she said, none of it matters. The only things that matter are the warm green eyes lighting her up inside, the arm holding her close, the thumb drawing circles on the back of her hand. She's not speaking to them—to the cameras, the audience, Keith, the producers. They all fade away, until it's just her and Cooper in the middle of their own universe.

"I've been scared for a long time, scared of giving my heart to someone, afraid they might break it. But when I thought of walking away, of never seeing you again, I realized something. You already had it. The moment we met, I gave you a little piece of myself. And with each passing day, I freely gave more and more, until eventually, I looked around and realized you had it all. Falling in love with you was so easy I didn't even realize it was happening until I was completely head over heels, but I know what this is now. I know what we are, and I'm sorry I ever doubted it. I'm not afraid anymore. I need you. So..."

Sam disentangles herself from Cooper and scoots back on the couch. She removes the ring on her finger and holds it out to him.

"The first time you gave me this ring, you didn't know what you were agreeing to," she says. "Now it's your choice. Break my heart if you have to, Cooper. I probably deserve it. Or be with me, the *real* me. No rules. No limits. No fear."

The studio is utterly silent, as if everyone is waiting on the same collective inhale. Cooper takes the ring between his pointer finger and his thumb, the brush of his skin like a match to sandpaper, setting her on fire. Her heart races. Yet he's utterly calm as he slowly twists and turns the gem, as if inspecting the cut. Suddenly, he tosses the ring high and deftly snatches it from the air. Beneath the brim of his hat, he wears an expression that can only be classified as sinful while he lifts his chin to look at her.

"I have one rule, Sam."

She gulps. "What's that?"

"I want your tomorrows." He tugs on her hand so she falls against his chest, then presses his lips to her ear, too quickly for the cameras to change angles as he whispers for her and her alone, "I'm a greedy man. I want them all. You say yes and every last one of them is mine. Understood?"

She leans back to look him in the eyes and places her palm over his heart. "They're already yours, cowboy."

"Well then..." He grins, slides off the edge of the interview couch, and drops down on one knee right there —in front of the studio audience, the cameras, and the ten million people watching at home. With her fingers clutched in one hand and the ring suspended expectantly in the other, he flashes those dimples, making her and about nine million other women swoon. "Samantha Rose Peters—I said this once, and I'll say it again—will you marry me and make me the happiest man in the world?"

"Well, I'm not sure I can promise *that*," she says with a wry twist of her lips. "We both know I'm a handful. But I will be your wife."

"Deal."

He slides the ring over her knuckle so fast it stirs a laugh, then she's in his arms and they're spinning. Applause rings out, claps and shouts and cheers. Then a loud *boom* echoes across the stage as an unholy amount of confetti and balloons rains down from the rafters. Cooper arches his head back to release a loud bellow as they come to a stop at the center of the madness, hardly able to see each other through the paper flurries. He keeps his hands at the small of her back as he lowers her to the ground. She tightens her arms around his neck and draws him down. They kiss long and slow, enjoying every second of knowing it's just the beginning as the romantic music blaring from the speakers hits a crescendo.

Suddenly, the spotlight shifts.

They're left in the dark.

Without even looking, Sam senses the cameras pan away. Good riddance. She has no intention to stop making out with the drop-dead-sexy cowboy who she can now officially call her fiancé. But then someone screams. And another person. And another in an excited chain of reaction that can only mean one thing—next season's lead has just walked out, and it's a good one. As a loyal fan of the show, she's dying to know who it is. Curiosity might have killed the cat, but it definitely kills the mood. She can't help it. She takes a peek.

"Ty?" The name pops out drenched in surprise.

"Ty?" Cooper rears back. "You forget to tell me something, Cuj? Since when are you on a nickname basis with Tyler Briggs?"

"Why?" She turns back to Cooper with a smirk. "Jealous?"

"Do I need to be?"

She snorts and pats him on the shoulder. "Down boy. It's not like that. Did I forget to mention that Winnie's older brother plays professional hockey? He and Ty have been best friends since they were kids. The three of them grew up together. They visited us in New York a few times. I can't believe he's doing this show. Winnie's going to lose her mind when I tell her."

"She's going to have to get in line. My ears are practically bleeding." He winces and looks up at the crowd of screaming women, then tugs on Sam's hip, turning her back to him with a grin. "Guess we're old news."

She cringes. *Not exactly.*

His brows immediately pull together. "What?"

Sam folds her bottom lip between her teeth, debating if she should wait, but it's like ripping off a Band-Aid— better to get it over with. "This is probably a good time to mention that I signed a contract with Nina, pursuant to your proposal on live TV, to film a new show called *Sam and Cooper: Happily Ever After?* about the two of us moving in together on your ranch."

"Cuj."

"It'll be great exposure for Emily's jewelry business. Did I mention I'm going to accept her CFO offer? Not for fifty percent, obviously. But I think sixty-forty is fair, and—"

"Cuj."

"It'll be the perfect way to launch your new photography business. I saw the website you put together after I left, by the way. It looks great, though I do have a few suggestions—"

"Cuj."

"Anyway, we start filming in six months during the next break between seasons. Oh, and in case this wasn't obvious, Nina is executive producing the whole thing."

"*Sam.*"

She gulps and leans back, trying to remain as casual as possible, which isn't the easiest thing in the world to do when a six-foot-two cowboy is fuming in her arms. "Yes?"

"Have you lost your mind?"

"Come on." She tilts her head to the side and fluffs her lips into that pouty expression that almost always lets her get away with murder. "You have to admit, it has a nice ring to it. *Happily Ever After.* Doesn't it?"

His glower deepens as he opens his mouth. She quickly switches tactics, cutting him off at the pass.

"Before you say anything, there's one more thing you should know."

He scoffs. "What the hell else did you do?"

"I left my underwear in the dressing room."

He drops his head against hers with a groan.

"What? I just thought it was an important piece of information you'd want to have before deciding your next move."

"You can't keep winning arguments like this."

"Why not?" She grins as he slides his palms down the

sides of her silk dress, checking for ridges that aren't there. He curses under his breath. She licks his neck. "It works."

"You're a fucking menace," he mutters as he bunches the skirt in his fists and pulls her closer.

"Maybe." She shrugs, playing with the hairs at the base of his neck. "But I'm your menace."

"You know what that makes me?" he asks as he takes a step back, then another and another, dragging them to a private little corner offstage. "The luckiest man in the world, Sam. The luckiest man in the entire goddamn world."

SIX MONTHS LATER

THE SECOND SAM ducks through the airplane exit to see Cooper waiting on the tarmac with his arms crossed and a too-eager expression hiding in the shadows beneath his ball cap, she knows exactly what he's planning.

"Absolutely not."

"Hear me out."

"No."

"Cuj—"

"What could the two of you possibly be arguing about already?" Nina calls out from over Sam's shoulder. "And can you give me five minutes to get a camera set up before you keep going?"

Sam rolls her eyes, smiling when she catches Cooper in the same act. She spent the past week with Emily in Los Angeles opening their first pop-up shop, assembling a new manufacturing team, and hiring a social media manager plus two new assistants to keep up with the rapidly growing success of Emily Ann Designs, which has taken off like a rocket since the season aired, and seems to be headed straight for the moon if her projections are correct—and her projections are always correct. She'd hoped to get some time alone with Cooper before they officially started filming their new show, but that was before her mom showed up unannounced outside of Emily and Jake's door with three lattes, a binder, and enough bridal magazines to restock a library. The woman is an unstoppable force. Luckily, that hurricane is completely focused on Emily. With her sister's wedding set for the summer, their mother is, for the moment, choosing to respect Sam and Cooper's plans for a long engagement. But it's only a matter of time.

She shivers.

At the bottom of the stairs, Cooper arches a brow. Sam just shakes her head. When she reaches the final step, he takes her by the hand and gently pulls so she falls into his chest. Instead of going in for a kiss, as she expects, he hauls her up against him with his arm securely around her waist and drags his lips across her cheek to her ear.

"Twenty minutes," he murmurs.

Sam leans back. He stares at her with a pointedly arched brow and holds her closer—close enough she can tell exactly what's on his mind. Not that it hasn't been obvious by the smoldering way he's been mentally undressing her since the moment she stepped off the plane.

"Twenty minutes?"

A dimple digs wickedly into his cheek. "Twenty minutes."

It's a compelling argument, especially when a tired voice asks from behind, "What the hell is in twenty minutes?"

Sam glances at Nina, then past her to the stream of producers, cameramen, and assistants waiting to disembark, all headed to the same place as her and Cooper. Her mom's surprise arrival in Los Angeles meant she pushed back her flight to the last possible moment and flew in with the crew. Sure, it was fun getting the extra time with her sister and her mom, but the change in plans left her with no time to be alone with her fiancé before the horde descended. Unless...

Sam turns back to Cooper and groans.

He knows he has her.

Dammit.

"Fine," she says, then jabs him in the center of his chest. "But *you* can't keep winning arguments like this either."

"Why not?" He twists his baseball cap backward with a wild grin. The fucker is taunting her. He knows how sexy he looks. "It works."

Before she can say anything back, he throws her over his shoulder and starts running.

"Where are you going?" Nina calls. "Stop! Wait!"

Sandals flap on pavement, but it's no use. Cooper has a foot on her and he knows where he's going. After about ten seconds, the pursuit stops.

"Don't just stand there, you idiot," Nina snaps instead. "Get a camera. Follow them. Now!" Then she shouts, "You assholes are going to be the death of me!"

Sam looks up from her perch and calls, "I thought Satan was immortal?"

Nina flips her an exasperated middle finger.

The sight is almost worth what's about to come next.

Almost.

Cooper turns the corner and there it is—her personal death trap, otherwise known as the official Kelley & Dunne helicopter.

I can't believe I'm willingly stepping foot in this thing again.

But the promise of an hour alone with Cooper before the film crew arrives is too good to pass up. He slides her into the passenger seat and tightens all the buckles before hopping into the pilot's chair. They're airborne before the film crew has time to set up. Even from this distance, Sam can tell Nina is muttering expletives as she lifts her phone to take a video while the cameraman fumbles over an open travel case. Sam wiggles her fingers in goodbye as they bank left, leaving the airport behind.

Cooper threads their hands together. "Home?"

Strange how that single word has the power to calm the nervous pounding of her heart. She turns to meet Cooper's eyes and squeezes his palm tight. "Home."

Finally, Sam silently adds, staring out at the rolling plains with fresh eyes. As part of the contract she signed with Nina, she had to delay her move to Nebraska until filming began so every single moment could be captured on-screen for the new show. Oh, she's visited. But it's different, flying over these grassy hills, taking in the expansive blue sky, studying that unmarred horizon with the knowledge that this gorgeous, untainted, untamed view is going to be her new normal.

Saying goodbye to New York was surprisingly easy. Sure, she'll miss the restaurants, and the nightlife, and the never-ending surprises that come with living in an ever-changing place like Manhattan, where every day carries the chance of discovering something new. But after seven years of leaving her apartment every morning with no sure sense of where the hours would lead her, she quite likes the idea of knowing that every night for the foreseeable future will end in the same perfect way—next to Cooper.

No, the only thing she'll really miss about New York is Winnie. They spent half an hour crying and hugging in their empty apartment after the moving trucks were gone, then got greasy dollar slices from the pizza place down the street before heading to the airport for the same flight to LA...but that's another story.

"Oh, I forgot to mention my dad wants us over for dinner tonight," Cooper says as the main house comes into view.

Sam gasps. "Does that mean he's forgiven me?"

"*Forgiven* may be a strong word..."

She snorts and drops her head back. Needless to say, Frank Kelley was not exactly thrilled to learn his ranch was about to become the epicenter of an entirely new television show. He was even less enthused when the trailers arrived and he realized it meant an entire production team would be moving in for at least eight weeks. According to Cooper, he spent a solid month muttering about it underneath his breath, but—and this is a big *but*—he didn't say no, especially if it meant his son would be here too. And apparently, when the first check hit those bank accounts, all signs of mumbling stopped. Turned out money was just as good a motivator as Sam predicted. While the payout for the new show wasn't much, becoming a public figure has been a different story. Cooper's already signed two six-figure sponsorship deals, one with a hat company and one with a jeans company, and he's in talks with some literary agents about a possible coffee-table book pending the success of the upcoming season. The old man is still having trouble wrapping his head around the idea of publicists, and brand ambassadorships, and the fact that his son now openly carries that Canon EOS 5DS with him everywhere he goes, but Sam is confident he'll come around—just as he came around on her. It took three dinners at the main house, and more afternoons on horseback than she cares to admit, but eventually, even Frank Kelley couldn't resist her charms.

"Did you tell him the news?" she asks.

"News?" Cooper frowns.

Sam can't hide her rueful grin. "The Best Kiss nomination?"

"Oh, for fuck's sake." He scrubs a hand over his face. "I thought that was a joke. You can't be serious."

"Nina wants us in LA for the award show in May."

"Dear god. I'm never going to live this one down."

Sam snorts. Turned out that little conversation they shared while Ty was being announced as the new lead wasn't exactly as private as they thought. Nina had a camera on them the whole time, capturing a rather racy backstage makeout session the network decided to surprise them with the following morning during their customary appearance on *Wake Up, America!* The woman is clearly an evil genius, because the hot mic moment went absolutely viral. It was the most watched clip from *Wake Up, America!* for the entire year, and it's been in every single teaser promo for the new show. The network already made an offer to extend their contract for another season, and they've been nominated for "Best Kiss" at the KTV Movie Awards this spring. Eventually, they both agree, they'll step away from the limelight. But for now, they'll keep riding that wave as long as it's working for them. Sam's never been one to turn down a good deal.

And one benefit to living in the middle of nowhere, she thinks as they touch down in the front yard, is that aside from the film crew probably speeding toward them far faster than local traffic laws allow, the media can't touch them here. It's up to them how much they want to post online, how much they want to be seen, how much exactly they want to share. The lines between public and private are drawn, and right now, as Cooper takes her by the hand and leads her inside, the distinction couldn't be clearer.

"There's something I want to show you," he says.

"If that's a come-on"—she smirks—"I think you could do better."

"No." He snorts and scrubs a hand over his face, muttering, "Fucking menace."

"What do— Ooh! What's that?" She pulls him through the kitchen door, lured by the sight of something new and shiny on the countertop. "Cooper Kelley, is that what I think it is?"

"What do you think it is?"

"I hope you know I have no idea how to use it."

"Well, I do." He shrugs. "I told you I'd make you a latte."

Warmth bursts across her chest, sending tingles down her arms. He's so nonchalant, so matter of fact, as if buying her an espresso machine and learning how to use it just so he can become her own personal barista for the rest of his life is no big deal. And maybe it isn't to him. But to her, it's everything—tangible acts of love that tell her so much more than words ever could. Promises don't mean anything if they're hollow, but Cooper fills them. Every day, in big ways and in small ones, he fills them until her heart is left overflowing.

Sam notices another new item on the counter. A grin pulls at her lips as she reads the title of the cookbook. "*The Art of Dim Sum?*"

"I'm expanding my horizons."

"*Ramen for Beginners*?"

"That shit was actually delicious."

"You didn't—"

Cooper lunges to stop her but Sam gets to the fridge first and hauls it open. Inside there are five plates filled with dumplings, shumai, and even bao buns. Behind them sit two containers of noodles. That warm feeling cranks up about a hundred notches, the burning almost painful if not for the fact that it's pure happiness pulsing beneath her skin.

"You made all this?"

"I have no idea if it's edible."

That's the last straw. She simply melts. "Cooper—"

"Save it, Cuj." He closes the fridge and takes her by the hand again. "They'll be here in about fifty minutes, and there's something I want to show you."

"Are you sure that's not a come-on?" she asks as she stumbles after him, still curious what other new surprises she might find in the kitchen. "Like, positive? Because, I gotta say, the second time around it sounds even more like one."

"Maybe your mind is just in the gutter."

"With you? It absolutely always is."

"Well, take a whiff of the fresh air for a moment, will you? This is important."

She stops pulling against him, sobered by the earnest lilt to his voice as they stop outside the first-floor guest bedroom. The last time she peeked in here, it was full to the brim with old camera equipment, prints in various stages of processing, half-broken frames, and about a million other photography-related things Cooper took from his dad's house after his mom passed away.

"You know how I converted that old barn into a studio?" He grips the doorknob and waits for her to nod before he spins it. "I took all the old stuff that was in here over there, and replaced it with this."

It takes her a moment to fully process what she's seeing—the empty bookshelves lining the walls, the desk floating in the center of the room, the comfortable couch tucked in an alcove with a reading light perched above each arm. Everything is pristine and white, just waiting for her to supply some personality.

Sam gasps.

"The couch is a pullout," Cooper says, his energy nervous. "So your sister and Winnie and your parents will always have a place to stay. There are hidden filing cabinets over there, and I got some electric run through the floor so you won't have to deal with loose cables. I thought about putting a few books up, but I figured you'd want to fill it with your own stuff now that you can finally unpack. If you don't like the desk, we can always get another one. I just wanted something here for you, so you—"

"Shut up." Sam puts a finger over his lips. "I can't believe—" She pauses to swallow, getting too choked up to speak. "I can't believe you did this. It's perfect. It's everything I ever dreamed."

She turns to take it all in again, pulling a deep, shaky

breath through her lips to calm the raw emotions surging up her throat. Water pools in the corners of her eyes. The sting only intensifies when she looks past the desk to a huge picture window with a view of the front yard, just as she imagined, as if he'd dived inside her mind just to bring this specific dream to life. He wraps his arms around her and pulls her back against his solid chest, holding her close as he nestles his chin in the nape of her neck.

"I know how much you sacrificed to come here. I know how hard this was for you. So I wanted you to have a little corner of this ranch that was entirely your own."

"Now that's where you're wrong, cowboy." Sam spins in his arms, sliding her hands to the back of his neck to play with his hair. "Moving here? Loving you? Choosing us? It's the easiest thing I've ever done. Getting out of my own damn way was a bit of a struggle, I'll admit. But we're here. We made it to tomorrow. And guess what? We still have half an hour to spare."

Sparks dance across his eyes. "Half an hour, huh?"

She starts back, but he's already two steps ahead as he grips her around the thighs and lifts. In no time at all, she's perched on the edge of her new desk, his shirt is off, and she's working his belt free. Cooper peppers kisses along the side of her neck as he makes quick work of the buttons down the front of her dress. With a victorious snarl, he pulls the cotton up and over her head. She hooks her ankles behind his hips and holds him closer, that delicious pressure mounting. When his lips return to her naked flesh, she drops her head back with a gasp.

"Be honest," she stammers as he tugs at the edge of her lace bra with his teeth. "Did you pick out my desk knowing it was the perfect height for this, or is it a happy coincidence?"

"I'm disappointed you even have to ask."

"So you're saying I was led here under false pretenses?"

"No." He pulls the cup all the way down, exposing her breast. "I'm saying when it comes to you, I don't do anything by accident."

"Oh. Is that so?" She grins victoriously as she fists his hair, thinking back to that first day in the Maldives and their argument in the bungalow about who was responsible for the fiasco of a proposal and the consequent makeout that started it all. "I *knew* you kissed me on purpose. Admit it."

He drags his nose up the side of her throat to stop at her ear. "You're goddamn right I did."

She yelps as he flings her onto her back, then erupts into a fit of giggles, her happiness too much to contain. Because he's right. Nothing about them has ever been fake or forced or fortuitous. They made every decision that brought them here, and here is exactly where she wants to be—mindfully, miraculously, and maddeningly in love with her cowboy.

* * *

358

bonus scene

Sign up for Kay's New Release Newsletter to read an exclusive bonus scene between Sam and Cooper!

The semi-smutty, super-swoony *wedding day* scene takes place after *The Love Lie*. If you'd like to read this extra bit of the story, just visit the following link to sign up :)

https://www.kaymariebooks.com/my-newsletters

Thank you!

about the author

Bestselling author Kaitlyn Davis writes young adult fantasy novels under the name Kaitlyn Davis and contemporary romance novels under the name Kay Marie.

While she's been writing ever since she picked up her first crayon, she spends more time these days with her "mom" hat on than her "writer" hat - and she wouldn't have it any other way! But she does squeeze in as much writing (and reading!) as she can. Storytelling is a vital part of who she is, and she can't thank her readers enough for keeping this beautiful dream of hers alive.

To learn more visit:
www.KayMarieBooks.com

Or follow Kay on social media:
Instagram: @KayMarieBooks
TikTok: @KayMarieBooks
Facebook.com/KaitlynDavisBooks
Twitter.com/DavisKaitlyn